D0854585

5 7 9 6 7 1   F.

LIDE, M.

— Command of the king —

This book is due for return on or before the last date indicated on label or transaction card. Renewals may be obtained on application. Loss of transaction cards will be charged at 10p. each.

Loss of Reader's tickets will be charged at 25p. for Plastic Type. 10p. for Manilla Type.

PERTH AND KINROSS DISTRICT LIBRARY

Mary Lide was born in Cornwall and educated at St Hugh's College, Oxford, where she read History. She has lived in the USA (where she was English Speaking Fellow at Ann Arbor), France, Denmark and Italy, and now divides her time between America and Cornwall. Her earlier novel *Ann of Cambray* won the New Historical Writer Award.

COMMAND
OF
THE KING

Mary Lide

GRAFTON BOOKS
A Division of the Collins Publishing Group

LONDON GLASGOW
TORONTO SYDNEY AUCKLAND

579671

Grafton Books
A Division of the Collins Publishing Group
8 Grafton Street, London W1X 3LA

Published by Grafton Books 1990

Copyright © Mary Lide 1990

A CIP catalogue record for this book is available
from the British Library

ISBN 0-246-13189-6

Printed in Great Britain by
William Collins Sons & Co. Ltd, Glasgow

COMMAND

OF

THE KING

INTRODUCTION

—

There was a time in the early years of the sixteenth century when Englishmen came to the conclusion that they were tired of civil war. The long-lasting quarrels between the two noble houses of York and Lancaster had exhausted them, and they wished for peace. They prayed and hoped that in the Tudor kings, who had finally gained the throne, they would find the means to achieve their aim. Yet such is the effect of civil war that former loyalties are difficult to break and old alliances die hard. Despite prayers and hopes, rebellions were frequent, and riots and conspiracies stirred up constant unrest. In a world that appeared as unstable as quicksand, people therefore began to rely on prophecy, on portents and witchcraft. Reports of a sorceress, a new one, aroused fresh interest (depending always, of course, how, and by whom, her gifts were used).

By origin she was a simple peasant woman, who, no doubt, would have remained content with her own local fame, had not the Convent of the Holy Sepulchre in Canterbury swallowed her and made her a nun. Her real name was Elizabeth. Like a hundred other country witches, she was round of face, sturdy legged, gifted in blending herbs and salves, which she sold for medicine. Had she not been persuaded to join the Holy Sisterhood, she would have lived out her life among the hopfields of her home, doing harm to no one. But God (or the Devil, depending whose side you take) inspired her, and gave her fits, during which, like Joan of Arc, she claimed she saw visions, heard voices and performed miracles (hence the Holy Sisters' interest in her). She also agreed to give advice to the king, the most recent Tudor king that is, who had inherited the crown a few years earlier.

Who persuaded her to meddle with kingship was at first unclear, or for what reason, but kings do not take kindly to advice, especially advice which runs contrary to their will. The Nun of Kent and her convent friends might have thought of that before she was pushed into seeking an audience with a monarch. And he, already beginning to change from the great lumpish boy who had inherited, he might have thought what punishment she would deserve if her prophecies did not please him.

The meeting took place in the early summer time, when the roses were in bloom and the fields of Kent were alive with game. The year was 1513. The king had most recently been in Westminster to plan a new war, not war in England this time, but war abroad, in France, where, like other former English kings, he felt he had a God-given right to rule. He was called Henry, eighth of that name, Henry Tudor, and he was desperate for some sign that this invasion would succeed, especially since an earlier one had proved so disastrous that he had threatened to hang his army on its return, down to the meanest mercenary. Why he agreed to meet with a sorceress is a matter of conjecture. Perhaps he still liked to give the illusion he was what he had been, a boy, who took more pleasure in dancing and hunting than affairs of state, and so pretended to see her for a joke. Perhaps he was curious; perhaps he had a superstitious streak; he may even have felt some bond with her; he might have argued that, like her, he was chosen by God (for if she had not looked to be a nun, neither had he looked to be a king; it was only when an older brother, Arthur, died, that the crown had devolved on him). But most of all the thought of his coming French campaign obsessed him, and he wanted its legality approved. In any case, whatever the cause, he allowed his friends to proceed and, under pretext of a hunting expedition, came to a country lodge, deep in the Kentish hinterland, where Sister Elizabeth waited for him.

Picture then this scene. The king, moody, petulant, partly sceptical, partly (the worst part) credulous, slouched in his chair, his polished riding boots pulled high over the strong legs of which he was so proud, his feet beating a tattoo on the floor of the hall where he had deigned to dine, his small eyes closed in thought (although whether he had God, or prophecy in mind, whether he was debating his plan of attack, or was simply digesting the last capon he had swallowed, let no man guess). Certain it was, he would not have come at all unless he had expected compliments, encouragement, praise, all the flattery to which he had become accustomed. Imagine his surprise, which turned as quickly to affront, when he was greeted with none of these familiar pleasantries; imagine his courtiers' consternation when he was met with homilies, with admonitions, lectures, counsel which, at best, might be termed motherly, and at worst bordered on insolence. There sat the king, growing even more restless; and there the Nun Elizabeth, plumped fairly down before him on a wooden stool, her feet in their rustic clogs planted as firmly as his were restless; her nun's habit stretched across her ample lap as if she meant to shell peas; her rosy cheeks beaming with self-righteousness.

'Beware, great king,' she is supposed to have said (although, since she was a simple country woman, used to speaking in a simple way, more like she had no knowledge of courtesy and addressed him by name, as she would have done one of her peasant clients in her peasant days).

'Take care, Henry, what you do. Your father gave us a taste of peace, we expect much more from you. Be careful where you put your trust; your friends are not always as friendly as they seem and your belief in them may be betrayed. These warlords with whom you play at war, this French invasion which you plan, may do you harm at home and may fail again. Instead, turn to peace. Make the king of France your ally; rely on Holy Mother Church to arrange a truce, whatever the cost. And last,' – here all agreed she waxed most eloquent – 'if God has not granted you an heir, perhaps the fault is yours, for flouting His laws. You have married where you should not, your brother's wife, contrary to church decree; perhaps God is punishing you.' And to compound her impertinence she repeated this last warning, her coarse country hands beating in time with the king's nervous scuffling (although had she remained the simple Elizabeth of village fame she might have welcomed a married life herself and certainly would have thought twice before blaming a man for his lack of sons).

How the courtiers felt, those warlords, to hear themselves abused when they had helped arrange the interview; how they, too, felt betrayed, fearful of anything that smacked of treachery; how they fell over themselves to stutter excuses, reproaches, blame – to explain all that would task the imagination: who faulted whom, who suspected what. At least the king heard the nun out, a courtesy he seldom granted anyone, and, in this case, revealed himself a marvel of patience. He had much on his mind these days. Hitherto hunting and feasts had occupied him, not politics. Now the intricacies of government were beginning to intrigue him. He had wed his brother's widow, that was true (although she herself claimed that the first husband had never bedded her); and he certainly still had hopes of a son. He had no ideas, as yet, of putting his wife aside, much less of looking for a new one. But he had also begun to tire of her, as is the way of husbands, kings or not. As for the war he planned, it was also true that he was jealous of the power of France, so jealous that he had attacked it once and was on the verge of attacking it again. Alliance with the French king would not have occurred to him. Finally, although he valued his friends, he had a malicious streak that liked to keep them on edge; he often smiled at them, but that did not mean he trusted where he smiled. He heard the Nun of Kent to the end, pulling at his chin where the thin wisps of a red beard showed; running his hands through his chestnut hair as if to part it from its roots. And when she had done and leaned

11

back, almost panting with triumph, he rose to his feet without a word, threw her some coins from the purse tied to his waist, and swept from the room in a storm of spurs. Not stopping to thank his hosts for their dubious hospitality, not bidding his companions farewell, he sprang on his horse, and whipped it out of the stable yards. In those early years, when he was young, they claimed he could tire eight horses a day, riding the poor beasts until they dropped, and could lose as many huntsmen along the way. Now he rode furiously, alone, making for his court at Richmond, where his queen expected him. What he thought of the Nun of Kent he kept to himself, until a later date proved, or disproved, the substance of her remarks. And those who were present at that meeting slunk away, afraid to speak (although in time, when certain events came to pass, they were to claim prior knowledge).

But there were others, shrewder men, who from the start felt convinced that the lady had been well schooled; what could a simple country woman know of courts and kings, be they English or French, what of queens, unless she had been tutored? Perhaps. She certainly had been taught enough of church affairs to know that among the king's advisers, the most powerful was a churchman, Wolsey by name, and are not church men, by profession, geared to peace, not war? As for friendship, she might have addressed herself to that subject more feelingly, seeing that *her* friends had given her such bad advice, forcing her to lecture the king on kingship, a breach of etiquette for which both she and they would pay a price. Well, the meeting had been arranged, and had taken

12

place; how much the king paid attention to, was influenced for or against by what she said, all that lay in the future, to be revealed. But in the early years of the sixteenth century, when England hoped much from its new king, that good dame of Kent may be remembered for temerity if not for tact. The rest of this story will recount the windings in and out, the effects and results of her prophecy.

CHAPTER 1

—

Vernson Hall lay far off from the court of kings, in the heart of the Devonshire countryside. That October day in the year 1512, its famous garden was already devoid of colour, the roses tattering into shreds, and behind the clipped yew hedges, the old grey house had huddled down, like a sleeping dog. The scene should have been a tranquil one, as calm as the western hills which sloped away on all sides, but Philippa de Verne, only daughter of the house, was blind to its beauty as she walked back and forth through the dew-heavy grass. Today, everything about her seemed on edge, even the air she breathed, and where her swinging braids struck the cobwebs across her path showers of raindrops fell in cold cascades. Her eyes, usually the colour of cornflowers, had darkened like a stormy sea, and her whole body, her whole stance, appeared caught between two things at once, between apprehension and defiance, between grief and fear. Her rounded face, still touched with childhood innocence, had begun to lengthen into adult awareness, and she held herself straight with an effort that was plainly visible. A watcher, a sympathetic watcher, had there been one, might have been touched by her valiant efforts to remain calm. For most of all it was her fear that showed.

Away in the distance she could hear the thuck, thuck, thuck, of the woodman's axe, rising above the more common sounds of kitchen and farm. That dull continuing scrape of steel against wood was like a blow to her own flesh and she almost felt the tree stumps bared like bones. She covered her ears. Behind her closed eyes her stepfather stood out, just as he had last night, legs apart, his stocky body decked in the silks which he liked (and which her father's property, her *real* father's property that is, paid for, the property that now should be hers). As if imitating a little courtier, he cocked his head at those falling trees, his jaunty cap pulled on one side. The same self-satisfied smile would cross his face and he would smooth his beard in the same smug way. 'What else is wood good for?' he would ask, gesturing to the avenue of oaks, old when Vernson Hall had been built. 'The very thing to build my house, my new house to fit these new times. Where else should I bring my new bride? How else should I spend *my* new wealth? And when you marry, as I mean to have you do, and send you far from here, what will your protest matter to anyone.' And he would smile, just as he had smiled last night.

Last night that stepfather, Thomas Higham, had summoned her, the first time she had met with him since her mother's death had orphaned her three weeks before. Master Higham had installed himself in the main room of Vernson Hall as if it already belonged to him. For

Philippa, that old medieval room had always seemed the heart of the house, with its huge fireplace and faded tapestries and sagging floors; she had always felt safe there, where generations of de Vernes had lived. To see Master Higham take it for his own, usurping her father's place (albeit her father had died when she was born), even to sitting in her mother's favourite chair, had given Philippa a strange sensation, like a coldness to the heart, like a warning.

Perhaps last night she had obeyed Master Higham's summons out of some sense of pity for him; to imagine him alone, bereaved and sad had disturbed her. Perhaps she had had some vague hope that she might comfort him, as he her, for all that he had always ignored her even when her mother had been alive. After all, she had told herself, three weeks is not long to grieve, and I myself have never felt so bereft. But Master Higham, Bully Higham as the villagers called him, had felt no need of pity for himself, and as little need for pitying her. Up he had jumped when she had come in, as bright as a robin in his crimson coat, no mourning garments for him, and no time for mourning. More than ever he had looked out of place in that room, with his broad solid frame straining at his gentleman's coat, and his broad solid legs, too short for straddling a gentleman's horse, a peasant tripping over a sword. And more than ever she had felt his dislike of her, held in check perhaps while her mother lived, now spilling out unrestrainedly.

Nor had he been alone. A man and lady had kept him company, one on either side of the hearth, so that Philippa had been trapped between them both, like facing two school masters at once. She had taken the

17

couple for a married pair, the woman of ripe, childbear-
ing age, a vigorous woman with thick dark hair and a
determined chin, as outspoken as her own mother had
been quiet. Philippa had not met the woman before but
the husband (or so he seemed) she had heard of. He was
plainly old, thin-shanked, scant-locked, his doublet
bursting over a paunch, his hand gripped nervously
around a tankard of ale. He was a companion of her
stepfather's, of whom the villagers had much to tell;
nothing sharper, they used to whisper, than Master
Simeon's long nose for ferreting out titles to land; nothing
faster than his legal tricks for cheating a man of what was
his. He and her stepfather had long been friends; wherever he went they claimed trouble followed close behind.
One look at him and his furtive stance and all those old
stories had come crowding back to put her on the alert.

Her first thought had been that, as a lawyer whose
ways were well known, Master Simeon must have been
summoned too, to give her stepfather legal advice. Or
perhaps he had come to advise her; was there her
mother's will to read or a last request to discuss? These
possibilities had seemed daunting enough, until she had
realized that Master Simeon was to appear in quite a
different sort of guise. And then she had been appalled.

When she had entered the room, knocking carefully
on the door to avoid offence, he had laboured up, with a
show of agility, doffing his cap with an elaborate bow,
and twisting his thin lips into a smile. That conspiratorial
smirk had roused her suspicions anew, as had her stepfather's accompanying bow. Master Higham had never
shown her courtesy before, why should he now offer it?

18

His unabashed encouragement of his old crony had soon revealed the reason.

'Come Master Simeon,' Thomas Higham had cried, giving the older man a nudge so that the contents of the tankard splashed upon the floor. 'No call to hang back; let's see your wit.' He had flapped his own cap as if shooing away flies. 'Master Simeon, stepdaughter,' he had introduced his friend, 'who craves a word with you.' And he had given another nudge, at the same time winking behind his hand at the woman, as at some private joke.

This attempt at pleasantry had been worse than his usual disdain. Philippa was used to disdain. And his urging on of his friend had seemed grotesque, as if Master Simeon himself had been uncertain how to proceed, and almost loath to start. Something her mother once had said seemed to ring in her ears. 'When Thomas Higham looks pleased, beware of him.' She had felt the blood drain from her face as she had looked from him to Master Simeon and back again, examining the older man more carefully. And what she saw had confirmed her fears.

Master Simeon had obviously dressed with care. His clothes certainly would have better fitted a younger man for they had hung about him in folds, the yellow hose wrinkling about his calves, the yellow lining of his cape emphasizing the yellow of his skin. His strange unease had matched ill with his reputation for sharpness, and showed little of his famed legal skill. And when at length he had begun to speak, his lisping formality had been equally ill-suited to his words, revealing him not so much as a lawyer, full of cunning legality, but as a suitor, bashful and shy.

'So, little mistress, it seems we are to be friends,' he had brought out at last, rubbing his hands down his sides as if to dry the palms, and swallowing hard. 'I hear,' he had stammered after a while, 'that you are in the market for a husband. Look no more; here he is.' And he had struck a pose that would have looked foolish on a love-struck swain. When that had failed to impress he had winked as if to make her his confidante. 'I have long been looking for a wife,' he had said in more normal tones, 'so why should not our two lives be joined as one? Together we could make a pair, you taking me and I taking you, so our twin needs be met.'

Philippa's own disbelief and shock must have shown for her stepfather had set down his goblet with a crash. 'Master Simeon is a God-fearing man,' he had cried, 'as honest a widower as ever breathed, and a wealthy one. He wants a wife. He will not refuse a maid who is not all she thinks she is.' And when Philippa had remained dumb, 'He is willing, unlike most men, to accept you as you are, dowerless, without family or influence. In your place most wenches would count themselves fortunate. Think yourself lucky he asks for you.'

Before Philippa could answer, the lady had stirred. 'Wait now,' she had purred. 'These men, God save us, have no idea how to woo. They are too rough. What they mean is that your lack of dowry only enhances your own worth. And so it does.' She had given the men a look from her hard eyes as if to say, 'Watch your manners.' To Philippa she had gone on, in the same soothing voice, 'But although God knows Master Simeon is old enough to take maidenly reserve with a pinch of salt, on your part a little enthusiasm would not seem out of place. Come child (the expression had sounded all the more grotesque since it was one that Philippa's mother had often used), come child, be sensible and accept. Besides, no doubt, out of his good heart, your stepfather will be generous and give you a little something from his own pocket to start you off, as good a beginning to married life as anyone's.'

Again, Philippa had been too startled to respond. Thought of a betrothal had never crossed her mind, certainly never with so old a man. But perhaps he appealed to her stepfather as a son-in-law. What would it matter that he were thrice her age? Master Simeon was someone her stepfather could rely upon, of his own rank and sort, someone who could understand his own needs, someone who probably had supported him before in some devious scheme. Master Simeon's role she now understood very well, and her stepfather's. But she still could not place the woman.

Forcing herself to respond, the words seeming to stick in her throat, Philippa had made herself curtsy her thanks, pointing out that as she was still in mourning marriage was out of place. As for her lack of dowry, she had tried to explain, there must be some mistake, for she was her father's only heir, now that her mother was deceased. But when she had questioned who the lady was, her stepfather had smiled unpleasantly; he might have been playing with his pot-fellows at hazard and had just produced the winning throw. 'I thought you would never ask,' he had said, almost triumphantly. 'Meet my betrothed. Meet the new mistress of Higham Hall. She

21

will grace my new house, which I mean to build when I have torn the old one down.'

And he had flapped his cap again and bowed.

'A worthy dame.' After a while Master Simeon had felt obliged to pipe up. He had been noticeably quiet during this last exchange, perhaps not liking the idea explicit in the word 'dowerless', and grateful to the lady for that hint of generosity. Now, regaining confidence, as if relieved the worst had been said, he had gone on in a wheedling tone, much as he might use to convince a recalcitrant juror, 'So, Mistress Philippa, no need to be coy. Your hesitation, although to your credit, has no place in this room. Your stepfather, your new step-mother, give their accord, and so must you. Why, even your blue eyes suggest compliance.' And he had wheezed out compliments, in a splutter of courtship, a grandsire aping a grandson.

Caught between them like a mouse batted back and forth, Philippa had felt the ground rock beneath her feet. Only some unexpected reserve of strength had made her realize that if she did not stand up for herself she would be overwhelmed. Defiance was new to her, but since there was no one else to rely upon she had made herself articulate. 'My eyes may be blue,' she had said at last, 'but they see clearly what is beneath my nose. Master Higham is free to marry whom he likes; that is none of my concern. But Vernson Hall belongs to me. Who else should it belong to? As for changing its name, it has been called after my forebears for over three hundred years; who would call it otherwise? And when I wed it comes with me, along with all my father's lands.'

22

At these words, Master Simeon had looked uncomfortable, shuffling his feet in their pointed slippers and rubbing his hands. She had heard him mutter under his breath, 'You said she would cause no difficulty. You called her lively, not shrewish. I am too old to welcome trouble in my own household, even if you have paid me well for it, and I certainly have no place for shrews.'

Her stepfather had silenced him with a slap on the back. 'Be a man,' he had cried. 'You are in too far to draw out.' And to Philippa, 'Keep a civil tongue,' he had said, 'or a whip will clamp it shut. Your claim to Vernson Hall ends when I marry to beget sons, or when you do, as I mean you shall.'

His repetition of his new marriage plan had sickened Philippa, to think that this woman would take her mother's place. But it had pleased the woman. She had leaned forward importantly so that her full breasts showed above the square-cut neckline, and had spread her skirts of rich taffeta, to make them rustle. When she had smoothed her lap one of the de Verne rings had shone on her finger like a challenge. 'My dear,' she had cooed, dove calm, 'I would not speak out of place. But as a bride I would like to have my new husband and new house to myself, without a great stepdaughter about, almost my age. Why, they will think we are sisters.' She had giggled falsely. 'Now, when I was as young as you,' she had preened herself, 'when I married my first husband, my father had to beat me every day until I agreed. How I cried!' She had pulled at Philippa's arm, adding in a confidential tone, 'But when that first husband died, see how rich I became. Master Simeon is as rich, and if you wait a while, so will you be.' And she winked in her

23

turn, as if to suggest that, woman to woman, they could understand each other on this point.

'I am no horse to be flogged,' Philippa had cried at last. 'Nor do I need to marry wealth. Find some other suitor if you wish me to wed. This one needs a nurse-maid, not a wife. Hire some other lawyer to do your work. For I do not believe a word.'

What an uproar had ensued. Even now, this morning, the shouts still reverberated like the falling of those trees. How her stepfather had howled; how his accomplice had looked pale and wiped his face as if regretting his offer; how the lady had scowled, every attempt at friendship gone. All three had begun to speak at once, such a jumble of lawyer's talk, of agreements and bargainings, of dis-positions, legal rights, king's courts, that she could scarcely disentangle them. They might have stayed argu-ing all night had not her stepfather, gritting his teeth in suppressed rage, pushed her from the room, promising further speech when she was in a 'gentler' mood, a reprieve that was meant to soothe Master Simeon as much as her. But the sleepless night that followed had not brought that change of heart; only, in the shiftings of predawn, a clarification of some parts. So that now, walking back and forth in the autumn garden of her home, she could begin to marshal her thoughts, as if to put some sense to them.

First, it was certain that her stepfather meant to marry her off, so that, in some way, he could keep her lands for himself. Secondly, Master Simeon was intended to be the means by which those lands were kept, and she as bride was to be the reward for his help. But thirdly, and most importantly, if she were the bribe, and if her stepfather had restrained his anger last night, so as not to frighten Master Simeon away, mayhap those plans were not as sound as he had made out. 'I know a girl has little choice,' Philippa told herself. 'I know my stepfather is stronger than I am. But he cannot force me to wed. And I do not have to give up my lands.'

Brave words these. The difficulty lay in turning words to deeds. Were I that boy he spoke of, she thought, I might succeed. As a mere girl what can I do? Is not a girl as good as a boy; does not a daughter have rights as well?

She thought, this house was sufficient for my father and for my father's father. It sheltered them all through their lives. My father died here in his bed. It should be good enough for me. But she also thought, my mother, God rest her soul, was never happy here, for all she used to say she was, and seldom complained. Yet the truth is that nothing went well for her since my father's death and she married a second time. I do not know why she wed as she did, but I do know she regretted Thomas Higham as her choice. And she was afraid of him. But that does not mean I have to be afraid; I do not have to show him my fear.

Down the garden path she went, quickly now, her mind made up, past the orchard and the vegetable plots, out of the small wicker gates that led to the back road, as if escaping everything that troubled her, as if to put it out of mind.

The back road was narrow, more like a track, trenched with rut of cart and plough. One way it edged around the park beyond the main gates to where, in a dip of the hill, the village of Vernson lay grouped about the church. She guessed that the villagers would be standing there at

25

their doors, listening, waiting for the trees to fall. Fear is what they were whispering about, she thought, fear that Master Higham will destroy them too, after he has destroyed Vernson Hall. They need someone to rely upon, they should be protected as well.

The left-hand track ran straight through open or common land, until it joined a main highway. Eastward, that highway led beyond her small world into a larger one, out of Devonshire, out of western England, across a kingdom. Usually she went no further than the edge of the common land, avoiding a thing that had once frightened her. Yet today she sensed that this was the way she must go, as if some impulse were compelling her.

It was colder in the open, and the wind blew fitfully. Her wooden clogs were not made for walking in and rubbed her heels and the dust made her eyes smart. Presently she came to the junction with the highway. She stared at it for a while, where it wound about and up and down in a thin white line. Then she turned aside, over a stile, and began to follow the direction in which it led, but on the inner side of the hedge. She had not gone back along the road itself, not since she was a child and had once passed a thing that haunted her. This way, shielded by the high thick hedge, she thought she could avoid seeing it again. Nevertheless, she kept her head bent and her eyes half-closed. Behind her lowered eyelids an image started out at her as she had seen it then, a strange bare tree dangling with fruit. There is a game children play on All Hallow's Night, bobbing for apples strung on a line and she had cried out at the sight, clutching the groomsman who had carried her, until, realizing what she was looking at he had spurred his horse around. Never had she gone that way again, to look upon the gallows tree with its fruit of men. But off the road, through the fields, what danger was there of seeing it, a thing so full of dread that she had never dared mention it. Off the road, who would look for her, a girl running away from home. In her heart she knew that soon both fears would join as one.

The soil of the fields was red and thick, the rich soil of a Devon farm. The mud clung to the sides of her clogs making them so uneven that she had to scrape them off. Her skirt hems were soon dyed a deep dull red; before her, flocks of seagulls took to the air, and settled back like snowflakes after she had passed. This is where the wealth of de Verne land comes from, she thought, not from cheating and stealing and legal tricks, such as Thomas Higham and Master Simeon love. This land is in my blood and bone. Even if my stepfather tears down my house and changes its name he cannot take that from me.

On she trudged, a small resolute figure, across those fields where since ancient times master and men had lived in accord. Ahead of her, the pasture stretched with its great sweep of grass. And beyond again, the last of those hedges where she would regain the road. She thought, a hundred years on from now, a hundred hundred perhaps, what will it matter, Master Simeon's and my stepfather's schemes? If a girl like me should run through these fields as I am doing now, she would follow the same track, keep to the same contour of the valley and hill, cross the same stream. Even we do not own the land; it owns us. She thought, now that both my poor mother and father are dead it is my duty to hold firm; I

27

must keep what was theirs for the good of everyone. Here is the end of my father's estate; beyond it stretches the whole wide world. Here is where I should make my stand. God grant me the strength to uphold it.

Partly afraid, partly eager, she began to run towards her future.

CHAPTER 2

—

Coming up that same east road, newly arrived at one of the little coastal ports, an entirely different group was approaching. They were as slow as Mistress Philippa was quick, although they rode on horseback. They were English, but far from home as their north-country voices showed, and they and their horses were tired. From time to time the poor beasts lowered their heads to the thick grass verges, and the men let them graze. They were mercenary soldiers, up for hire; or had been. Their swords and pikes were sharp and clean and they kept their breast-plates on, although they themselves were dirty, travel-stained, their faces unshaven, their feet wrapped in rags. Many had been wounded, yet they still held to some semblance of discipline, maintaining a sort of casual watch. But they had that glazed look of men not sure that they had returned to England, from that French hell that had buried them. These were the remnants of the king's first expedition, those he had sworn to hang if he could lay his hands on them. He had no need to threaten them; defeat had already done most of his work for him.

If these men thought of anything they were longing for plates of hot food, goblets of good strong English ale, and clean soft beds, with a willing wench to share with them. The last thing they expected was to have a wench tumble in their midst.

Brisk walking through those autumn fields had helped restore Mistress Philippa de Verne's spirits. She swung her scarf loose, hitched up her skirts out of the mud, kicked off her clogs and hose to feel the autumn grass between her toes. Let Thomas Higham try to demolish my house and marry me off to steal my land she thought, that does not mean he will succeed. And giving wing to her thoughts she scrambled down towards the last hedge, a thick west-country hedge, banked with turf and briars. Finding a gap she thrust through the bramble canes, until she pitched headlong onto the road, under the hooves of the leading horse.

It shied and snorted, backing away, jarring the others in the line, unseating one man, and leaving another grasping for his reins. Those closest to her snatched for their swords; those in the rear shouted encouragement; the fallen man rolled and clasped his wounded arm, bellowing in outrage. Crouched in their midst Mistress Philippa covered her head with her hands to avoid being trampled on, and stared about her in alarm.

'Now, by Christ,' the wounded trooper finally found breath to gasp, 'this is too much.' He tried to lever himself up, his square, northern face streaked with mud, his round eyes hard. Shooting out his good arm he grasped her ankle fast. He meant of course that to be tossed on his back by a maid was a final insult, but his fellow soldiers were quick to take his meaning in another sense. Snatching stealthy glances round to ensure their captain was not in sight, they began to laugh. 'Not too much for me,' one cried, while another, slapping his horse to make it side-step wickedly, rephrased the jest. 'Or if for you, not for us,' *a willing wench*, and here she was, a gift from heaven; no wonder they all sat up straight and their eyes gleamed. Those who were young (as most were, raw recruits, culled from some border farm or country village) licked their lips, flicked back their hair, grown overlong and full of lice. The older men put up their swords and unbuckled their belts, preparing for action. Food, ale, sleep, suddenly those needs could wait. After the whores of Guienne, a clean English one would be more than welcome and would serve as proof, nothing better, that they were safe in England.

They were dirty, hungry, anger running beneath the surface. For six months they had seen good comrades die unnecessarily; even their own generals had abandoned them. Unpaid, forced to find their own way home, no wonder they felt God meant them to enjoy themselves. The wounded man still held Philippa's foot; another grasped her by the arm; a third, coming from behind, caught her by her long hair and whistled as he saw her face. 'Marry, come up,' he crooned, trying to take her chin between forefinger and thumb. 'We means no harm. You'll not refuse us, certain sure, soldiers of the king, returned from foreign parts. Don't we deserve some recompense, better'n what he planned for us? Shouldn't it be an honour to greet us?' And he spat and cleared his throat, already savouring that welcome.

31

Pinioned hand and foot, terrified by the milling horses and hot-eyed men, Philippa remained crouched like a hare in its nest. Her eyes had grown wide, her skin pale; her breath came in great gasps. She had never seen men like this in her life and she struggled desperately to pull out of their reach. Their hard mouths, suddenly gaping into smiles amid the stubble of their beards, reminded her of hounds, all froth and teeth. The hands reaching for her were claws. It began to dawn on her that she herself was the quarry and in a panic she started to scrabble back towards the hedge, trying to snatch her skirts away, trying to shake herself free of that cruel grip, crying out to let her go.

The man Philippa had tossed on the ground had begun to grin, a sly grin, bright with anticipation. 'By rights of capture the first turn be mine,' he howled. *First turn.* First turn for what? Fear twisted her innards in a knot, starting the sweat upon her face. It dawned on her that for all her boasts that she was as good as any boy, dreadful, shameful things hung in the air simply because she was a girl. These laughing men were not laughing any more; dreadful shameful thoughts were hidden behind their eyes, and she was far from help. She began to struggle in earnest now; the more she struggled the more they seemed pleased, roused by her terror as they had been by her beauty, until the one who claimed first turn advanced purposefully, pushing her backwards with his foot and fumbling with his netherhose. As he threw himself down on her she tried to fight him off, holding tight to the bushes and screaming, turning her face to avoid his hot rough breath, twisting her body to avoid his.

Half a mile down the road, hidden behind some trees

where he had stopped to help one of his men, their captain heard that scream, and swore. He had been uneasy at letting the rest of his troop proceed, although at their slow pace he should have had no difficulty in catching them. Today, more than usual, he had been watching them like a hawk. He knew how close they were to breaking point, but after all they had suffered he did not mean to let them break, not on this last part of their journey home. With a savageness born of weariness he heaved himself on his roan horse with as much agility as his broken ribs allowed, and swung into a gallop. He had been dreading a confrontation of some sort. Mercenaries are never popular and rape on a country lane would not endear them. He cursed again the stupid female who had let herself be caught; he cursed the fools among his troops who had let temptation get the better of them. He burst into their midst, flailing about him with the flat of his sword as if he would hack them all apart.

His men recognized his anger and concern, having come to know the mixture well. They scrambled out of his way, trying to pretend nothing had happened, putting on that air of injured innocence typical of soldiers everywhere; all, that is, except the first man, who still remained crouched over the woman he meant to have.

'Stand back.' The rough fury's edge in the newcomer's voice was terrifying. 'Leave her alone.' A string of soldier's oaths followed, a violent clattering; the captain leapt to the ground with an agility that belied his wounds. Hurling himself on the crouching man he knocked him aside with one hard blow.

'Nay,' the trooper had wind enough to howl. 'She

came willing-like, so willing she threw herself in front of me. Ask her.'

Still gripping the branches she had wound about her fingers Philippa was obliged to look up. She was staring at scuffed boots, crusted with dirt, their sides slashed as if by spears or pikes. Above them rose long legs, encased in equally dirty hose, above them a doublet, mud-caked too, that once might have been velvet trimmed, now stained and flecked with rust, pulled awry over an even filthier shirt, all topped by a face on which anger was written in every line. The large dark eyes smouldered with rage, the long mouth was tight with it, the black hair, dark as a raven's wing with a raven's blue tint, was stiff and caked with it. But the face itself was surprisingly young to be a captain to this crew, unshaven, with long locks curling down to his ears, and sun-bronzed skin, shadowed beneath those fierce dark eyes with lines of fatigue and pain.

'There's no need to ask.' Philippa let her voice out with a rush. 'Do I look as if I tumble in the dust with men?' She tried to pull herself to her feet, with as much dignity as she could, although the words came out in puffs and she still was shaking.

The dark eyes narrowed for a moment, then unexpectedly, seemed to smile. She could see he was taking in what his men had not, the way she spoke, the fine clothes beneath the mud, the velvet edging, the lace. And beyond all these things, the youthfulness, the inexperience.

'Alone?' His question mocked. 'Where is your escort, where your maids? Where are your shoes?' He began to grin. 'You ask overmuch indulgence of my men. I might have made the same mistake.'

His mockery made her gasp. 'How dare you?' she cried. 'Captain or not, deal with these scum as they deserve. Punish them, or I shall demand justice myself.'

He rammed his sword into its sheath but did not move, his legs apart, planted firmly on either side of her skirts.

'Courtesy if you please,' he corrected her. 'These are men, my men in fact, and I am responsible for them. We have returned from fighting for your well-being, mistress, and are in no mood for silly games. If you plan to offer solace as a woman might, at least make up your mind to be quick and quiet.'

He shot a look at her. 'And if you've the wish to be gone, then go, where you belong. But for God's sake leave the ordering of my men to me.'

He strode away. She could hear him, quieter now, sending some back to retrieve their companion left behind, sending others ahead to search out lodging. His disinterest suddenly bothered her. In a day so full of mishap, it mattered that he should not misunderstand her. Free to scramble away, instead she went up to him and grasped his arm. As he rounded on her, 'Aye,' she said, 'knock me down, you and your company seem good at that. But show me some courtesy in return. No one has accused me of falsehood before. I came through that hedge there, about my own affairs. I never knew your men were here. I have as much right as they to be in this place, upon this road. No, more, since all the land behind it belongs to me. The road you stand upon, the hills, the woods, all border de Verne property.'

The dark eyes narrowed again, and the lips tightened in a soundless whistle. Then the mouth twitched. 'Am I to understand, lady,' he said, with a wryness in his voice that she found equally infuriating, 'that you wish me to apologize because my men did not recognize you? If this is de Verne land, who the devil are you?'

She drew herself up to her full height, not much beside his, especially since she had lost her shoes. 'I am Philippa,' she told him, proud as a peacock herself, 'only daughter of Edward de Verne, once lord of Vernson Hall and the village which bears his name.'

There was no doubt of his surprise. His eyes (which were not so black as she had thought, more dark brown than black, fringed with long black lashes) showed a momentary hesitation, and he ran a perplexed hand through his hair so that it stood on end. 'De Verne land,' he repeated, looking round, as if he expected to see the name carved on the trees. 'Then you must be "Sweet Ned's" child.' He gave her another long look, then smiled, a wholehearted, open and generous smile. 'There was a brave and noble soul,' he said after a pause, in which he seemed to be thinking of what to say. 'And he died bravely, before the world, as he was a Devon gentleman.'

She had never heard her father spoken of in that way. 'Sweet Ned' had a pleasing sound, but as for his death, 'You are mistaken, sir,' she told him. 'My father, God rest his soul, died here at Vernson Hall, of plague they say, the same year that I was born. But he was a Devonshire man, Edward de Verne, and perhaps a sweet man, although I do not claim that, never having heard

36

him so described. But certainly he was my father, as my mother lived to tell.'

The young captain's eyebrows contracted into a thin line and his mouth tightened to snap out some reply; he looked down his nose at her in a haughty way that seemed characteristic of him. 'Edward, the last lord of the house,' he repeated impatiently. 'There cannot be two men with the same name, and this, I presume, is Devon land; certainly not two in Devonshire.' He would have said more but stopped himself, tugging at his shirt as if the collar had grown too tight, almost as if he were debating with himself. Finally discretion won. He limped back to his own roan and hauled himself into the saddle with an effort that this time was plainly visible. 'Well, Mistress Philippa de Verne,' he drawled. He had a pleasant way of speaking when he wanted, she thought, and his smile could almost be called attractive. 'I beg your pardon. It seems that twice we have mistaken you. But if this is de Verne land, and if you are its mistress I think you might show my men hospitality rather than revenge. They have had a long hard journey so far, and a long hard one to come. It would be a Christian kindness to shelter them.'

He spoke formally, no longer the rough soldier but a gentleman, and his voice had a persuasion that was hard to resist. But there was still something hidden under those courtesies which puzzled Philippa. She knew hospitality was due to travellers, but how could she bring them home? Her stepfather's parsimony was notorious. As was her habit when in doubt she gnawed her thumb, unaware of how innocent her indecision made her seem,

37

and how young. It caused the captain to smile again, and, for a second, a look came over his face, as if he were allowing himself the luxury of appreciating her soft skin, her wide-set eyes, the brightness of her hair for all that it was snarled into ringlets; as if for a moment he let himself imagine the delights his men had dreamed of.

And what of those men? Intent on making herself known, Mistress Philippa had paid them scant heed, but their captain had been aware of them, even when his back had been turned. He sensed the uncertain mood of the younger ones and knew that Philippa's hesitation had given them the opportunity they had been looking for. Their leader was the man Philippa had unhorsed. He was glowering, his square-jawed face suddenly stiffening into ugly lines, biding his time to make a move.

'Scum is it?' he now shouted, his voice thick, his north country speech pronounced. 'Who be she to call us scum? De Verne is a name I recalls as well as you.' And his fellows, muttering behind him began to step forward, closing ranks.

The captain remained calm. 'Now lads,' he told them, as casually as before, although his look grew sharp. 'We are nearly home, no use to lose our senses over a woman. As for you, John of Netherstoke, there will be plenty more as good. What is one more to you?'

But to the girl he snarled an aside. 'God's my life, but you're the fool, not to run when you had the chance. Get behind me, quick, before we are caught in an open brawl.' And without giving her time to resist, he dragged her off her feet, pulling her willy-nilly over the rump of his horse so that it kicked, forcing her to cling to him in a flurry of petticoats, pivoting round all the while to ensure no one could creep up unawares, shifting his belt

38

so that the hilt of his sword swung within easy reach.

It was too late to stop the malcontents with a show of force. One cried, 'One wench perhaps, but it seems she's yours, not ours.' While that John of Netherstoke, still nursing his wounded pride, shouted, 'Your commission ended overseas; here in England we be quit of it. De Verne land means traitor's land. Shall a traitor's whelp get the better of us? We've had a belly full of traitors. And what's loyalty given us, except the threat of a hanging when we returned? I knows my rights. I claim that wench as soldier's due, let no man say me nay.'

There was a hush. Philippa could feel a tension running down the captain's spine and along his sword arm, as it seemed to tighten almost instinctively. Yet he leaned forward in the saddle, as if trying to reason. She sensed rather than heard the involuntary grunt of pain this movement caused but his voice remained unruffled. 'Who bleats about conspiracy?' he asked. 'We left treachery behind in Guienne. When we sailed from France I swore that I would lead us safely home and I do not mean to be forsworn.' He suddenly thrust out his hand imperiously, signalling out John of Netherstoke. 'And you promised to follow me,' he cried. 'I'll bring you back to your mother in one piece, although whether we carry you in a sack or you ride in on your own, is up to you. Knot up your tongue, John of Netherstoke, or by Christ, I'll hang you in it myself. Mount up. We feed tonight at Vernson Hall; judge if the de Vernes be true or false when you have downed your first jug of Devonshire ale.'

He flashed a look about him, crowding that roan horse forward now to make the little group of men retreat. He waited a second time for Philippa to respond, a second

39

time openly offering her a cue she could not misunderstand. She knew what was expected of her but shame kept her quiet.

Silence gave the malcontents the chance they wanted. They began to shout, disappointment fuelling their rebellion's fire. 'Nothing give, nothing have,' one screamed, while their spokesman, John of Netherstoke, leapt forward and clasped her skirts, tearing at the flounces to drag her off, clawing at her, until his captain's balled fist at his throat made him reel aside, gasping for breath, his legs buckling under him. The roan horse reared once more, pawed at the air, forcing the other men away. Then the captain gathered up the reins, and with a violent curse breasted through the hedge, tearing the top apart in a shower of dirt. Left behind in the road the soldiers bunched in dismay, not one daring the same leap. Shouts, recriminations, threats died away as horse and riders thundered up the hill towards the ploughed land ahead.

Terrified by this fresh outbreak of violence, Philippa caught snatches of his oaths, Christ's balls, the least of them, what a simpleton she was, dear God, without the sense she was born with, not even the decency to offer hospitality, were they lepers? Well, he might have known, women ever misery. And what a greater fool was he, to risk his men in argument. God's life, but they had done her no real harm, not as great as the harm she did, to undo their fellowship. She felt the injustice of it like a knife, and yet at the same time realized there was some truth to what he said. But before she could tell him so she sensed that he, in turn, had calmed down and was regarding her quizzically over his shoulder, almost amused. Now it so happened that, terrified of being thrown to the ground she had been clinging to him all this while, and even, as he slowed, had continued to wrap her arms about his waist, hanging on for dear life. A gasp of pain forced her to pay attention as he prised her hands loose.

'Have you never sat a horse before, nor ridden with a man? You squeeze me half to death.' His wry grin made her blush. She pulled away, so abruptly she would have slid down the horse's tail had he not caught her to bring her upright. Held against him like that, so close she could feel his breath upon her cheek, Philippa had another chance to look at him. She had not noticed before the pallor underlying the sun-brown of his skin; nor the slash on his forehead beneath the curls. She had not realized that the specks on his shirt were not from rust but blood. 'Dear God,' she could not keep the dismay from her voice, 'you are hurt,' remembering suddenly the halting limp, the involuntary gasp. He returned her look levelly. 'It is a soldier's lot,' he told her, with the same wry smile. 'No more than what my men have suffered. I told you, mistress, they were brave. But if you, on the other hand, are, as you say, heiress to Vernson Hall (and I think you are, for you are very much like your father in hair and looks, and perhaps in smile, although you have not yet smiled at me), I wish you had welcomed us. It would have made things easier for them and me, and would have avoided this unpleasantness.'

Once more she hung her head not sure how to reply. And when she glanced up she saw he was watching her with that same concentrated concern that seemed to be

41

habitual to him. 'Or is it,' he asked, more softly, 'that the mistress of the hall has run from home? In which case, we will set you down at your gates and bother you no more.'

Her downcast expression, her repeated gestures of indecision, gave her away, and touched him despite himself, for in truth he was tired and not much in the mood to play at nursemaid to some silly girl, not while he had his men to gather up, their confidence to rewin, their own journey to complete. He sighed. 'Come then, show me the route to the back door; 'tis too cold for wandering far barefoot,' and kicking his horse forward he headed for the closest hedge, looking for a weak place where he could rejoin the road, for the moment abandoning his companions.

When she saw what he intended she clutched him tighter than ever, his wounded ribs forgotten. 'Not by the road,' she cried. Her face had gone milk-pale, and tears were trembling on the edge of her thick eyelashes, although she had shed none before. 'Keep to the fields on this side of the hedge if you please.'

He eyed her, a thoughtful appraising look, as if to ask, 'What game is it that you are playing?' When it became obvious that no pretence could have counterfeited such terror he curbed his impatience in a way that afterwards surprised him, and resettled her arms so that they did not press him so hard. All he said was, 'Lady, my horse is too tired to push through those ploughed fields ahead. Nor do I have all the time in the world. My men will be waiting for me to return. They rely on me you see, and there's a fact. But since you have obliged me to leave them so precipitously I should take it as a courtesy to be rid of you as soon as possible.' Again he gave a wry grin. 'I mean you no ill-will, you understand,' he said, 'but the road is shorter and easier. The quicker I leave you the quicker I go back for them. So, why not by the road?'

Her voice had grown so soft, that he had to catch her by the chin, forcing her head up. 'Why not?' he repeated more sharply. 'Mother of God, what's amiss with a simple highway that it forces us to go sliding through the mud, like ploughboys?'

When she gestured frantically, her voice gone beyond horror, for the first time he looked clearly in the direction she was pointing at. And there, coming over the line of bushes was the gibbet, black and stark, its chains rusting emptily away, where it had been standing all those years before.

He held her close then, letting her burrow her head into his arms, comforting her at first almost absentmindedly as he would a child. Her mouth was just beneath his own, he could touch it, gently to begin with, then more passionately as he felt her respond. All the frustrations of the day, hers and his, were suddenly in that kiss, as her lips parted to meet with his, as her arms went around his neck to hold him close. 'Take me with you,' she was saying between breaths, 'do not leave me here. I cannot go back home.'

He felt her young body arch against his, pliable, ready for his. He felt his own body move to meet hers despite his wounds. And torn between wanting her, not wanting, he continued to kiss her ardently, and as eagerly she kissed him. In the end he pushed her away, holding her off with something between a sigh and groan. 'Come, little mistress,' he said with a half smile, that was more at himself than her. 'It is not often I have such an opportunity, and I wish I could stay to enjoy it. But go I must. And so must you. Love on horseback is not exactly comfortable. And although I would do you no harm, it might not be good for you.' He smoothed her hair again, cupping her face between his hands. 'So let me take you back to Vernson Hall to your friends.'

'I have none left,' she told him, openly honest, her honesty clear like flame, touching him again despite herself, emphasizing her youthfulness. 'Let me come with you. I would not even expect to ride with you, just keep you in sight. I would make no demands on you, just thank you for your protection. As I thank you now for what you have just done for me.'

He smiled, the same half smile. 'I wish you could,' he said, 'but you know it cannot be.' He unclasped her hands that were still holding him. 'We must part,' he told her softly but firmly, 'but do not think too harshly of me.' He hesitated. 'And do not judge the past too harshly either,' he said. 'We cannot change it. I tell you this from my own experience who have already lost so many companions in this king's war that I cannot bear to lose another one. That gallows-tree back there has not been used in many years, and God willing, will not be used again, as long as the house of Tudor keeps the peace as it promised to. Better to fight abroad, say I, than fight our fellow countrymen.'

She tried to wipe her eyes, tried to appear calm, although her chin still trembled. 'Are you a Tudor man?' she asked him finally, seriously. Her little attempt at pride touched him as much as her tears had done. 'Yes,' he said. 'But my family was for Lancaster first as yours I

44

think was for York. That was over long ago.' He straightened in the saddle. 'And now,' he said gently, 'we'll take you back.'

He turned the horse away from the hedge, and re-directed it towards the ploughed fields, wading resignedly through the red mud that mired it to its hocks. The gallows with its black outline, like a half-completed cross, sank back behind the hedge and was lost to view. And slowly almost regretfully he brought her to the gates which she had left, it seemed, hours ago. And there he set her down.

She detained him one last time. 'And if,' she asked almost shyly, with a smile that had both sweetness and longing in it, 'I should wish to thank you, what name shall I ask for?'

He smiled back. 'In the king's court,' he said, 'I shall use my father's name. He was Lord Richard Montacune, of Netherstoke, in Northumberland, a northern shire. My men and I left from there, over a year ago, and there I return, God willing so. But to my friends, I am known as Dick.'

Now it was his turn to hesitate before taking up her hand, holding it loosely between both of his. 'I would that we were friends,' he said. And as she continued to look at him, 'Come sweetheart,' he said almost helplessly. 'A kiss is not so great a thing, that it means the end of the world. There will be plenty of others in time.' She suddenly flashed her full smile at him, like a burst of sunlight. 'Oh,' she said, simple as a child, wise as a woman, 'I did not mind. It is only I wish you would kiss me once again, so I should remember you. And so that you might have something to remember me by.'

And laughing now himself, with an effort that caused him more pain than he cared to admit, he stretched down and lifted her so he could. 'Now then,' he said, 'fare you well. But if I may presume one last time, keep you safe at home. There are many soldiers on the run these days. And the Tudors have long memories. My men and I will ride on; we'll not trouble you again. Tell your stepfather to guard you well. Pray for me.'

He lifted her hand to his lips with a courtier's gesture. Then resolutely touching his horse's sides he sent it trotting down the way he had come, not turning back although she almost hoped he would. And she was left alone once more.

CHAPTER 3

———

Long after Richard Montacune had disappeared, Philippa stood listening. The steady clip clop of his horse's hooves drummed like a heartbeat. Clear as glass she had an image of him: lean tall body, lean strong face, warm eyes beneath the frown. In a little while, she thought, he will ride up to his men bold as brass. 'Gather up your gear and mount,' he will say. 'Are your boots jelled?' And he will clap John of Netherstoke on his sound shoulder and tell him again not to be a fool. 'Put aside your sulks,' he will humour him. 'Shall a country lass outwit us, when all the French army could not?' And he will grin, chivvying them along, until, like fractious children, they will follow him. How far off is that Netherstoke, she thought; how many days to reach there? I wish that I were one of them. *Pray for me.* God keep you safe Dick Montacune, she thought. God bring you safely home again. And God keep me safe as well; God protect me from my stepfather's wrath. A sense of premonition, like a foretaste of what was to come, sent its shiver down her spine.

She began to run. The gravel spurted up behind her heels like hail stones; her bedraggled skirts left long sweeps from side to side as if a rake had been dragged across the surface, the tall fir trees stood like sentinels. All seemed as silent as the grave; no one about, even the woodcutters paused in their hewing down of trees that were old when the house was built. She saw no one, the maids somewhere about their work, the men in the yard, only her mother's nurse left alone, rocking ancient bones before the fire. Making for her own room under the eaves like a ship's prow, she opened the main door. Inside the passage-way Master Thomas Higham was waiting for her.

He must have been standing there, watching for her in the half-shuttered light, like a fox in its den. A scrape of flint and candles flared. 'So,' Master Higham said, pretending to brush a speck of dirt from his cloak, 'you have returned. You have been gone long enough.' And in a whisper worse than a shout, 'Harlot, have you no shame?'

His hand with the de Verne ring he wore bit into her flesh, but Philippa forced herself to stand still and face him. There was no way to dissemble where she had been, and had she tried, there on the stairs, hurrying from field and barn, came the servants to tell their tales. And behind them, appearing on cue, was the bailiff, her stepfather's favourite, with his crooked grin and crooked walk, making sure all knew who the informant was. Almost wearily Philippa thought, my stepfather has been waiting to play this out, as if dislike has been in the making for years. Why does he hate me so?

He was all in green today, a shade to grace a man half his age, and, caught as she was beneath his arm, Philippa could see his face clearly. She recognized the fleshy self-indulgent mouth, the glinting eyes, the scowling frown. But the pretence was new. However much he might scowl or let anger show, underneath he was pleased. And it was that secret pleasure that was most frightening.

As if he guessed her thoughts, he took a step forward, pressing her back against the door until the hilt of his little knife was caught at her ribs. 'Who were those men?' he howled. 'What one brought you back? How long have you known him?' And like an actor on a stage he turned to the waiting crowd on the stairs and shouted, his voice always too loud for his size, 'A whore, just as I always said. Blood will out. And what decent man will have her now?' And in self-righteous wrath he brought his hand down on her cheek so that the ring scored a long red mark. But behind the mask of self righteousness he was grinning.

The force brought Philippa to her knees and when she tried to rise her head spun round. Pride urged her to defend herself; caution told her silence was safe. Suddenly all the events of last night, all the events of this day, came into focus, as if she had been looking at them upside-down, and now, unexpectedly, at last they made sense. And it was her stepfather's secret pleasure that gave her the key. She stiffened her back and said the first thing that came into her head, making herself watch him for effect, making herself respond to him.

'Your spokesthing,' she told him, pointing at the bailiff who had been leaning against the railing post, enjoying a scandal he had revealed, 'could have rescued me, if he hadn't been scrambling for safety first.' Her voice was

49

cold. Years of breeding were in that voice, as if her forefathers spoke through her, all those who had been lords here when Master Higham's kin had been peasants. 'What did he see that was so bad? If you want the truth ask the man who knows. Ask Lord Richard Montacune.'

The effect at first was gratifying. Thomas Higham's disappointment was obvious; clearly he had hoped for denials and tears, and he scowled in earnest while his bailiff began to splutter excuses. It dawned on Philippa that he had hoped that his bailiff had told the truth and that too was a thought to chill.

'She lies,' the bailiff hissed. 'I saw them part. They have been lovers, that I swear. Only lovers act so indecently.' He made a smacking sound, puckering his lips against his hand, making the servants grin, turning a delicacy into its mockery. 'As for his being a lord, did he look like one, with his ragtag crew and his tired horse? Scratch beneath his airs you'll find a thief, waiting to murder us in our sleep. And she,' he pointed at Philippa, 'led him on.'

'He has already gone.' Philippa tried to explain. 'I told him there was no hope of hospitality here. I told him Vernson Hall was no place for gentlemen.'

Her scorn must have been apparent even to men as thick-skinned as Master Higham and his bailiff, but afterwards she was to regret having belittled them. Her stepfather began to splutter; his eyes bulged; if looks could have killed he would have plunged his dagger into her heart. 'Lord, lord,' he cried after a while, trying to control his rage, 'any vagabond could claim a rank and any stupid slut believe him.'

That thought seemed to renew his confidence. He

50

plunged into a new attack. 'So while you turned up your nose at better men, refusing Master Simeon, you were planning to meet this ruffian! No wonder you spoke so tartly last night. How long have you known him, I say, and how many times have you met?' And in full flight of fancy now he howled again, 'Slut, who thinks to wed where she pleases. Isn't that what you said? Let me tell you, madame, that a whore has little choice and no hope of sympathy.'

Again that thought pleased him. 'I am master of this house,' he cried again. 'All you have comes from me. Marry as I order you or I brand you as wanton for everyone to scorn. Then find out what scandal is. Then find out what de Verne pride is worth, a whore, tainted with the mark of treachery.'

Something about his words recalled the ones of Lord Montacune. An idea began to fill her mind, blocking everything else so that she could only fix on it. It spread until it seemed to encompass the world, rising out from some dark place where it had been hidden, full of thoughts so deep they stifled her.

'It is not your lands that I shame,' she managed to choke out. 'I do not even bear your name. But Richard Montacune knew me.' She raised her chin. She could not know that to the watchers she seemed almost her father's self, with his same fair hair and dark blue eyes, outfacing her enemies as once he had outfaced his. 'What of my father, Edward de Verne?' she cried, 'how did he come to die that you should speak of treachery?'

And all through the house there rose a cry like a mourning cry long overdue.

Miles to the north where already the rain had come to

shroud the moors that stretched in purple waves to the distant hills, Richard Montacune started round, as if he heard. He had been thinking of her as he rode along in the driving rain, and the memory had been like a ray of light. He could not get the feel of her out of his mind, the softness, the warmth, like a kitten. 'Why Mistress Philippa,' he was saying to himself, 'there was no need to tell me who you were, with your head in the air as if you were a princess. I knew you all the time. Your face, your smile, your look were all familiar. I saw your father look like that once. And he saw me.'

His hands looped round the slippery reins were blue with cold, and shelter seemed a long way off. Behind him his men plodded on just as she had imagined them. *Not that way* she had cried. God pity her, he thought, when she finds out. 'I told her her father met his death as a gentleman,' he told himself, 'I did not tell her I had seen him on the road to death.'

Now the gates of memory opened wide for him. He too was a child, brought to London by his uncle's men, soon after war had caused his own father's death. He had been standing with them, bewilderedly, until one of the guards had thought to hoist him up above the crowds, to watch the west-country rebels carted past. High in the air, he had had an unimpeded view of them, poor wretches, too terrified even to pray. Edward de Verne came last, the only lord among a group of peasantry, not one worth a king's revenge, out of their depth in conspiracy, not knowing completely what conspiracy was.

What madness had made Edward de Verne try to overthrow the Tudor king and restore a Yorkist line? Why had he risked his life and the lives of his poor followers? 'I saw her father pass,' Richard said to himself. 'I watched him, in his torn and sodden shirt, until the cart lurched round a corner, throwing him off-balance against the rails; in my dreams I still watch him. I did not see him die, but others did. I hope I make as brave an end.'

They brought him last to the place of execution but he faced the executioners first. 'I go before you,' he told his companions, to give them heart. 'As I led you in the past so shall I lead you to the end.' And he smiled at them, and smiled at the butchers who would murder them. 'Sweet Ned' they called him, like a child himself, believing in some old Yorkist dream, fighting the same old civil wars. Yet lacking the greed that makes traitors out of most men; believing what he had been told, out of some old loyalty. And who even in the hour of his death had time to spare for a frightened child.

God in heaven. Richard Montacune jerked awake as his horse stumbled, the ache in his ribs worse than before, the driving storm, the mud, bringing him back to the present. Who could forget 'Sweet Ned'? he thought. Not I who saw him pass and witnessed his last smile to me. Nor the Tudor king who had his remains brought back to hang on the gallows near his home. His story has been a thread woven through my life. Seeing his daughter today made me feel that she too was part of it. He thought, she would not seem so out of place, even in my own castle at Netherstoke. It would be good to have such a girl waiting there, although to tell truth I have never thought of wife or child before, and lack the means to keep them if I did. Soft arms, although they gripped too hard; soft young body, moulded to your back; little

53

breasts just budding to shape, lips soft as silk. Dear God, he thought, a man could go mad imagining such things. Yet if all were equal in this unequal world, I'd risk much so she and I might meet again, as I think we were meant to meet. I'd not mind having her smile at me. God give her courage, he thought, such as perhaps her father had; God spare her from the cruelty of men who would use that knowledge to do her harm. As for Philippa, so for him, a shiver of apprehension ran down his spine.

In the doorway of Vernson Hall, Master Higham smiled. 'So now you know,' he said softly, savouring the thought, 'what your mother tried to keep from you. I told her it would never work. Why else do you think she married within weeks of your father's death if not to try to hold on to his lands?' He smiled again a wide-lipped smile, full of delight. 'And why else should I have married her except to keep them tight, so Henry's men shouldn't claim them first. Traitor's land is lost land, miss. If I've got it thank Master Simeon. And thank him too, for his generosity to you. He's waited long enough for repayment. But,' and now his eyes grew cold, he stiffened like a hound, 'you never, ever, will lay your hands on it. Your father disinherited you when he put his neck in that hangman's noose.'

Years of hatred suddenly burst out like bile. 'He thought he was a king himself, with his little army, with his fair hair and handsome face that all the women doted on. What did it do for him? And what good did it do your mother to yearn for him, or what good me, who never stood a chance with her? And what good you, you silly fool, playing into my hands like this? Take Master Simeon and be done with it.'

54

But although she felt the ground reel, although that hatred sucked her under into darkness, 'No,' she shouted at him again. 'No, no, no.'

Thus the battle between them began, one which she had known from the start must be hard and would test her strength. Isolated from neighbours and those who might have been her friends, she was cut off from everyone. Within the house itself, her stepfather's servants had replaced the de Verne ones who might have been loyal to her for her father's sake. And in any case, what sympathy could she hope for, a mere girl, disobedient to a man's will, a disgrace which the world would condemn. She thought, but other people do not give up, even when things look dark. She thought, my father did not. Nor did Richard Montacune. She thought, true I have only one kinsman left, my mother's brother, a sea-captain, perhaps drowned years ago, in any event someone I do not know and who does not know me; I cannot rely on him. Again brave words; they could not hide how alone she felt.

'No, is it?' her stepfather screamed. 'We shall see what your no means. Kept in your room until you agree, you'll sing to another tune. Master Simeon will seem a blessing in disguise before we've done.' And on the stairs, over-seeing the servants, the new wife-to-be held her hands up in pretended shock at a stepdaughter's stubbornness.

The third day of imprisonment there came a scratching at the door, a tap, tap, tapping such as the wind might have made. It sounded like a drum in the silence. Philippa could not have sworn that it was the third night, by then both day and night had become one. Fear had been replaced by hunger, and hunger by despair. Had not this sound roused her she might have sunk into a lethargy. She started up. The great oak door to her father's room was doubly barred and its thickness made hearing difficult, but when she pressed her ear against it she could make out a voice, itself as thin and scratchy as a file. 'Lady,' the voice was whispering, 'lady, be on guard.'

No one called her lady in that house and she knew of no one who would, yet its use heartened her. 'Tonight I saw your stepfather's paramour,' the voice went on. 'That whore came into the kitchen when she thought herself alone. She had come earlier when we sat at meat, and had sent all the maids away on some pretext, all chores that could have waited until morning. She wanted to get us out of the way. But I took care she didn't see me left in my chimney piece, and, to be sure, I didn't tell her that I was there.'

Philippa had begun to recognize the speaker, her mother's old nurse. And she knew what chimney was meant; the huge stone fireplace in the kitchen, large enough to roast an ox, with its stone seats cut into its sides, where a man might hide himself. The old voice went quavering on; how had that old dame found the strength to creep out to whisper through a keyhole in the dark? But although the voice was feeble, the sense was firm. 'When she thought the room empty the whore pulled out a phial beneath her robes and sprinkled the contents on a loaf of bread. With my own eyes I saw her crumble the loaf to bits and pour fresh milk on it. She left the whole to steep before the fire, inches away from my feet, where I sat among the pots and pans and soot.

"Tomorrow morn," she ordered when the others returned, "give her that. Let her feast on slops." Away she went, nose in air, and when they had done with grumbling, for as mistress she is hard on them, when every jack straw of them was snoring fast, up I wakes and makes for the stairs. I loved your mother, lass,' she said, her voice unexpectedly assured, as if there were no doubt of that. 'In her old home in Bristol town, you would be safe; she should have returned there herself when my lord died, if pride had not held her back. I would have left for there long ago had it not been for her. There'd still be a place for you.'

Out of breath, she leaned against the door-jamb and wheezed. 'When my dear mistress first was wed it was for love, against her father's wish, out of her class. But he, your father, would not be denied. Her dowry was large from ships and trade. Should've been large enough for de Verne needs, although he said the wars had impoverished him. For there be other things you need to know.'

She put her mouth to the crack and whispered. 'In Vernson there is a rose garden that everyone praises; sailors say they can smell it out to sea. But I remembers another rose garden whose flowers brought grief. They say two lords were fighting for the crown, and wanted to pick a rose for their emblem. One side picked white, the other red. White for death, white for mourning, red for blood and war. Your father chose the White Rose side. They call it the Yorkist side, and they say some of its kings once ruled. I only know your father found his death supporting them. But when the wars were ended, when all those great lords were gone, who got the

57

crown?' She gave a cackle. 'Why a Tudor princeling did,' she crowed. 'He found it rolled under a bush at a battle's end and popped it on his head quick enough to make himself a king. And your mother gave her money to your father to keep him safe. Instead they hanged him and stuck his head upon the gallows tree. Lord, how she wept. And then she married Bully Higham fast, to keep the rest of those monies safe. But a loveless marriage is an offence to God. So it was for her and so for him. And will be for you if you don't watch out.'

Her message delivered she shuffled off. Philippa heard her footsteps on the stairs; then all was still again, nothing except the wind against the shutters, and the rain thrumming on the roof. She was an old crone, living on scraps herself, relying on pity, yes, and on forgetfulness, since those who would have remembered her would have turned her out of doors. But her message was both unexpected and frightening and must be acted on. And her wish, that Philippa try to find her mother's kin, touched some chord that somewhere in this loneliness there might be help. But if she were to have her uncle's help, she must go looking for him herself. And before her stepmother poisoned her.

Certain that no one had overheard, not giving herself time to think, hurrying herself into her warmest clothes and knotting her shoes about her neck, Philippa climbed onto the broad window seat, set under the roof like the prow of a ship. The night outside was dark with wind and rain but that would hide any sound she made. She knew there were creepers hanging on the wall and hoped they would bear her weight. The wind blew the rain in gusts against her face and the branches shifted and swayed. In bare feet she crept down the wall, flattened against the stones like a fly. The darkness hid the void below and the solid earth felt as unstable as sand. Yet she found strength to run towards the barn, snatching up the first saddle she could find, and choosing the nearest horse. It was one of Master Higham's hunters, his favourite (which pleased her later when she found out). In haste she saddled it, hung a small sack of oats in front and led it away from the house.

She went on foot at first, past the litter of fallen trees. The darkness was so complete that no one could have seen her through the driving rain and almost instantly the house disappeared. And when she came to the park gates, using a fallen log to mount, she gathered up the reins and thrust along the left-hand road at a gallop, like any other fugitive. And as the horse thudded over the frozen grass of the common land and came to the high road in a clatter of hooves, she sensed, beneath the fear, some ripple of excitement. Somewhere she passed the old gibbet with its creaking arms, but there was no reason to avoid it tonight, no need to remember a past that had been put to rest. And so her journey began.

In later years, in other times, Philippa was to speak often of that ride, always marvelling how one so gently reared could have survived. She would recall the details with a mixture of amusement and surprise. 'Perhaps I was my father's daughter in more ways than looks,' she used to say. 'For as I moved steadily on towards the border, that ride began to take on aspects of other rides, becoming the symbol of other escapes. So when I skirted sleeping farms where dogs howled alarm, I tried to think as my father would have done, or when I glimpsed the outline of a town and made a detour to avoid its walls I sensed a comradeship with Richard's men. The horse was strong and young; I was no weight, we made good time. And when with the dawn I had the sense to leave the road and make my way across country out of sight I might have been making journeys all my life. I tied the horse to graze and, burying myself in my cloak out of the wind, I slept, almost as peacefully as any mercenary, armed with sword and pike. Not quite perhaps. I still was young and inexperienced. If I had known at the start how long the road, and how difficult, I might not have gone off so readily to find an uncle I had never met. And if I had known that I left home just at the time Richard Montacune reached his, I might not have appreciated the irony.'

'I shall not recount all that journey,' Philippa used to say. 'That first night was repeated many times. I confess that only then did I begin to appreciate the difficulties that Richard Montacune had faced. But neither lack of food nor sleep, nor even cold and loneliness bothered me as much as the thought of pursuit. Master Higham's rage when he found me gone, and his best horse gone, haunted me. I started at every sound, and, afraid to ask the way, often wandered in a circle. When hunger drove me to seek food I stopped at isolated farms whose peasants would not recognize the value of the trinkets I traded. Once I found a clutch of eggs which I swallowed raw; another time, too cold to care, I slept in some sort of shed where a store of apples had withered almost to the core yet still tasted sweet. And when at last I came within sight of Bristol, by too many detours and side-ways to name, I was almost surprised that I had reached it at all.

'In those days Bristol was a fine and prosperous place, a great trading port, north and east of Vernson, the pride of the west country. My mother had been born there, and there I hoped my uncle still lived. Once, it had been famous for its cod fishermen; now many of its sailors had crossed the Atlantic Sea to the New Lands which they say lie at its end. Such a man was my uncle, Captain Harvey. It seemed he was well known. For when I asked for him the guards let me through the gates although I must have seemed a vagabond indeed, riding a horse too good for me. I might have found my uncle's house without asking, though; it was the largest one, centred in a line of tall thin buildings facing a wharf, resembling the spars and masts of the ships that rose in front of it.

'For a while I dared not approach but sat on my horse, seeing it through my mother's eyes, until the servants inside began to point and whisper. What they thought of me I never knew but the effect upon my uncle was disastrous. He appeared almost at once, as if he were on the lookout for me, a stout, broad-shouldered man, showing his age in his grizzled hair and beard, although in all things else the years had been kinder to him than to my mother. Yet there was something of my mother in the way he braced himself, and he had her eyes, blue grey like a wintry sea. He stared at me as sailors do, used to vast distances. "Well, niece," he said coldly, "I would recognize you even if your stepfather's man had not been here looking for you."

'This greeting was not exactly welcoming, and mention of my stepfather's man terrified me, "A small lame man, with a shifty look," he went on, "who claimed you had stolen off in the night with your stepfather's horse. I told him I knew nothing of that. She'll not come here I told him, what am I to her or she to me? But here you are, turned up like a piece of driftwood. And he'll be back." He stood with legs apart on the white steps of his house, as if on the deck of his flagship, reminding me, if truth be told, of my stepfather himself. They shared the same solidness, that same truculence, above all, the same dislike. For dislike there was and my uncle made no attempt to hide it.

'But he was an honest man as my stepfather was not. "Niece," he said, as if he owed some explanation, "when your mother was your age she was the most gentle of maids, as merry as a bird which sings all day long. Or so I thought, until your father rode into her life. My father, your grandsire, was a seafaring man, a trader of wool and hides; had he wanted he could have bought up Vernson Hall and stuffed it into one of his own money bags. Your mother told him she must have Edward de Verne as husband, or die, and that he himself, and I, who once had been her favourite, were nothing compared with this marvel of nobility."

'Here was the same bitterness that my stepfather had shown. It spilled out of my uncle now, in a flood, old unhappiness, old regret, old hostility, which I was not prepared for.

'"I warned her," my uncle said. "I argued that the marriage would never last. Your father sloughed off the coils of matrimony soon enough and replaced them with the coils of conspiracy. And when he died your mother married a second time, an even worse match, not caring what it did to her, or to us, as her kinfolk. I am not likely to be involved with Vernson Hall again."

62

'But when I told him of my stepfather's plan his expression changed. "Get you down," he told me, his eyes never flickering from my face as if to learn it by heart. "Advice is free for everyone. And I see you are my sister's child. I cannot keep you here. My family has suffered enough because of yours. But what I can do, I will."

'So it was, the first part of my journey done, I found I was obliged to go on. But true to his word, before I left, my uncle gave me help. It was of a practical sort, advice from his friends, letters of credit to London acquaintances, even introduction to lawyers who might get my lands restored. All spoke to the same theme. As ward of the king I and my lands would be free of Master Higham; otherwise I might never succeed. And to become ward of the king I should have to find the king myself, and his court, in London.

'"Yours is a difficult situation," my uncle told me bluntly. "Your father's fault was grievous, and your stepfather's tricks to hold on to his lands were devious. All agree that finding ways to present your case will prove as hazardous as steering a passage through a sand shoal. But if luck favours you, you may find the means to throw yourself on the king's mercy, and beg for forgiveness in your father's name. Once the taint of treason is removed, then you may get your lands back. If not," he shrugged.

'It was not an inviting prospect, but again I had little choice. He was a hard man, my uncle, but a just one. He gave me passage on one of his ships, to avoid pursuit, but he never could take me to his heart. And neither could I him. We parted with mutual respect and little liking. Yet I think I could have liked him once, as my mother had when she was a little girl, free to roam among her father's wharves and ships.

'As chance would have it, I left on one of those small trading ships, just at the very time Richard Montacune set off on his travels again. His purpose was more forthright than mine, looking for a new war to wipe out the stain of defeat. But we were both enthusiastic, resolute, and in our unequal ways, stout-hearted. He was a man of course, accustomed to hard knocks, not exactly cynical, but not dreamy-eyed. I was a girl, used to country ways. I might have had justice on my side, but it certainly was not royal justice. And when we both reached the king's court, neither of us found what we were looking for.

'Before I left my uncle tried to warn me. "My voyaging days are done," he told me, standing stiffly on the pier to watch me embark. "But when I was younger I sailed to the New World with the Brothers Cabot. I do not brag about what we saw, but on my return I was hailed as a great navigator and found favour with the Tudor kings." He drew a breath. "That court is a cesspit," he cried, "where the scum of England sink or swim." He gave me his hard uncompromising stare. "In the sea," he said, "there are creatures with smiling snouts, full of teeth. They swim beneath the surface with sharp black fins, waiting to attack. The young king's court is filled with them. Remember that. They will lie in wait for you. And remember that the king may become vicious too, for all he smiles at you." He meant well by his advice, I am sure, and it showed him in a less harsh light. If I never followed it nor met his friends nor asked for help, it was not my fault, nor his. And perhaps in the end it was better that I never did.

'I set sail then in the late afternoon, going down the wide estuary with a following tide. The wind was strong enough to blow us through the Bristol Channel towards Land's End; then along the Cornish peninsula and the southern English coast. The vessel was not a great seagoing ship, but old and small, used for inching around headlands from one little port to the next. It changed its cargo at each stop: wool for tin, tin for grain, grain for hides, and its crew was as simple and homespun as the goods they carried. It was then I learned what a lookout was and from the prow of the ship kept watch for the sheer Cornish cliffs, whose rocks lie under the water like black pointed fins. I saw the small fishing villages where my father had found his men. The sight of their poverty made me realize what exactly it was he had done to make them follow him. Battered finally by fresh storms that kept us land-locked later than we meant, we came by slow degrees to the mouth of the river Thames and dropped anchor within sight of London, months after I had left home.

'By now it was early June. When the moment came to disembark I was almost loath to leave. The little ship, with its cramped quarters, took on the appearance of home, and the crew seemed my only family. They set me on dry land as they had been ordered, and rowed their skiff back to their waiting ship, as if relieved that their duty was done. I watched them with a sinking heart, as they hoisted the patched sails, retracing their route westward again, and so found myself alone, on the river bank, clutching a bundle of clean clothes, my uncle's letters of reference tucked in the waist of my gown, a vast city spilling about me on all sides.

'For the first time I think the realization of the immensity of my mission swept over me, this asking of a king's pardon, for my father and myself, a mere nothing when spoken aloud, that encompassed within itself a magnitude of difficulty. I had no reason to doubt the honesty of my uncle's friends, whoever they were, nor their friendship for him. But could they win me an audience with a king who sounded anything but trustworthy? And having won it what was I to say on my behalf? As for the king, he might as easily refuse; or send me back to my stepfather in disgrace; or worse, reminded of my father's offence, take offence again and so seek new revenge.

'So there I was, set down amid the bustle of a city that made Bristol seem smaller than a village. Like any other country lass, I was bewildered by its variety, caught up in the many city currents that seem to run as fast as those at sea. Although the streets teemed with folk, I never found one to ask the way; all seemed too intent upon some purpose of their own; all seemed bent on hurrying in the same direction. For lack of anything better I followed them, idly at first, then after a while swept along as in that sea current, helpless to turn aside. And presently, in the distance, I began to hear a hum, a kind of insistent clamouring, that sharpened and intensified as I drew near, resolving into one constant shout, one single cry, "The White Rose, the White Rose," as if a thousand voices were shouting in unison.

'By now I was jammed in such a crowd I could not have broken away had I wished to. The thought of any

66

sort of garden, any flower, seemed preposterous in those dark and stinking streets, and for a moment a wave of homesickness swept over me. It was replaced, instantaneously, with feelings of a different sort. I remembered another kind of white rose that was the emblem of the Yorkist side; the white rose my father had followed. White rose for grief, for death. Fear suddenly leapt into my throat, hot as vomit; had not the mass of people held me up it is possible I might have lost consciousness, suddenly aware of the press, the heat, the stench of those unwashed bodies close to mine.

'I repeat, I had drifted along with the crowds, without an idea where they were going, and I suppose I must have imagined that we were far inland. Now I realized that the river had looped round, for there it was again, grey and dank, lapping at wooden pilings that lined its banks. As we emerged into a square I saw the shadow of a great bridge span hanging almost over us. I did not recognize it, the Tower Bridge where so many traitors' heads had hung, nor the Tower beyond it, where my father had lost his life. I only knew that its shadow cast a shadow over me so that whereas a moment before I had been stifled, now I felt cold. And all the while the shouting continued, the same mourning cry that I had heard in my house.

'Suddenly there was a stir in the square, a ripple, a thrashing, like trapped fish. The crowds in front began to push back, attempting to fan out into the smaller side streets, while those behind continued to push forward. The chanting had stopped, turned into shouts, to screams. Above the bobbing heads a group of horsemen began to show themselves, some dressed in blue, some in red, all well-mounted and determined. The sun glinted from their armaments and their horses' harnesses. Their uniforms, the way they thrust their horses into the crowds and struck with the butt end of their spears increased the crowd's panic. People began to fight openly with each other to escape. I felt danger closing in on me.

'I turned to run. But I had left running too late; the horsemen had already blocked off most of the square and were driving those left towards its centre. I tried to find a way out, my bundle long lost, my uncle's letters scattered underfoot, nowhere to go except down one of the remaining lanes which led to the river edge, no escape from there. I pulled my cloak over my head, retreating as far as I could, then, pressing myself against the wall, waited, in the hope that no one would notice me.

'Someone did. He came towards me on foot, one of his men holding his horse at the entrance to the lane. I could hear him slipping over the heaps of dirt, his spurs dragging in the rubbish heaps. Like a rat caught in a trap I waited for him, head down, back to the wall, the river edging past my feet. And there he stood, staring down at me, as in my thoughts he had done a hundred times. His blue doublet was gold laced; his breast plate gleamed; his face, under its heavy helmet was smouldering with a familiar rage, and his dark eyes flared. All I had breath enough left to gasp was "Why, Lord Montacune, such coincidence," before he took and shook me hard so my teeth rattled.'

CHAPTER 4

———

'Coincidence, coincidence,' Richard Montacune snarled.

With each repetition of the word he shook her hard, so that her neck appeared to snap from her slender neck. 'Do you know what coincidence means? See those men?' He forced her chin around so she could take in the half-empty square, the milling prisoners, the circling guards. 'See those red and blue coats, do you know whose colours they are?' At her obvious bewilderment, 'Those in red are Wolsey's men, Wolsey's "wolves", and in case you have forgotten, he is the most powerful churchman in England, one of the king's chief councillors. The rest in blue like me, serve his rival, the man who captains us today. There he is, on that black horse, Charles Brandon, the king's best friend, newly created duke. And why is he made duke; whose name and title is he about to usurp; what is his duty here today? Don't tell me you don't know what coincidence is.'

Philippa's eyes widened and her face grew pale. It wore the same expression of innocent defiance which had startled him in that Devon lane and had kept him company for many a night afterwards. But today was much more dangerous. With one of his soldier's oaths he dragged her to her knees. 'Listen to me,' he cried. 'Today we attended an execution. The victim was called the Earl of Suffolk, who was imprisoned in the Tower for more than seven years. This morning he was suddenly dragged out, paraded through the streets, displayed to the public, and then beheaded on Tower Hill. It is his name the people shout, the White Rose; he was the last of the Yorkist line. And hearing those shouts, the king has ordered us to round the people up as traitors to the crown.' He almost groaned. 'I cannot tell you why that man was condemned to death,' he cried, 'except that he was who he was, cousin to two former kings and perhaps a threat to the present one. But the man who had the task of mounting guard on him, Charles Brandon, has just been created Duke of Suffolk in his place.' He let go Philippa's arm, so she sank back in the mud. 'And that is why the crowd shout a name that has not been heard these twenty years,' he whispered, bending down. 'And that is why we take hostages, to make an example of them. Try explaining to the king, mistress, that your appearance is coincidence. Tell him so, when he hangs you as part of a Yorkist conspiracy.'

Philippa began to speak, but fear dried her mouth and swelled her lips so she could not open them. All she could stammer was, 'I arrived by chance,' as if chance explained everything. All she could think of was that a wheel had come full round and here she was, in the same place where her father once had been. 'I came by chance,' she repeated, 'looking for a king's pardon. If this is what king's justice is, God spare us all. And God forgive those involved with it.'

She tried to round on Richard Montacune. 'And what coincidence brings you here?' she cried. 'Was not watching my father die enough? Is this your plan for making your way in the world? Is this how Lancastrians find fun, killing Yorkist men?'

Her reproach was lost on Richard for he was only half-listening. He knew without looking what was being done in the square, and the consequence. It seemed to him that she still seemed unaware of the peril that she was in; worse, he himself had no idea of how he was to disentangle her. 'Dear God,' he thought, wiping the sweat, the walls of the narrow lane so close they seemed to drip. 'Christ's bones, grant me the wit to save her from herself,' suddenly afraid for her as he never would be for himself.

His companions' impatience was mounting. The day was hot, their work distasteful, they were anxious to be done. Several had begun to peer down the lane; one, in a red coat, was obviously debating whether to venture in. There was little time left to explain what rumour said, how the king in Westminster Hall, come to town to discuss his French campaign, had miscalculated the crowd's response. Expecting them to shout for him, listening for the usual 'Long life to Harry Tudor,' Henry had been appalled to hear instead, 'God save the Yorkist White Rose.' Nor how, careful not to let chagrin show, he had pretended to listen to his councillors' discourse, toying with his dagger hilt, as if nothing was amiss, not even when the peace party begged him to put aside his war plans. He had left the quelling of the mob to his closest friend, to whom it had amused him to give charge

71

of a troop recruited from both sides, demonstrating royal impartiality. And there the hostages were, in the square, tied together now, all those whom the guards could catch: the blind, the lame, the mad; the ones who had not the sense to know whose name they cried; the young, the innocent, all whose little deaths would be an offering to appease Tudor nightmares. 'As for me,' Richard wanted to shout, as if answering Philippa, 'I am just a soldier, looking for a war. Do you think this the war I sought?'

The guardsman who had been peering down the lane had made up his mind. He began to stroll towards them, pulling at the sleeves of his red coat, poking with his scabbard tip at every pile of dirt to prise up some fugitive, as unconcerned as if he were planting beans. 'What's amiss?' this man now cried, rubbing his forehead with his cuffs. 'If you've done, haul that one out; no need to linger in this heat. We'll soon clear up this lot.' He laughed. His laugh, as if to say, 'Not even good for sport,' was the last straw.

With a howl Richard Montacune leapt at him. His own disgust was all in that leap. It so overwhelmed the man in red that he stumbled out of the way, not even daring to unsheathe his sword. Richard brushed past him, eyes blazing, his own blade swinging dangerously, his free hand clamped about Philippa's arm. He stormed into the square, sending another red-coated soldier sprawling, backhanding him into the mud, and tossing his sword after him. The remaining guards drew back warily, but Richard shouldered his way through them, making for the rider on the black horse as if he meant to bowl horse and man aside. Behind him, Philippa came running to keep up, trying to pull her cloak's hood over her face, despite the heat, to avoid being seen, trying to make sense of a scene that overwhelmed her with its violence.

Charles Brandon was waiting at one side of the square in the shade. He bestrode his horse with the easy grace of a born horseman, and his thin face with its aquiline nose and dark beard was turned aside, so that he seemed to be disclaiming all responsibility for what was being done in his name. Philippa of course did not recognize him, but to people of the court and town he was famous, the 'great commoner', the 'ordinary man' without title or lands, who had risen to become the intimate of lords and kings. What his opinion would be of the way his title had been acquired had not been asked, but the new duke's narrow eyes wore an air of scorn, as if challenging criticism. He was older than Richard, perhaps having some thirty years, and he rode hand on hip, with a kind of arrogance. But even his enemies admitted his charm (although they said his inability to resist a pretty face was a further sign of his lack of sense).

Stopping just in time before his headlong march brought him on a collision course, Richard drew himself up short in front of his captain and patron. He caught a breath. In a tone of voice that suggested he and the duke were not strangers, at the same time motioning to Philippa to remain silent, he said, 'My lord duke, my lord duke, I crave a boon.'

Now, he may have known that on the very day a new dukedom had been assured, a new duke might have preferred to have heard the title used in a different place and different way, by men closer in age and rank, rather than by a youngster, asking for a favour, and showing not one ounce of humility. And clearly the duke recognized him, nodding in a distant way, perhaps not so irritated as if Richard had been a stranger. 'I crave a boon,' Richard was repeating (although 'demand' was what he meant). 'You once were kind enough to say I did you a favour when I arrived at court. Now I claim one in return.'

The new duke might have preferred respect. 'What?' Charles Brandon's roar frightened his horse and made it rear. He fought it to a standstill. 'You bargain for me, do you,' he shouted, 'like some geegaw at a fair. God's bones, but you're proud, to claim as right what I gave as gift. What cause makes you act so bold?'

Without a word Richard pushed Philippa forward, removing her hood. Her face had regained its colour, and her golden curls, her blue eyes, her panting breath made the duke's own eyes gleam. He opened his mouth to speak but Richard forestalled him. 'I owe this lady as much as you owe me,' he said. 'When she is free, so we are quits. Let her go. She has done no wrong, to that I swear, except be in the wrong place at the wrong time.'

The duke looked at the girl curiously. But she was not looking at him. She was staring at the lines of prisoners, the flush fading from her cheeks and her eyes darkening in sympathy. Perhaps the duke was touched in spite of himself; perhaps on a day when compassion seemed to have been lost he welcomed some simple sign of it. But Richard's words certainly revived some memory. His second roar was almost as loud as the first. 'What,' he cried, 'you risk my liking, nay, my friendship, for a mere wench? Mind your manners, lad, before I clout them back.' And, for a moment, his dark face darkened as if he meant to make good his threat.

But Richard held his ground, his fixed look showing he would not give way and after a moment the duke backed a pace. 'Aye,' the duke snorted, turning to Philippa. 'Look your fill. What your lover asks is imposs- ible.' And to Richard, 'Wolsey's "wolves" hang on every move. You know what their master will report if he thinks the king's commands are ignored. And where, for God's sake, would you take her, even if I gave her to you? Where would you hide her; where, in barracks or city, would she be safe, if Wolsey's men are hunting her? Where would you be safe yourself?'

Philippa's clear high voice cut into his speech almost with her former child's clear honesty. 'If he were my lover,' she said, 'how could I wish him ill, to be the cause of lost friendship? But what harm have they done?' She gestured to the prisoners. 'Let them all go free. I for one would never have killings on my conscience, never, never, never.' An indiscretion Richard tried to stifle, clamping a hand across her mouth, although he knew what she said was true enough, and perhaps needed to be said.

Her words intrigued the duke. At any other time Richard knew he might have given good advice as to the care and treatment of maids as he had in the past. 'I like a wench with spirit,' he might have said. But today he was on edge, anxious to have a distasteful duty done, careful that there should be no mistakes. Now he took a closer look at the girl. Despite her countrified clothes she seemed a lady, no street strumpet. He pursed his lips. Richard knew what he was thinking. 'If this lordling has

75

his heart set on her presumably he knows her worth; perhaps she is highly placed, someone, therefore, as king's representative, I had best be chary of.' Giving one of those sidelong glances that made men claim he had eyes in the back of his head Charles Brandon began to assess what options still were left to him.

Most of the guards had withdrawn to the edge of the square and were waiting there with their hostages. Only a few of Wolsey's men lingered, licking their chops, expecting to be tossed this last juicy morsel. Sight of them made up the duke's mind. He knew what was expected of him, and he was more than capable of ruthlessness. But the lady's predicament had affected him, and he liked her fire. But most of all he resented the presence of Wolsey's 'wolves' making him feel in thrall to them. Why should he fear Wolsey's influence any more? A duke was the equal of any Archbishop.

'Take your freedom if you wish,' the duke spoke first to Philippa. 'But if you persist in lecturing me, then follow them.' He jerked his thumb towards the prisoners. Next he turned to the guards. 'Ride on,' he cried, 'captives to the Tower. We follow in our own good time.' But to Wolsey's 'wolves', a challenge of his own, a defiance. 'Today you obey me. I am master here. Ride on yourselves.'

What the effects might be on him personally he chose to ignore. But when the retreat had begun, when the screams for pity, the shrieks, the confusion had quieted, 'There they go,' he said. 'God rest their souls. God pity them. Their king will not.'

Philippa's little burst of energy was gone. She clung to Richard's side as if her legs had given way, so that, sick

76

with pity himself, he tried to shield her from the sight. The duke watched the miserable procession pass without further sign, merely turned his head away, looking out into the distance. When Wolsey's men, the last to leave, had mounted with a show of reluctance, 'I am all sorts of fool myself,' the duke began, speaking quickly from the corner of his mouth (a trick he had, which men claimed he had learned to prevent his enemies from eavesdropping). 'But there is only one place I know of where Wolsey will not dare hunt for you. That is in the royal court itself, under the royal nose.' He suddenly spun round with a clatter of hooves and steel, addressing Richard directly. 'Tonight the king will lodge at Westminster. Use this to gain you private audience to the court.'

It seemed that once he had made up his mind to help nothing was enough for him. First he fumbled beneath the lacings of his breastplate to produce a scrap of silk. It was a lady's scarf, of the sort a man might wear as an emblem of her favour, pale cream in colour, worked with beaded pearls and gold, a fragile possession for such a masculine-seeming man. A faint scent still clung to its folds. 'The lady who gave me this,' the duke was continuing, speaking in the same secretive way, no doubt from habit, since the square was almost empty, 'the royal lady' (he emphasized the distinction) 'will take your mistress to her care. At least while the court is here. And do you, mistress,' addressing Philippa, in more formal tones, 'show the scarf to her and ask her aid. Use my name. But as she is young and fair, as gentle as she is innocent, tell her nothing of yourself, not how we met nor where; nothing that would cause her pain. Let her shelter you as is her pleasure and as her kind heart will have her do. And thank God, today, that Charles Brandon has in mind to spare one poor unfortunate.'

He looked her up and down, and for a moment a smile curled his thin lips, softening the angle of his face, giving attraction to his narrow eyes, so that the claim of his charm seemed justified. 'And thank God', he told her softly now, to her ears alone, 'for beauty and for purity, as I thank God myself.'

He swirled round on Richard, 'As for you, my lord.' His voice was cold, punctilious. 'Let no one call Charles Brandon an ingrate. It will not be wise to approach this royal lady openly, indeed, it may be impossible. I give you this to show you a way to her own rooms.' He leaned down and wrenching off a leather strap from the saddle, rapidly pricked a kind of rough design with his dagger point. 'Follow this map,' he said. 'The path winds beneath the undercrofts to an inner yard that not many know about. Ring the doorbell there. Whoever answers say merely that you have been sent with a message for the princess, and he will take you to her. So much I do for you.'

He was gathering up his reins preparatory to leaving, pulling on his gloves, settling his stirrups, and spoke rapidly. 'Henceforth I know you not. I have twice repaid my debt; two favours for the price of one, and the day may come when I shall expect a like favour in return. Until such time you have made your claim of me and so now I am done with you. Make your own peace with Wolsey's men; make your own way in the world; I never lift a finger more. I do not dismiss you from my guard, and you ride with me to France as was agreed, but that

78

is all. Since this moment's time, your advance is all your own.'

He saluted Philippa with a graceful bend of his head, put spurs to his black horse which had been growing ever more restive, and let it bound away, following the direction that the soldiers had taken. Like a backwater after a storm had passed, the square sank back to quiet; and like flotsam cast upon a bank, Richard and Philippa were left alone.

Richard recovered first. Philippa was still clinging to him, and he drew her aside, trying to find a clean block of stone out of the sun. Someone had left him his horse and he fetched it, returning to stand in front of her, unfastening his helmet and running a hand through his curls making them crisp about his ears. 'Well, Mistress Philippa,' he said, as if he had been doing battle on her behalf (which in one way he had). 'Luck spares us a second time. Thank God for that.' He slung his breast-plate over the saddle bow, taking his time, for the truth was now he had her safe he was not sure what to say to her. But she had much to ask of him. 'How are you and that lord friends?' she cried. 'What is he to you or you to him, that you trust him? What favour does he speak of? And that lady, royal or not, who is she? How came you here in the first place?' She drew a breath, 'Are you glad to see me?' she cried. 'Oh, what horror were those men about that you could not prevent them?'

He sighed. 'Gently, gently,' he said, 'about to smother me with words again. Learn to hold your tongue, Mistress Philippa, else grief will come of it. Great lords do not relish scolds.'

'I suppose you count yourself a great lord these days,'

79

she wanted to cry, 'with your fine blue coat and fine horse. You forget I saw you when your luck ran low. You did not brag about your fine friends then, Lord Montacune.'

She bit back a reply and said nothing. She certainly did not mean to quarrel with him and certainly he had not meant to quarrel with her. After a while, shyly she put up her hand to pull at his sleeve, while he, contrite, began to speak. Her, 'I never,' and his 'I only' seemed part of the same thought, and seemed so natural that they almost laughed, hers being 'I never meant to discredit you,' and his, 'I only meant to help.' 'I said you would be better off at home,' he said at last. 'What made you leave? But I also told you to rely on me. Call me by name.' He tried to coax a smile. 'I told you what my friends call me,' he said.

He felt her slight body begin to shake, as he had felt it once before, and her voice came out muffled. 'I have made harm between you and that lord. And if I have acted as scold, then I have made trouble betwixt us both.'

'Not so, sweeting.' He wanted to comfort her, the endearment coming awkwardly, the endearment not strange itself, but his sudden urge to use it. 'If truth be told, it galls me sore to be beholden to anyone, and I would rather make my own way by myself, or not at all.' He looked at her, suddenly bursting out, 'When we meet, you seem to land me in a fix, first with my men, now with the duke's; if I were wise I should hope we never meet by chance again, lest I face a king's army next time.' He grinned. 'Yet, for all that, I am right glad to see you.'

He looked at her, this time really looked, seeing her as

80

the duke had done. He became aware of the closeness of her; he had but to stretch out his hands and he could clasp her round the waist as he had often thought of doing. He could draw her up against him, feel the silkiness of her hair, her pale face pressed to his own, her lips against his, as now they were. 'You found me after all,' he was whispering, 'didn't you ask to follow me?' And she, 'I prayed for you, and hoped that you would remember me. I believed that we would meet again.'

'Come ride with me,' he was whispering, 'we should not linger here. And when we get safely to the court let me show you how I thought of you.' He started to lift her up to the saddle, lingeringly, letting his hands slide beneath the folds of her cloak, to touch her long legs underneath, where her skirts had bunched. That naked flesh was like silk, the skin smooth. He wanted to pinion her against him, his body aligned with hers. He wanted to press himself on her as she strained towards him. And he thought now I know what it might mean, never to let go.

But he set her sideways on the broad saddle, swung himself up behind her, settled his hands around her waist. 'Hold on,' he told her, 'it is not far.' And with a smile, 'This time you may squeeze as tight as you please, I'll not complain.' And he lifted one of her hands to hold between his own.

Now as they rode along they began to question each other, trying to fill in the gaps in their lives, trying perhaps to assure themselves that in the meanwhile they had been in each other's thoughts. Philippa's story was soon told. 'God's mercy girl,' he exclaimed when she was through, 'I marvel that you survived.' He looked at her with new respect, until a fresh concern jolted him. 'But if it is your father's memory you want to clear, tell no one. If I had known that was your plan I'd not have accepted help from the duke so readily.' And a worried frown crossed his face, at the thought of her past dangers and the possibility of new ones.

'And you?' It was her turn to laugh at fear. 'What makes your adventuring so different? I thought you back at Netherstoke where you belong, you and your men, safe in your own home.'

'So you did remember me,' he teased, 'down to the very village we came from. We should be flattered.' And he watched her blush, as if strangely pleased. But as she was insistent, to satisfy her and help pass the time he began to tell his tale. It was a simple one at that: either to stay at home, and starve, or seek his fortune at court. And what a morass he had found there, that cesspit of her uncle's words, where everyone pushed his fellow down, while trying himself to climb ahead; he might have been left to drown, had not this same Charles Brandon come to his aid.

Sensing her look of distress, 'Nay, I can manage without him if I must,' he said. 'If fortune favoured me once she will again. But the way we met was strange, you see. For Brandon came to count on me, as I on him, and such comradeship is rare at court, although fighting men cherish it.'

He gave a rueful laugh. 'I thought to set the Thames on fire,' he said. 'I never realized that for every one like me there were a score, all jockeying for a place, the Tudor world jam-packed with us, a new breed of men on the make. Little chance then to use my father's name to rise to the top, in a court where only novelty counts.'

If there was a hint of bitterness he hid it well. 'So there I was,' he continued, 'without friends, without money except what my mother could spare me, without prospects, a parvenu like the rest, come to Richmond to try my luck. Richmond is where the king normally resides,' he explained, 'a new palace too, newly rebuilt; sometimes I think the past and its old loyalties are quite forgot. Now it so happened that the day I arrived the king had ordered his horses put on display, a new breed too, brought from abroad, and since I may claim to know horseflesh as well as anyone I went to see them myself, with some hope, I suppose, of using my knowledge to good account.' He grinned. 'I never thought to have used it so soon,' he said.

'All the courtiers were out in force that day,' he went on, 'among them, Wolsey's men, their coats as bright as cardinal red (a church office I hear Wolsey covets for himself). If I had had any idea of joining them one look at them soon changed my mind. In any case, the thought of serving a churchman, sworn to peace, sat uneasily on my military conscience, the more so since it is said he only chooses handsome youths, having an unnatural hankering for good-looking boys. Besides, it was then I met Wolsey's chief opponent, the man you know as the Duke of Suffolk, although he was a mere Charles Brandon at the time.'

He cocked his head at her and as she smiled expectantly said, 'He was conspicuous because of his height, the only great man to mingle freely with the commoners. But he walked alone, with none of the usual circle of court hangers-on, as if the court itself was avoiding him.

I thought that odd for one who was the king's champion, and so did the crowds, until a little groom with one leg (who claimed to know all the gossip, and perhaps he did, having worked in the royal stables himself until a fall had maimed him) took upon himself to elucidate.

'"Poor sot," he lisped, jerking his thumb at Charles Brandon. "There he stands, the king's friend." He sniffed. "Fine thing, a king, to turn a friend into a laughing stock. Just look how Wolsey's 'wolves' have come to jeer." He sniffed again. "The truth is, Henry's spent a fortune on these new Flemish nags of his," he whispered, "and has ordered Brandon to test 'em. Henry wants to prove to the world, and to himself, that he's bought a bargain. So he's told Brandon to ride one in a joust."'

In answer to Philippa's questioning look, Richard explained patiently, 'To joust,' he said, 'a man must have an opponent to ride against. But no one was willing to partner Brandon that day. And when I saw the horses themselves, I saw why Brandon's friends kept themselves apart.

'The stables at Richmond are also new,' he went on, 'better built than most men's homes; Montacune Castle could benefit from such repairs. The king has housed his purchases in style. But when the doors were opened to let those horses out, laughter rippled through the crowds. I almost laughed myself. I know the qualities of a war steed, and a little of jousting skills, although now it is a sport only the rich afford. I swear I had never seen stallions like these. To begin with, they were huge; so tall most men would have needed a ladder to clamber on and so wide they needed two grooms to prod them along, like plough horses, fit for Flanders mud, certainly not intended for riding on. Soon everyone was grinning, Wolsey's "wolves" among the rest. And then I caught the look on Brandon's face.'

He said, 'It made me realize just what a predicament he was in. He was glancing about him with that curious look he has, as if trying to find where his friends were; as if assessing his chances. Not many I thought. For if he failed to ride, or did not show those horses' worth, his failure would rebound upon the king. And kings do not like failure.

'I began to look at the horses more carefully, trying to see them with Brandon's eyes. Under their chestnut coats there was not an ounce of fat and their muscles moved without effort. True, they would never be fast, but it occurred to me that jousting horses require less speed than ordinary war-chargers. What they do require is sure-footedness and the ability to carry weight, such as a man with full armour on. Brandon himself is tall and heavy; so is the king. I began to see some purpose behind the king's choice, and I sensed Brandon thinking as I did.

'He was standing in the sun, his nose quivering like a greyhound's (which his enemies say he resembles), as if he were scenting out the mood of the crowd. I think he saw disgrace facing him, unless he found someone who would ride as he meant to do, not in open fight to win, but to display the horses' qualities rather than his own. I thought, he needs to prove these are the best jousting horses in the world; if not, farewell to favour and championship; farewell to friendship with the king. And when he looked at me, I knew for sure our thoughts were the same.'

Richard gave another laugh. 'I knew I was all sorts of

fool,' he said. 'I had not even noticed how the crowds had thinned. Most had made for the jousting grounds to get a good seat; the rest carefully avoided Brandon's gaze. If I had not been so raw and green I would have done the same. I did not remain deliberately, as men since have said. God knows, it was not a situation into which anyone would willingly have thrust himself. Curiosity alone kept me there, and fair play. Fair play that is, to man and beast.'

He rode on thoughtfully for a while, before explaining, 'There is a look,' he said, 'which I cannot describe, but which passes sometimes between fighting men, when their backs are to a wall and they need someone to trust. Brandon gave me a look like that. I think he read my feelings as I read his. "You, lad," was all he said. "I do not know you but you look well-schooled. I seem to lack a partner today; will it please you joust with me?"

'At any other time that offer was one most newcomers in my place would have given their sword arm for. Imagine, matching with England's champion. On the other hand, I saw that our reputations would be linked, not only to be made to look fools, but to risk the king's wrath. God's life, a man must be a fool indeed, not to know that disadvantage outweighed the good. Yet I agreed.

'The rest is soon told. I have said I know a little of jousting technique, not much, but enough to get by; even at Netherstoke we have our champion. I cannot say I felt at ease perched on that great stallion, double the size of my father's old war horse. Nor can I say I rode with confidence; I may have looked "well-schooled"; in fact, the horse was to teach me.

'When I saw the jousting field I tell you I prayed not to disgrace myself. It was a long stretch of turf, with a wooden barricade down the centre, and balconies where the courtiers lounged, making bets, and stands for the commoners (all a far cry from our meadow lands at home). I tell you, without that horse I would be a dead man. It had a strange flowing gait as if it went through air, yet its weight kept us anchored to the ground. All I had to do was to sit tight and concentrate on thrusting back.

'We ran five passes. Each time my lance was shattered but I hung on. I know I would have fallen except for that horse. And after the last bout, when the crowds were silent with respect, when I was still reeling in the saddle from Brandon's blow (but in the saddle, mark you, not under it), Brandon wheeled back to me.

'He thrust up his heavy jousting helm (I should explain we had ridden lightly dressed, without all the armour true jousting needs, with only helmets and practice wooden spears). "They wager on us," he said evenly. "Shall we wager on ourselves? We have proved the king was right; these horses are bred for this sport. So now, this time, let us prove which of us is the better man."

'Without jousting armour, wood lances can prove deadly; and a man can die on a jousting ground as easily as on a battlefield. But my blood was up. And Brandon was fair; he gave me the right to refuse. "My lord," I said in formal style, my breath coming hard, for his last pass had caught me under the ribs, laying open that old French hurt. "My lord, I have no monies to spare, not even to bet upon myself, but willingly will I match with you."

'So we rode a final time, for ourselves. Down the lists I came, mounted on a horse that I would wager my life on; and down on the opposite side he came, the master champion. His lance jabbed me as he passed. And then indeed I did ride on air. And when I came to myself, sprawled on my back, surrounded by a group of onlookers, I realized that on the other side of the barrier, Charles Brandon was stretched equally prone upon the ground. It was a lucky thrust on my part, and when he had recovered, which he did first, he came to tell me so. He had a lump on his forehead, big as an egg, and his eye would blacken but he looked self-satisfied. "That must be French work," he said, pointing to my scars. "Well, lad, you are in good company. Guienne needs to be avenged and so it shall, this spring. I marvel that any of you returned from there alive. So why are you fresh here at court, if not looking for the chance of revenge? You shall have it, in my company. But now, what will you do with your earnings, the first, I trust, of many spoils of war?" And he shook a little bag of coins before dropping it into my lap. "The odds were on me, lad," he said. "But I put the wager in your name. I downed you, boy, fair and square; pricked you out like an oyster from its shell. As clean a fall . . ."

'"And I downed you," I said.

'We looked at each other and laughed, so hard my side began to throb. Well, laughter is as good a way as any to start friendship, and so ours did. And that is how I met Charles Brandon, who now is made Duke of Suffolk, and that is the "favour" I did him.'

Richard could see Philippa's sympathy was aroused. He seldom spoke about himself but he had wanted

88

suddenly to tell her what his own plans were. And when with loving words and caresses she had assured herself that he was not still hurt he felt to some extent he had explained himself. Her next question was not so easily handled.

'And the royal lady the duke spoke of?'

'Ah.' Richard kept his tone cheerful. 'She is someone I have *not* met. From all I have heard of her she is just as the duke described. She is the king's younger sister, more like her mother, Elizabeth, in looks and temperament than her Tudor heritage. Have no fear of her, Mistress Philippa. In any case it will not be for long. We'll soon think what to do with you.' But here again he spoke more cheerfully than he felt, although even he could not have guessed how long and intricate the way before that 'soon' was reached. (Nor, being a discreet man himself, did he add what else he had heard of this Tudor princess; hints only, murmurs, that put a slightly different look to what the duke had said of her.) But since it was nothing to her great discredit, he kept quiet, not wanting to alarm. Although he did sense an indiscretion on the duke's part, to speak of her so openly. It was true he had never met the lady in question, but he knew more about her than perhaps even the duke himself realized.

After the joust, he had been brought to Brandon's rooms, where he had found his new patron stripped down to his shirt, boots on table top, at ease, like a soldier himself, instead of a great courtier. Such informality had pleased Richard. At first that is. Gradually he had noticed how his host began to drink himself into carelessness, displaying a wantonness of thought and

89

speech, which his enemies castigated as stupidity but which his friends felt added to his charm. 'Drink up,' Brandon had begun to hiccough. 'I shall not forget what you did, nor will my king. He'll love that I was unhorsed by a boy scarce dry behind the ears, and he'll love more that we bested those blackguards who thought to see us bested. The king has plans for those horses, lad. He means to breed them to others for a touch more speed, to produce a new type of cavalry, heavier, powerful, like a machine. But he'll love best that we proved him right and you shall tell him so yourself when you meet.

'Your father was a Tudor man, I think,' he had added later in the night, when ale continued to loosen his tongue, 'and so was mine. My father never did a better thing than die at Bosworth Field. He was standard bearer to the first Tudor king, and he had the sense to perish in front of the king's own feet; not even a Tudor could fail in gratitude. Most of my father's exploits were in the field of love, not war (a virtue I seem to have inherited) so my thanks are doubly due, that in his final hour he did well by me. Although he left me no estates and although I am a simple country man, from boyhood I was brought up with the Tudor princelings. You have a title, lad, but so one day shall I. We know each other, my Henry and I. I know his teasing, goading ways, to keep those closest to him off-balance. I know how it amuses him to reward loyalty by handfuls; how he likes to make a test of friends. Today was such a test for me. But he can be generous. If he is pleased so in the end will he please me; he will grant me what I want.'

He had leaned forward drunkenly. 'I knew you had the look of luck, Lord Montacune,' he had cried, waving his tankard. 'Toasts go down better in good country beer, so hear mine. God sot that weasel, Wolsey, with his knavish tricks and cunning eyes; God sot his friends who are my enemies. God grant that the king see fit to reward me as he should. God grant me the nobility that I should have.' He had begun to whisper then, eyes crossed, in an effort to make sense. 'A title lies waiting for me in the wings, and when I have it, when its rents and lands are mine, then Charles Brandon will be the equal of the master he serves.' And as if this talk did not smack of treachery he had made things worse by crying out what common sense should have kept hidden, spilling out his secret wishes on a gush of ale. 'Once I am duke, nothing will prevent me from seeking the greatest reward of all. What if I be wed! Wives are easily put aside, and the royal princess already looks upon me as a friend. When I woo her, as perhaps I mean to do, I shall be more than her equal. Since she is young, her affections are not yet ready to be plucked, but even so she yearns for me. I swear she would do anything I asked. It is but a question of time before that affection shall bear fruit, ripe for the picking; and when it does, Charles Brandon means to be the one to pluck.'

Indiscretions, these, of the grossest sort, better never thought of, not meant to be shared with every passing stranger. Certainly not for a mere lad's ears. But that was Brandon's way, his strength and weakness, and he guessed Richard never would betray him. So it was now, in answering Philippa's questions, Richard spoke as sincerely as he could, without revealing all he knew. 'I have not met this royal lady myself but of course the duke has. If he entrusts you to her care you should rely on her. And in truth her help will be better than none. But keep all hid, until I can come back for you.'

By now they had emerged from the narrow streets into a wider thoroughfare leading in a straight line towards the palace of Westminster. It lay at the end of an avenue, a grey mass of stone, seemingly veiled in a mist of heat. In normal times this part of the city would have been filled with bustling life, but today was not normal and emptiness seemed to engulf them with a faint suggestion of alarm.

Richard sensed danger before Philippa did. He kept turning back, searching, for what he could not say, and his hand twitched towards his sword hilt, as if to assure himself it still was there. Something still seemed to nag at him, some unfinished thing. He became conscious of her scrutiny, and when she half-turned as if to look herself, his colour rose. And yet there seemed no cause for unrest. The streets were deserted, the palace lay ahead; a hundred yards or less would bring them to the small side-turning leading to that private entrance. He drew out the duke's map and tried to study it, attempting to memorize the faint dagger marks that showed the twists and turns through the passageways. But when he spoke again, it was not of that at all.

'When you talked of your stepfather,' he said, almost abruptly as if the words slipped out, 'you told how cruelly he drove you out. But,' he hesitated, 'you did not tell who it was you were meant to wed.'

'Not anyone of importance,' she answered him. 'And he, poor old fool, was bribed. As for me, I want no part of wedlock until my lands are secured.'

This answer seemed to disturb him; he shifted rest-lessly, as if fumbling for words. 'And when I have returned from France,' he said at last, 'when my own fortune is made, what if I ask then for the king to give me right to act as your champion? What if I fight your stepfather for you?'

She bit down a smile, for the thought of Master Higham with a sword amused her. 'Perhaps,' she said, demurely. 'And I would thank you if you did. But first, I should thank you for today. I owe my life to you. After this war is done will be time enough to talk of him. But I do not like the sound of war . . .'

'A nothing,' he said. 'And would not your prayers keep me safe as they did before? You said you prayed for me every day; was that so?'

He watched her from the corner of his eye, and saw her look aside and blush. Once more the awareness of her washed over him, the scent she used, the texture of her skin and clothes, the feel of her hair. His hands were still clasped loosely around hers on pretext of holding the reins, but his horse could have found its own way without guidance. Against his chest he could hear the thudding of her heart, just as he had done before. And as before, perversely the thought of parting even for a day irked him. He wanted to say, 'For my part, I do not find it strange we meet again. Rather, it seems inevitable. Each time has been in consequence of some event; each event has had a bond of its own; perhaps that is coinci-dence, but I think it deeper than that.' But he said nothing, still not certain how to express himself; merely kicked his horse forward. But now as he rode he began to whistle beneath his breath, perhaps unconsciously. It was a northern ballad, so old its words were known to everyone, a haunting melody, and hearing it Philippa too began to hum with him.

Perched in front of him, close to him, she had only to lean sideways to touch him. She too had not said all she felt. 'Yes,' she had wanted to cry, as if in answer to a question. 'I know how you feel. When things looked dark, when the way was long, you gave me strength to continue. Yes, I came to London, hoping to restore my father's name and repossess my lands, but that was not the only cause. Yes, I believe we were destined to meet. Fate has shown us that much charity. What we make of it is yet to be.' The tune seemed to keep time with her thoughts; seemed to pick up the beat of the horse's hooves; seemed to match her own breathing. They might have been riding together over his native moors, and for the moment that grim fortress disappeared, the cobbled streets turned to grass; in a sudden burst of light June seemed to flower about them in the richness of a full summer day. And she thought, with a queer aching, must we part again so soon?

> There was a knight sought out his lady fair,
> Trela, trela, trela,
> She waited him, her castle within.
> His enemies without set up a shout,
> They had him fast into their snare,
> Trela, trela, trela.

CHAPTER 5

The palace of Westminster, where the king had been sitting in council, was old, a vast overstructure of stone that hid the foundations of a more ancient fortress. Today the king was in residence although he seldom felt at home there, preferring to stay in the Tower when he came into his capital (but even he realized that the Tower was not the most auspicious residence today). Richard pointed out the royal flag, with the green Welsh dragon that was a sign of Tudor birthright.

It fluttered over the gate towers where the guards in their livery of green and white paced smartly back and forth on the battlements. 'The great gates are locked today,' Richard said, 'because of the disturbance. Usually they are left wide open, so everyone can go in and out. The king is proud of his popularity. Without this map we'd be hard put to find our way. There's the entrance, just ahead.'

He gave a sigh. 'The princess keeps her own court,' he began to explain. 'They say the king dotes on her, and cannot be parted from her, not for a day. So that is why she is here with him.' He gave a grin. 'As perhaps I cannot bear to be away from you.' He turned to smile at her. Philippa saw how his smile died. She too looked round. 'Who are they?' she cried. 'Are they Wolsey's men?'

A scant hundred yards behind, issuing from the narrow streets, almost parallel to where they had come, some half dozen riders were spilling into the full sunlight. If the red colour of their coats had not given them away, their shouts, their naked swords, their sudden surge forward would have done – Wolsey's men, closing for a kill. And nothing between them and their quarry, nowhere to hide, a wide empty street and the locked palace gates.

Seeing them, Richard dug his spurs so hard that his horse bounded forward as if on springs, jerking Philippa against him. Had she not had her fingers hooked in the horse's mane she would have been thrown. They took the distance to the side entrance in a stride, at the last moment skidding skilfully to make the turn, almost bringing the horse to its heels. Darkness seemed to engulf them as they disappeared, swallowed up in a kind of tunnel way, running deep underground.

Richard had recognized at once he had only one chance, and that was to outrun their pursuers. So, in spite of the semi-dark, the uneven terrain, the twisting path, he rowelled his horse on as fast as he could, its hooves beating out a staccato that echoed hollowly. When for a moment he surged into light, he thrust the leather strap at Philippa so she could keep sense of where they went. He hoped his sudden burst of speed would throw Wolsey's men off the track, complacent as they must

96

have been in thinking they had him caught. But he did not know what lay ahead and feared he might be running into a trap. And as he surged up a last incline and burst through a gap in the wall her cry told him what it was. 'Here is the courtyard, just as the duke described. But there is no way out for you.'

She was clinging desperately with both hands, unaware that she had knocked her head against him, starting a cut across her cheek. She did not try to wipe the blood away, perhaps she never felt it. For as Richard now hauled on the reins to bring the horse to a stop, skidding it round in the entrance, behind them, following them up those same dim tunnels, came the steady thrum of other horses after them.

Richard ignored these obvious sounds of pursuit. He thrust the horse forward again. He had come funnelling into a kind of inner quadrangle, irregularly shaped, open to the sky, surrounded on all sides by the same high walls. The lower levels were built of rough grey stones, hand hewn and worn, so that in the gaps between the masonry scrawny wild flowers grew. The upper levels were pierced with a row of windows whose uneven panes caught the sun and reflected it down in slanted stripes. They might have been standing at the foot of a wide chimney shaft looking up at a row of stars, with as much hope of escape.

To their right was an old portico, its row of pointed arches almost like a church. At the furthest end, half hidden by a smother of vines, was a door, beside which a bell rope was newly hung. There was Philippa's escape if she could get inside in time. But where was Richard's?

His horse snorted, tossing its head so that foam flew in

97

dark patches on the ground. Its steel shod hooves sent sparks off the stones, like portents. It might almost have been smelling battle, and when Richard stretched for the bell rope, a deep echo seemed to reverberate underground, like a drum. But nothing could drown out the other incessant thrumming.

They listened. Then Richard unclasped Philippa's hands and lowered her to her feet. He felt for the scrap of silk and knotted it loosely around her neck. 'Wait there,' he ordered her. 'Pull at that bell rope until it breaks. Keep out of sight. Let nothing, nothing,' he emphasized the word, 'tempt you out. And keep hold of that scarf at all costs.'

He gave these orders in an even voice at the same time unhooking his helmet from the saddle, and reaching to check the girths and stirrup leathers. When he drew on his leather gloves as if preparing for some task ahead, 'Stop,' she cried at him. 'Leave your horse and come with me.'

He snatched a glance at her. 'What should I do among a group of women?' he asked, trying to make her smile, all the while working his sword back and forth in its scabbard. 'Besides, I am rather fond of my horse. You see to your task, which is to pull on that rope; I'll see to mine.' And he turned to ride off.

'Wait,' she cried, trying to run after him along the portico. 'I can't leave you. What can I do to help?'

'Only not hinder me,' he said, reining back. He gave her another quick smile. 'Come sweeting,' he said, more awkwardly. 'I am only creating a diversion until you are safely inside; that done, I'll fend for myself. I told you I was a soldier. I don't mean to brag, but surely one

Montacune can take on six wolves spoiling for a fight.'
And he grinned again.

She wanted to cry, 'One cannot fight six,' but she did
not dare. She ran alongside him, hanging on to his
horse's reins. 'Well then,' he said, almost exasperated,
'Give me your cloak; wrap it round my left arm, so, to
form a shield. Now let me go, else they will be on us
before I am in place.'

Despite the jesting, the easy confidence, she sensed his
urgency. She drew back. 'God save you,' she cried. 'God
succour you.'

He did not reply. She watched him clatter over the
rough stones and station himself in the shadows beside
the entrance. He had snapped his helmet on but not yet
fastened it, and was leaning forward, listening intently.
She had never seen him look like that, cold, appraising,
professional. She thought, he has already put me out of
his mind. I have never seen men prepare to fight or ride
as this man does. She thought, little good that does him
if he cannot break away. He has already risked his life
for me once, and now he does again. But were he alone
he could escape. And she thought, with the same sense
of cold despair, he cannot fight all of them.

As if he guessed her thoughts he shouted to her, one
last time, not turning round, his voice muffled now by
the helmet. 'Quick, quick, pull on the rope,' just before
the first horse came clattering through the gap. Edging
backwards towards the door, feeling for the bell beside
it, Philippa was unable to look away, although she
wanted to. The first horseman rode at a gallop. Dazzled
by the flood of light after the dark, he never saw Richard
waiting for him. And like a whip uncurled Richard swept

down with his sword, at the same time flinging the cloak across the horse to blind it. Horse and man fell in a rolling heap, blocking the way for the second horse which went stumbling over the first. A third, too late to stop, blundered into the second sending its rider against the wall within reach of Richard's sword and a spume of red splattered out. Three down then, in the first instance, two riders motionless, one scrabbling to his knees, slithering snake-like out of harm's reach. And behind him, yet another three, pouring through the gap, trampling over their fallen companions in their eagerness.

Unable to move, Philippa remained rooted to the spot. The jangle of harness, the clang of steel, the choked-off screams, all seemed damped down, as if a mist enshrouded them. The silver of that stabbing sword, that gush of red, had turned to grey; the falling men never touched the ground, the horses never finished their fall. She thought, this is not happening, but her eyes were open; the little courtyard still was dappled with light, and the upper windows still twinkled in the sun. She did not know she had gnawed her fingers to the bone, never felt the draught at her back, until a hand gripped her tight and drew her within the door, and slammed it shut.

She was in a kind of hall, which might have once been part of a church nave, the darkness thick and damp, blocking out all sounds. She began to struggle with the cowled figure who held her tight. 'Let me go. He is alone. I must go back to him.'

The man ignored her, and continued to glide along on sandalled feet like some monk, pulling her behind him. His mutterings might have been prayers, his long gown a monk's habit, sweeping over the rough paving. Surely this must have been some sort of church, a sanctuary perhaps, whose reputation lingered on in memory. She glimpsed dim oratories whose dark monuments flickered in the pale taper light; there was a familiar smell of stale wax and incense and the altar coverings gleamed momentarily in gold and red. Then she was climbing up narrow stairs, along winding corridors still in the dark, obliged to run after the figure who ran in front of her. A door was thrown open. She entered a world of light, so bright, so full of people, animals, birds, that she was stunned.

The room was large, newly decorated in sumptuous style, lined with windows through which the sun poured. The door was guarded by men dressed in royal livery; pages skipped about with plates of fruit, a bevy of serving women started from their embroidery frames like a flock of pigeons. In their midst, seated on the floor, her dress billowing round her like a sail, a little compact figure seemed smaller by reason of her composure. She was a scrap of a thing, with a mass of ruddy hair, but the face that turned expectantly had a determined chin and a nose that was formed for tilting haughtily; and the voice had a ring of authority which contrasted strangely with the first fragile appearance.

Like a moth drawn to a candle flame Philippa ran towards this seated figure, her own voice with its cry for help seeming to come from some other throat. She clutched the fluttering folds of silk dress as if to cling to them.

'Help, help, help,' she heard herself scream. 'They will murder him.'

The little figure on the floor rose briskly to its feet. Upright, the princess, for so she was, topped Philippa by a head, for all that she seemed so slight and small. The brilliance of her clothes, her jewels, all revealed her royalty, to say nothing of the command in her voice when she suddenly questioned Philippa, 'That scarf, where got you that?'

Not waiting even for a reply, perhaps misunderstanding Philippa and fearing that 'him' was that same Charles who was her brother's favourite, and her own, she spun round so abruptly that her wide skirts knocked a table aside as she ran towards the windows, letting her silk slippers drop from her narrow feet. She knelt in the embrasure, craning to look out.

'Wolsey's wolves,' after a moment she cried in an excited voice. 'Six of them, see them in their red coats. Three on horseback, one afoot, two dead. Who is the man they fight?'

Again not bothering for a response, 'Brawling beneath my walls,' she cried. 'I'll not have that.' Then, with a display of energy typical of the Tudor line, as if drawing a sword and exhorting an army on a battle field, 'Get rid of them. I'll not have them skulking around my private yard.'

Her guards had been hanging on every word. They eyed each other expectantly and on the instant were gone, snatching swords and pikes from wall-racks, clattering over each other on the stairs. 'Now,' said the Tudor princess complacently, 'we shall see what we shall see. One against four is not just. Let Wolsey's men cope when the odds are turned.'

She tucked up her voluminous skirts, making room for Philippa, and beckoned to her ladies to approach (which they did eagerly, chattering with each other vivaciously,

102

casting sly glances at the newcomer when they thought themselves unobserved; they might have been gazing from a balcony down on a stage, so much they cared, their comments more suitable for a play than real life).

Philippa ran after them and peered down. From this high angle she had a clear view, and the reds and blue were so bright, the figures so distinct that they might have been painted miniatures. Richard Montacune had been driven from his first vantage post, where ambush had given him the edge of surprise. Now, he was backed against the portico, ringed by the remaining horsemen, while the one on foot was trying to crawl under the arches behind him. He had not given up although he was surrounded. His sword danced in and out as if it had a life of its own, and even as Philippa watched he parried a blow, charging out and pivoting back, forcing the others to withdraw. The blow was such that only superb swordsmanship had deflected it, and taking advantage of the lull that followed he wheeled round to drive back the creeping enemy who was trying to hamstring his horse. But he obviously could not keep up the pace and already Wolsey's men were calculating counter-moves to draw him into the open where they could break through his guard. And seeing again what the end must be, Philippa gave a cry of anguish.

He could not have heard, but he pushed his helmet up as if he did, catching breath. As he wheeled once more she caught a glimpse of his face, almost indistinguishable beneath the mask of dirt and blood. She at least could recognize the straight hard look, the determined set of the chin, the level gaze, that looked through danger to its outcome. Then he rammed the helmet down, levelled his sword like a lance, and settled down in the saddle, leaning forward in his distinctive way. She heard his cry, perhaps the battle cry of his northern forefathers when they prepared to attack. And hearing it, his enemies raised up a cry of their own, and began to spread out, waiting for him to charge. They had him caught, nothing but a miracle could save him now, and their shout turned to a howl of triumph. A third cry made both sides halt in their tracks.

The princess's men came at a trot, stamping along the portico, either issuing from the door that Philippa had used or from some other one not visible from where she stood. They held their pikes at a slant, treading down the crawling figure as they came, sweeping round to circle the rest of Wolsey's men. Their green and white uniforms made a cool contrast to the red coats, and when they had hemmed the three horsemen in, they stood with their pikes raised like a hedge bristling with spikes. Seeing such opposition, even Wolsey's wolves drew back, in turn bunching against a wall, arguing uncertainly among themselves. Left outside that spear wall, Richard must have realized he had his miracle.

Wolsey's men were within the hedge; the princess's men had their backs to him; the way out was clear at last. Seeing his chance, he took it. But before he left he glanced up once, perhaps to ensure Philippa was gone, perhaps out of curiosity, made aware that he was being overlooked by some change of light, some darkening of the window panes. His coat was ripped, the blue doublet hanging in strips, the breastplate straps were severed and a slash ran red along one arm but he was not so hurt he could not throw up his sword by the hilt, as if in salute.

Then he too was gone, making for the gap in a swirl of dust, leaping his fallen enemies in a flurry of hooves.

'Bravo, bravo,' the princess crowed, sitting back and clapping her hands. 'My guards will hold the others at bay until he has had time to get clear away. When they are sure he has escaped, they will let Wolsey's men leave. The Duke of Suffolk will take good care of him; just as the duke expects me to take care of you.'

All this was spoken nonchalantly, as if she were used to having strangers burst into her midst and welcomed such diversions. 'What if they search for him?' Philippa's concern was not readily put to rest. 'They know at least whom he serves. They must know where to look for him.'

The princess was not offended by such insistence. She smiled, as if pleased at displaying her superiority. She had a strange smile, revealing a line of small teeth which jutted crookedly over her lower lip, a defect that enhanced her apparent frailty. 'Of course not,' she cried. 'What excuse would they use? Fighting is forbidden here at court. My father made that the law, and my brother upholds it. Although all great lords still have their retinues and dress them in their own livery, they do not keep private armies as they once did, and they do not flaunt their numbers as Wolsey does. My brother once cut off a man's sword arm to keep the peace, and all *he* had done was unsheathe a sword. So imagine what the penalty is for using one! No, Wolsey is not likely to complain to my brother that he breaks the king's own law. Nor will his men. They'll scuttle off, you may be sure, without a word to anyone. So you and your friend,' she emphasized the word, 'your rescuer is safe; safe enough for you to tell me who he is. And who you are.'

'Thank God,' Philippa found she had been praying aloud, her eyes closed, fists twisted in her lap, all her energy concentrated in that prayer. When she looked up she saw the princess eyeing her speculatively. It occurred to Philippa for the first time that here was Tudor royalty in the flesh, daughter of a king, sister to the reigning sovereign. Philippa's own safety depended on her good will. She sank into a curtsy, gaze fixed meekly on the ground. 'Your grace,' she began, not certain how to address the royal lady the duke had described in such glowing terms, 'Your majesty . . .'

'No ceremony, I beg,' the princess cried, waving her hand patronizingly. 'Here, all are friends, especially anyone who is a friend of the duke's.' Her gesture encompassed the other ladies in the room, who tried to look agreeable although since she soon had them acting like servants, bringing warm water and clean clothes, they could not have been pleased. When she had dismissed them out of earshot, she placed herself in a carved chair, so large she seemed dwarfed by it, like a child playing at judge. 'Now,' she said when Philippa's needs had been taken care of, 'you are free to speak. Answer my questions, one by one.'

Her attempts to glean information could hardly be called childlike. They were persistent and shrewd. And when Philippa resisted except for her first name, 'So,' the princess pouted. 'If you refuse, so could I. I could say I will not keep you here. I could send you out into the streets for Wolsey's men.' She stared at Philippa. She had been running her hands through the folds of the scarf, tying it in bows about her dog's neck. Now she knotted it and pulled hard, making the poor creature choke. 'I could call my guards,' she said. 'I could have them question you.'

Her change of tone was sudden and alarming, but Philippa's common sense kept panic down. 'We did the duke a service,' she said at last, 'at least, the young man did. And the duke promised your help in return.'

This reply silenced the princess. Then she gave a little laugh. 'Very well,' she said, sounding more pleasant, 'I shall keep you for a while.' She laughed again. 'If you had some evil purpose in mind,' she went on ingenuously, convincing herself, 'if you meant harm, I imagine the duke would have discovered it. If he vouches for you, then I accept you as you are. Besides,' with a flinty side glance that showed she was not as simple as she seemed, 'besides, if you were evil, I think you would look less harmless than you do, and would try to seem more so. And you would flatter me, like these other ladies. You'd not refuse what I asked, now would you! In fact, I like that about you.' She untied the scarf and flicked Philippa with it. 'My brother allows me to select my own retinue, so when I marry I will know how to control a household. I shall make you one of the ladies who serve me. When we go to Richmond you come with me.'

She gave her little smile, that might have been childish mischief, or spite. 'You may not have told me much about yourself,' she said, 'nor who that young man is, but your silence gives you away. He means more to you than you admit.'

At Philippa's blush, 'Just so,' she crowed. 'I know about such things by instinct. Even my brother calls me his queen of hearts.'

She suddenly looked at Philippa in a shrewd way that belied her silly chattering and made her knowing and hard. 'Why are you afraid?' she asked suddenly. 'You have a look in your eyes as if you are trying to hide. It makes me wonder what it is, or what you are. For what is there to fear here, unless you bring it in with you.'

She seized Philippa by the hand, and made her turn round on a scene as domestic as that in her own home when her mother was alive: the late afternoon sun streaming through the windows, the little dogs stretched before the fire, for all that the day was warm, the cages of bright coloured birds chirping along the walls, even the guards, recently returned, lounging unharmed and gossiping with the ladies, everything tranquil and harmonious. 'At Richmond,' the princess coaxed, 'no one would know you, and Wolsey would never think of searching for you. Besides, the court is so jam-packed with people, looking for a stranger is like hunting for a needle in a hayrick. And life there is never dull. Sometimes my brother and his friend, the Duke of Suffolk, play at tennis and we watch. Or they joust. I gave the duke this scarf at a jousting match.' She flicked the scarf again in Philippa's face just as she had done to her little lap dog. 'And the duke wore it, preferring it to any that his own wife gave. His wife is old and sick,' she said, 'but the duke is a valiant gentleman, like a knight of olden times. Once,' her eyes grew round, a trick she had, as if a child remembering a nameday treat, 'at my betrothal feast, my brother and he challenged a hundred men, and outfought every one.' She clapped her hands, as if delighted by Philippa's surprise. 'You did not know that I was to be wed,' she cried. 'Where do you live? I

108

thought all the world knew. One day I shall be married, to another Charles, who will become an emperor. I shall be his empress, better than a mere queen. But I think that now my Charles, Charles Brandon that is, has been made a duke, he will be the equal of an emperor. Wolsey will have his work cut out to best him now.' She grimaced. 'Wolsey is only a butcher's son,' she pouted, 'with a long grim face and yellow teeth, just like a wolf, a wolf's head on a priest's body. One could be frightened of him.'

She cast another look, her prattle suddenly taking on another meaning. 'If people say we Tudors are vindictive,' she cried, 'I say that Wolsey is worse. He hates everyone who is higher born than he is.' She gave a little giggle. 'And that means practically everyone. But we keep a lady at Richmond, whose husband was executed for treachery. He led a rebellion for the throne, pretending to be the real heir and his poor wife thought he was a prince. We gave her a free pardon, though, and she lives there freely, as merry as the rest of us. And then there is another rebel, whom my father treated equally kindly, making him a scullion although he could have cut off his head.'

She took Philippa by the wrist, as if to caress her, as if petting a lap dog, which must be alternately hugged and pinched, smiling at her all the while as if pretending her words could not have more sinister meanings. Or was it that she was listening for a quickened heart beat as a sign of guilt? Philippa felt her colour rise. It seemed clear that this little lady was no fool, although sometimes she wanted to appear so, and her discourse, although often shallow, a random mixture of importance and trivia, hid deeper levels than she wished to show.

One other thing was obvious too. She did not mean to let Philippa go. Philippa never knew why – because it pleased her royal whim; because she liked to collect strays, stray cats, stray dogs, birds with broken wings, and wanted to add a human to her collection; or because she wanted to please the duke. No matter that the guest was reluctant and the other ladies felt aggrieved, the princess persisted in her attentions, perhaps all the more so because of that reluctance, which was new to her.

She had Philippa dine at her right hand, sharing titbits from her plate like one of her pets; she lodged her in a small ante-room close to the royal bedchamber; worst of all, she used Richmond as a bribe. But when she slept the other women-folk seized the chance to point out her fickleness, as only other women could. Their scandal spared no one, ranging from criticism of Philippa's country dress, to whispers of the duke's liaisons. They certainly showed little loyalty for their mistress, revealing her as thoughtless, perhaps cruel, and certainly self-centred, like all the Tudors, although she tried to hide it.

No wonder Philippa tossed and turned all night, fearing she had exchanged one trap for another.

Yet it was also true that in this strange unlikely way, she was being offered the chance to do what her uncle and his friends had advised, that is to seek out the king, under the protection of the one person who surely might influence him. On the other hand she did not need the other ladies' warnings to tell her what she could see for herself, that when the princess tired of the novelty there would be the end. Besides, the princess's inconsistencies bothered her, by turns kind or spiteful, speaking in one breath of her own marriage plans, the next revealing her attraction for a married man whose affairs, to say the least, were notorious. These were things she could not reconcile, nor could she get at the real person underneath. Nor could she trust the princess's word. And a king who hanged hostages for revenge or cut off men's arms to 'keep the peace' did not seem 'kind' to her.

There were other things to remember from this strange long day, things to do with someone else whom she was glad to think about. And if she left the court where would he find her again, how could she find him? Was it only 'coincidence' that had brought them together again? When she remembered how he had greeted her her cheeks burned. But afterwards, he had been kind; afterwards he had embraced her as a lover might. She sensed that underneath his jesting ways there ran true feeling. She thought, it is true he is a lord, but he also is an adventurer who has to make his own way as best he can. Perhaps he greets all ladies as he greeted me, but I think not. For I believe he feels some bond with me. She thought, I know the princess is correct, and I feel more for him than I am willing to admit. She thought, I wish next time we meet I could greet him as a lady should, no more lying in the mud like a serf. Mounted on a horse of my own, wearing silks and brocades, would he be proud of me, would not I seem his equal?

By now her thoughts had blended with sleep. And as she slept, it seemed to her that she was riding in a large meadow, along a river bank, surrounded by a group of men. They all wore black, like judges, and they were grimfaced as if judgement sat heavily on them. Richard was riding towards her and he seemed weighted down as well, as if his armour burdened him. He held his sword

111

hilt up. But she could not decide if he were asking for justice or responding to some challenge. The river was in spate. The current flowed so rapidly that it lapped the banks, undermining the verges which fell in clumps. As the water rose it eddied into whirlpools that threatened to sweep her away. And when she awoke, her face was moisture wet, as if she had been weeping for some sorrow all night long.

The next day saw the court prepare to leave, as the princess had promised, an upheaval this, as if Richmond lay ten thousand miles distant. The king himself sent word that since the day was hot, the roads baked to ruts, he had ordered out the royal barge to convey them hence. This sign of loving courtesy pleased the princess, but the next seemed to plunge her to despair. The king also said that he would not accompany her. He was in need of exercise he said, wearied with sitting all day long; and tired of his councillors who bothered him with advice. Instead, it pleased him to go off hunting with his friends, although apparently those councillors begged him not to leave (something the princess did not quite dare ask), warning him the French war still hung in the balance, and too many details had been left to chance. He laughed their objections aside. 'Not if I lead the expedition myself,' he was supposed to have said. 'Not if I myself go to France. Last time my generals wasted my army and lost me the war. If there is a next time I mean to win. Even if that means risking my own life.' And he had grinned at the consternation that aroused, shouting for his horse and causing his courtiers to rush about, no time to lose, the best hunting in the world in those

Kentish woods. Let the French gnaw their fists, waiting to see which way he would jump.

Now it may have been that the princess had expected that the king would accompany her and was chagrined that he had changed his mind, not liking to share him with anyone. But when rumours of his real intent to visit a Holy Shrine were spread abroad it was never clear exactly what the princess had thought. It could have been that Mary had grown suspicious of her brother's plans; perhaps the Duke of Suffolk, being privy to the king's mind, himself had whispered a word of warning in her ear. The duke must have been all for war of course, as became a younger man and a soldier; he might have harboured doubts about this Nun of Kent, fearing the influence of his rival Wolsey in this affair. The princess herself never mentioned any of these things, and most likely, neither he nor Henry ever spoke of them to the little lady whom the king certainly seemed to keep more as a playmate than a confidante. All this too was conjecture. But the more Philippa saw of the princess, the more her own suspicions grew of what the princess really knew, and what the princess really felt.

In any case, unable to change or alter her brother's mind, and perhaps unwilling to reveal her true anxiety, instead the princess let her disappointment show in many petty ways, like a spoilt child herself. She fussed over her menagerie, insisting that it be cared for first, obliging pages to run to and fro with yapping dogs tucked underneath their arms. She had her own ladies trail up and down, using them like menials, packing and unpacking her boxes of jewels, while sweating grooms stuffed carts with loads of gear, with dusty tapestries, pillows and bed linens, with plate and clothing, as if Richmond were a desert, lacking all comforts. By the time the ox-carts had been loaded to the rims, and the barge had been brought to await her embarking, she had exhausted everyone.

But once the barge was under way the princess brightened. 'Come sit with me,' she cried to Philippa, patting the seat under an awning, as for a favourite hound. 'A river trip is what we need to clear the mind. See how the people shout and point. This is the largest barge in the world. Look at those swans in our wake, they belong to us.' And she leaned back and closed her eyes, letting the sun warm her face. 'When we reach Richmond you shall dance and feast with us as if at home,' she whispered. 'And one other thing.' She smiled cunningly. 'When my brother returns, so will the duke. And he will bring your young man with him.'

It seemed to Philippa that a monarch, off to war, would have scant time for feasts or balls, nor, remembering the last interview with the duke, did she have great hopes of his bringing Richard with him, but she held her tongue. And indeed, when the city walls were left behind and the barge glided on in glittering triumph, the meadows that stretched as far as the eye could see, the small villages dotted about, the rich dairy farms, all suggested a land of milk and honey, brought to prosperity and peace by its king.

Only one incident marred their passage through this fair-seeming countryside. At a place where the river narrowed and was lined with trees, so low-growing that the oarsmen were obliged to ship their oars and pull themselves along by the fronds, a small stone bridge spanned the stream. There was a sudden loud clattering. A group of horsemen was making for the bridge and, seeing them, the princess leapt to her feet and began to wave her scarf, the scarf that Philippa had returned. On the bridge itself one of the horsemen paused. He was dressed in hunting gear (as were the other men, all richly accoutred), and mounted on the black horse that Philippa recognized. Another man rode beside him, equally tall and broad, big-boned, his chestnut hair only partly covered by his flat-brimmed cap. This second man did not stop, drove his grey horse forward as if time was too precious to waste. Philippa caught a quick glimpse of dark eyes, like the princess's, only smaller and close set, a full red mouth pursed to pout, and cheeks that were broad and flat where the princess's were thin. Then he was gone, his men spurring after him. And although the princess still waved, neither he nor the duke acknowledged her and never turned back. After a while the rowers bent to their task; the barge slid under the arch, and, in disappointed silence, the princess and her retinue continued on, through a countryside that no longer seemed so fair.

CHAPTER 6

—

The princess had talked non-stop about Richmond, in her effort to make it seem a paradise. 'It was rebuilt,' she had explained. 'The old palace was called Shene but it was burnt to the ground when I was a little girl. Richmond is a Tudor name, you know, a title my grandfather held. My brother has spent a fortune building it.' She gave her little giggle. 'The joke is,' she said, 'that my father was a miser. And when he died my brother opened his coffers wide and let all that gold spill out. Ambassadors from other lands visit us sometimes. They come to sneer, pretending that nothing in England is worth their interest, but they stay to admire. As you will. And Richmond is only one of the royal residences! My brother owns fourteen. But Richmond is his favourite. And when he returns you will see how he makes himself at home, like any other country gentleman, no airs or graces for him.'

She pattered on. But nothing could have prepared Philippa for the sight of Richmond. From the white scoured planks, stretched end to end along the bank so that the ladies could disembark without muddying their shoes, to the high brick walls, tall windows and gate towers with their token battlements, it had the air of a royal residence, befitting a Renaissance prince.

The banks were lined with people. Philippa soon realized that although they welcomed the princess and cheered, their real purpose was to advance their own cause. Some had engaged acrobats to amuse her. Others had hired a troop of musicians to play her favourite madrigals, while yet a third group, disguised as nymphs, had perched themselves unsteadily upon a raft which floated down towards the landing stage. The princess was used to such excess. She smiled distantly, but there was no doubt that this welcome pleased her and she allowed the courtiers responsible to kiss her hand. Such is the power of flattery that even Philippa felt it. But she also noticed how many people there were; surely among these crowds one could be lost. This lack of identity had exasperated Richard Montacune but it gave Philippa confidence. She felt more secure in the heartland of her father's enemy than at any time since she had left home; although not for long.

This boisterous welcome restored the princess's good spirits. She prepared to dine with the queen, alone, since the king was not expected until nightfall, and as she dressed she took time to give a commentary on the treasures that the palace contained, from the great four-poster beds to the new-fangled Italian tables and stools and the very rugs upon the floor, imported from some Venice warehouse. She also gave all the gossip, suddenly brisk and efficient, as if this was a task she liked. 'The queen is Spanish,' she explained. 'And since my mother's death she relies on me to keep things straight. Her Spanish ladies are stiff and dour, and speak only Spanish with her so she trusts me to choose the English ones. I am good at that. I told you my brother prefers smiles to sour looks, and so he too likes my choice. And if you smile he is bound to like you.'

She let that thought sink in. 'Queen Catherine is older than he is,' she confided, 'and he married her to keep his word.' She looked at Philippa as if to say, See, I told you he was kind. 'She was married first to Arthur, my older brother who was heir,' she continued. 'And when Arthur died my father would not let her go back to Spain but kept her prisoner, neither maid nor wife.' For a moment her smile faltered, not a happy example for a princess who wanted to show her family in a good light. But recovering, she went on, 'God's will be done. My younger brother, Henry, took my older brother's place, and married his wife, so she became Queen of England after all. Her lands and revenues in Spain were too valuable to let slip, and now they still belong to us. And Spain has become our friend. In the same way, when I wed, the lands and riches of Charles, the emperor-to-be, will be assured to us, and he too will be an ally.'

But when night came the king still had not returned. His queen, who, in fact, was in mourning for her last stillborn child, retired to her chambers to weep and spent the night in prayer. She was a small, sallow-skinned woman with pale lips and a furrowed brow that was hidden by the close-fitting caps she wore, a complete contrast to her vivacious sister-in-law. 'We Tudors are different,' the princess rattled on. 'We prefer to have fun.

118

But then, I would not like to have been kept here, far from home, if my husband had died.' And she shivered as if for a moment the reality of grief cast a shadow on her.

The morning brought the king back. But a furious black-browed king, spurring a tired horse, riding alone. The court was soon abuzz with rumour, the king's ill-humour of concern to everyone. Gone in an instant was that jovial giant, that golden boy, that chestnut-haired youth whom everyone admired. What had caused his gloom was never clear and seeped out only gradually after his companions had returned. Among these was the great duke, who looked crestfallen himself, trailing in the king's wake, with the other courtiers, to the disappointment of the princess who, by turns, was alarmed and angry that her 'fun' was curtailed.

Even to Philippa it was obvious that the king was miserable. Instead of hunts and jousts, he went alone, sulking along the palace drives or riding furiously, as if the devils in hell were chasing him. When he was not on horseback it was said he devoted long hours to prayer, and after Mass was heard, often remained on his knees, with his queen, in their private chapel. What the royal couple prayed for was God's to know, but a living son must have been high upon the list. And if the king prayed for guidance in this French invasion, or for victory, he did not say so. Nor did he discuss his meeting with the Nun of Kent with his friends; he certainly never mentioned her to his family, and his family suffered with him. Especially the pleasure-loving princess.

Gradually however Henry came to learn two lessons which his peace-loving churchmen had not known about, although his councillors could have told him so. One was that once war preparations have been put in motion they tend to acquire a life of their own; the second, that it is easier to prevent a war before it starts, than stop it once it has begun. Hourly it seemed, messages arrived, with news of musterings of troops, with lists of armaments, with demands for provisions. The royal fleet had already been ordered to prepare; should it stand to off shore, or return to port; how many horses should be commandeered, how many guns? All these were questions which the king, as commander of the troops, had to decide but which he had left unsettled. In short, the courtiers whispered among themselves, the king had put a machine to work, and, like a wheel that runs downhill, nothing could hold it back, unless he himself put a brake to that wheel. And that he still was undecided about.

'You see,' the princess tried to explain, for in truth like everyone else she was puzzled by the king, never having seen him in this mood before, 'Wolsey and the churchmen want Henry to make peace with France, not because they believe in peace, but because they want to make France their friend. France is a large and powerful country, and they are afraid of it. Wolsey even has his ministers preach peace sermons in London. But the duke says the war is necessary. We Tudors have a claim to the throne of France and my brother should make good his claim. Besides, France defeated us last time.' All these were arguments that Philippa had heard before, although in truth not one made sense. But she too had learned enough to keep that thought to herself.

In the end Henry made up his mind for himself. He steeled his conscience against the church (for he was a devout man as his sister had explained) and had the church serve him. 'Very well,' he cried. 'Wolsey is a great organizer of his affairs. Now let him organize mine.' He sent a message ordering him to become his master of supplies, which the courtiers thought a great joke. He sent his envoys thundering out of the palace gates, with lists of musterings, with times and dates; he himself ordered out his stables and paraded his Flemish steeds, selecting those he would take with him. When neighbouring villagers appeared, armed with pitchforks and scythes, he inspected their ranks as gravely as if they were the flower of his guard, commenting loudly to his friends that any English peasant was worth ten French lords. And when he had ordered bread and ale for them and thanked them for their support, he had his court prepare a feast, more than a feast, a banquet, of some twenty courses, to whet his appetite, and to celebrate his victory in advance. More to the point, after the feast, his queen was to arrange a masked ball with songs and dance, in honour of their parting. Once assured that Wolsey was committed to his cause, Henry prepared to amuse himself.

The court blossomed in the excitement. Gone in a flash were those secret tears and prayers. The queen set her women stitching new frivolities, putting aside the flags and banners which they had been working on. To give her her due, when her husband was in good spirits and attentive to her she tried to match his mood. She determined now that she and her ladies would outdo themselves to please. At great expense and effort she had elaborate masks made, decorated with long pink plumes, in honour of the Tudor pink rose which mixed both red

121

and white. The colour enhanced the queen's olive complexion, giving it a glow it lacked (although less becoming to Princess Mary, whose red hair clashed). But the princess professed to be delighted. 'Shall we not look elegant?' she cried. 'All of us alike, a garden of pink.' And she had laughed, her lisping laugh, confident, of course, that everyone would know her, mask or not, for the costumes were flimsy enough for the royal ladies to be sure their royalty would not be ignored.

Masked balls were new to Philippa, as indeed were all dances and feasts (why would her stepfather have spent her money to please her?). She would have been content to have remained a spectator, had not the princess conceived another thought.

She pulled Philippa aside and began to whisper to her. In the past days the princess had paid her scant attention. Now, seeing her interest, Philippa was on her guard. 'You cannot refuse,' the princess was coaxing, at her most ingenuous. 'The scarf saved you, so you should return it. Say it comes with my prayers; no, better still, let him guess. That will add to the joke.'

She was speaking of the silken scarf the duke had returned, and since she had recognized it at once, Philippa presumed the duke would too. It was true that the princess had had no chance of returning it herself; the king's preoccupations had kept him and his companions apart and there had been no time for casual meetings as in the past. But the princess's idea rang false. On the surface, it appeared harmless, a joke that would appeal to a child, but underneath was a lack of decorum, a rashness, which could be misconstrued. But when Philippa tried to explain her misgivings; pointing out that

122

this 'joke' could bring hurt to the princess, to say nothing of the duke, the princess laughed.

'Pooh,' she said. She cocked her head on one side. 'You talk of difficulties because you are afraid.' She began to pout, drawing her bottom lip over those small protruding teeth. 'When the feasting is done and we ladies retire to arrange our dress, you are to seek the duke out. You remember him.' And when Philippa hesitated, more sharply still, 'He would be shocked to learn what an ingrate you are, after all I have done for you. And after all he did.' She gave her little moue, as if to say, 'Of course I do not know the details, but I could always find them out.'

Put that way, with the familiar flicker of ambiguity, quibbling seemed ill-advised. Actually it was the princess's last argument that persuaded most. 'You would not want the duke to leave for war without some gift from me,' she coaxed. 'I want him to have it to bring good luck.' That appeal touched Philippa's kind heart and so reluctantly she agreed.

In the normal way she would not have dined in royal company, for the king, like most men, chose to eat with his family and close friends, and even the banqueting hall at Richmond could not seat everyone. Only at the feasting's end, when the dancing began, would all the courtiers join in, all, that is, who could squeeze and push inside. Before that, the ladies would withdraw while the gentlemen, like men everywhere, would remain to talk or drink or play at chance. So while the ladies tried on their masks, not without much giggling from the maids who helped them, Philippa donned a mask of her own and waited for the princess to tell her what to do.

The princess had dressed in haste. She threw a pink cloak over Philippa's gown, tied the fastenings with her own hands, and, making sure that the mask was in place pulled her towards the hall door. 'Now,' she said. She thrust a little package at Philippa and opened the door, one hand to her mouth, either to stifle her own giggles or doubly to ensure she was not recognized.

Philippa found herself at the entrance of the largest hall she had ever seen. She was the only lady there, for behind her the princess kept her hand upon the latch so no one else could enter. By now the menials had begun their work: most of the tables had been stacked, the benches removed; scraps of food had been piled in baskets for the poor, only the floor underfoot was still ankle deep in straw and refuse. The candles had almost guttered out, needing to be replaced, but the dim light was an unexpected blessing.

The king was seated at the main table with his drinking friends. Tonight he had drunk well. His face was flushed, and he himself was boisterous, over-talkative, making up for those previous days of silence. His arm was round one of his companions, while both bawled out an indecent love ditty. Between him and the rest of his courtiers were the ladies' empty seats, and at the other end of the table, closer to the door, the duke was engaged in conversation with his friends, laughing at some joke.

Philippa hesitated. The duke was not alone, yet she sensed she would never have a better opportunity. So while the servants continued to sweep the floor and the stewards circulated the wine, she tiptoed towards him, her slippered feet making no sound. It should have taken only a moment to lay the little package in front of him, and it would have done, had not the king chosen the same moment to hiccough. The royal chorus missed a beat, faltered out of tune. In the ensuing silence, the duke's exclamation of surprise rang out over-loud.

The king swung round. Wheezing for breath, wiping his eyes with the back of his hand, he did not miss a thing. 'What's wrong?' he cried. 'What makes Charles start like a hunting hound?'

He hiccoughed again, watching with his small dark eyes that suddenly took on the look of an animal, by turns furtive or aggressive, hesitating between retreat and attack. He gave a beady grin. 'And who is the lady there with him?'

When the duke did not reply, he grinned again, looking round him as if to say, 'There, I have him trapped.' But as the silence lengthened, so did his face start to darken ominously. Philippa felt her heart begin to thud. She sensed danger in the air, breathing down at her. A cloak of velvet, a mask of silk, the dim candlelight, suddenly these things seemed too flimsy for disguise, and the little package felt as large and heavy as a case lined with lead.

The duke was quick. Years at court now stood him in good stead. He clasped her arm and spun her about so she was facing the king. From the side of his lips, she heard him hiss, 'Be still,' as he bowed to the king, free hand on hip, seeming completely at ease. And showing the careless disregard which his friends called bravery and his enemies foolhardiness, he began to unfold the length of silk, deliberately making sure that the king saw what it was, although he was careful to keep its colours and texture concealed, as the dimness of the hall allowed.

125

He actually beckoned to a page to bind the scarf round his sleeve; then shook his arm vigorously to make sure the knot would hold, nodding meanwhile to the other courtiers as if to say, 'What a fuss over a scrap of cloth.'

His frank smile made a favourable contrast to Henry's shifty one. And, to top his performance, when all eyes were still on him, he drawled an answer to the king's question. 'A gracious lady, my liege, whose gracious gift I mean to wear to war, as I have ever done in peace.' The smile was calculated perhaps but then, what had he hidden or attempted to hide, only a lady's favour, presented in person by a lady to a lady's man.

Afterwards, with a sudden spring, he leapt onto the table top and beckoned to the servants to bring more wine. 'A toast,' he shouted impulsively. 'Lords all, I drink to victory.' The epitome of gallantry, he hoisted up his goblet, and one by one the other courtiers hastened to follow suit. 'To our great king,' he cried, 'the lord of war, who leads us at the charge as he ever leads us here at home. Health and long life to him; God grant him a safe and joyous return.'

Fine words these, obliging everyone to repeat the same toast, an old courtier's clever trick, saying all, revealing naught, evading the real issue.

Henry, drunk as he was, may have decided not to push too hard. After all, on the brink of war he could not alienate his chief general. He gave a royal snort, either of disappointment or relief, and snapped his fingers for another round of wine. Having failed to embarrass his friend, the king turned his attention to the next best thing. 'Tell your ladies we need prayers,' he hiccoughed. 'Victory lies with God, not in ribbons. But you still have

126

not presented the lady to us.' And he pointed to Philippa.

While the duke had so cleverly captured all men's attention, he had, perforce, let go of Philippa and she had seen her chance to withdraw. The guards let her pass, smiling good-humouredly themselves (for the duke's amorousness was well known and there was no reason to suppose that, having changed his name, he had also changed his habits). She had her hand upon the latch before she realized that someone held it firm on the outside. And before she could break the hold, the king's remark turned all attention on her again.

For an instant the duke's own poise deserted him. Then he sprang down as quickly as he had sprung up and, approaching Philippa with easy stride, caught hold of her, digging his fingers in hard, as warning. 'Here my lord,' he said. 'See for yourself.' And laughing lightly, as if without a care in the world, he drew her towards the king, and then stood back, arms crossed on his chest, a handsome wanton, whose only fault was his liking for the ladies.

Close to the king Philippa could see what her mask and the natural dimness of the room hitherto had blurred. She recognized the height of him, and the wide expanse of embroidered shirt, for he had thrown off his doublet and over-gown, preparatory to dancing. He was sweating heavily. His chestnut hair hung in lank curls, and when he stretched out his thick hairy hand, she was surprised at the calluses on the palm, like a peasant's. She expected him to rip off her mask, but instead, with a smile that was almost the copy of the princess's, he fumbled on the table for his own, a black, heavy contraption of cloth

127

which hid his face, from scanty beard to the roots of that flaming hair.

'Now mistress,' he said, words coming out hollowly, 'we both are strangers, concealed from each other, and from the world. If you hide behind a mask, so can I. When you uncover, so will I.'

He spoke in courtly style, although he swayed upon his feet, rocking back and forth on his heels, leaning all his drunken weight on Philippa's shoulders, so that she bent under him. But, with unconscious imitation of the duke's strength (or perhaps intent on matching it), he leapt onto the dance floor, dragging her as his partner. Trampling over the mounds of debris, he swung her round, holding her by the waist. The dance was a French one he was fond of, the steps fast and elaborate, and, lacking music at first, he sang the air aloud in a hearty baritone.

Startled by his outburst of energy, the musicians had been caught unprepared. They had been craning over the gallery, safe out of reach, so free to stare. Now, snatching up their viols and lutes, they began to fiddle for dear life, scraping so hard that the strings snapped. The younger courtiers, equally unnerved, jumped back to give the king space; others ran helter-skelter to haul whatever ladies they could find to partner them. The servants came scurrying with new brooms and pails; taper boys ran to replenish the wall-sconces. Only the wiser, older men stood in little groups and looked ill-at-ease. To start the dancing without the queen was an affront which her Spanish temperament would resent. But there was no way now to stop the king, bent on pleasing himself. Nor any hope of turning it into a jest, unless the queen herself did. And the Princess Mary, her own jest gone astray, stood at the door, her hand still on the latch, her eyes rounded in dismay.

The king danced with gusto, with much stamping and hearty leaps and swirlings of his partner so that her feet left the floor. His hair stood in spikes, and the strings of his shirt had come undone, revealing a white, hairless chest, upon which a gold medallion hung. He was proud of that medal. The Pope had given it to him in honour of his piety and when he caught Philippa to himself the design left an imprint on her cheek, Defender of the Faith, carved in Latin. But Henry was not feeling like defending anyone today, rather he was on the lookout for attack.

Meanwhile the other courtiers had brought more ladies back into the hall, in an effort to minimize the king's indiscretion. The musicians continued to thump and screech; the new candles flared as the boys relighted them, the shadows of the dancers crossed and criss-crossed, a swirl of black and pink, the effect being all the queen had hoped, although she was not there to enjoy it. Philippa of course had never seen such a spectacle. The thought that she was dancing with the man who held all of England in his hand, who held life and death over her, made her lose her footing and stumble. But the king merely tightened his hold, as if all this energy had sweated drunkenness out of him. He certainly was sober when, with great stealth and skill, he began to steer her out of the press towards the darkest part of the hall where the candles were still unlit. A low archway led into an obscure alcove, and there he paused, twirling her about one last time so he could thrust her in. Sure that they were alone he let the bulk of his body block the arch.

She came to a standstill against the wall. Violent movement had tumbled her dress and the pink cloak was ripped; worse, the mask had begun to slip, held in place only by its feathered plumes. The king himself stood athwart the arch and observed her from behind his mask. If exercise had worn off his drunkenness it had not diminished his curiosity; quite the opposite, he was really curious now, but in a different way. Where before he had wanted to test the duke, now he genuinely was interested in her. He had seen enough to make his senses race, and he tightened his thick fingers about her waist, giving warning of his intent.

Pressed as she was against that wide expanse of chest, Philippa could smell the wine upon his breath, and see his fleshy lips, feel the excitement mounting in him. 'By St George,' he was breathing, 'no wonder Charles tried to hide you from me.' And he shifted his bulk closer, so that her curls brushed against his chin, and her body was folded against his.

'Who are you?' The king was nuzzling her hair, touching her here and there, moving, shifting, like a greedy child with a new toy. 'You must have a name. Give me it or I die.' He groaned, in a parody of courtly love, all the while pressing her with his hard muscles, hard chest, hard groin.

In an effort to keep him at a distance and break his embrace without his noticing Philippa kept her body rigid, drawn back from him as far as she could. She wanted to cry out or push him away but she knew instinctively that to insult a king in his lechery would be an offence, which he assuredly would not forget. Better to endure it than offend. So when he held her against him like a doll, when he rubbed himself upon her, like a horse scratching itself, she tried to detach herself from his indignities. She knew what loving meant perhaps, but little of violence and carnal needs. And there was no disguising the king's desire, nor his greed.

He thrust one knee between hers; felt for her breasts with his large hands; stroked her down from neck to navel as if he owned her. 'By Christ,' he said, 'those eyes are blue as a summer storm. I would see them plain; strip off and reveal yourself to me.'

Whether he meant the mask alone, or wanted her to remove all her clothes, the order was a royal one, and desperately Philippa searched for some way to refuse. Suppose I tell him no, she thought; will he rear back outraged? Will he shout for his guards? Will he do what he wants anyway; who could stop him? Straining now to break away, by sheer good luck she hit upon the one strategy that intrigued him, using his own ruse to pretend she did not recognize him.

'My lord,' the ambiguous title came easily to her tongue, as did the flowery speech, 'tonight, by the king's command we have all concealed ourselves, and by his law we have placed ourselves under the spell of anonymity. I, for one, would not break that spell, nor flaunt the laws that he has made. Tonight we are not ourselves.' And she made herself curtsy to him.

He drew back, for a moment surprised and perhaps intrigued that she had not recognized him. Not many women refused him anything. He liked the idea of power, even power in such small demands, but he found he also liked having it challenged by so slight a creature. Her quick response made him feel more quick, as if in some flattering way she was complimenting him. Devious himself, he admired the same quality in her. So for a moment he could stand looking at her with a flash of genuine admiration.

'You must have a name, girl,' he said, speaking in more normal tones without hyperbole. He began to tug off his mask. 'Everyone has a name. Where do you come from?'

'The country, my lord,' she began, when he broke in, 'So far away, I suppose you have never heard of us.' He started to laugh. 'If you have kept Charles dangling on a string,' he said, 'you must be new to court. Not many women resist him long. We are in the country here, child; where do you think Richmond is?' She could tell he was grinning. 'Well, I will make a bargain with you. If I tell you my name, you must tell me yours.'

He was playing with her of course, allowing her her little pretence. And when she did not answer, sensing an indecision in her that made her seem not entirely insensible to him, he leaned towards her to whisper. 'Suppose I ask as a man, not as a king; suppose Harry Tudor begs.' He expected of course that she would cry out in alarm or mock surprise; certainly she would not refuse. In actuality, his more honest approach showed him in such a different light that Philippa was almost touched. She felt herself drawn towards him by the force of his personality as before she had been repelled. And he was perhaps equally drawn to her. 'You tremble like a leaf,' he said. 'I shall not hurt you.' And he put out his hand to remove the remnants of that fragile mask.

132

He meant things sexual of course and, thinking like a man, may have reckoned she was about to give in, while she was thinking of him in his kinglike role and hoping she could confide in him. Sensing another victory then, he began to grin, and catching her to him in almost a genuine display of affection, he began to turn her around, so that he could slip his hands under the lacings of her gown.

What saved her was a simple thing, or rather a simple shout. The courtiers took up the cry, 'The queen, the queen'; the music stopped; the dancers floundered mid-step. Catherine of Aragon billowed into the room, every inch a queen, her face set, as if it were a mask itself. Had someone warned her what was happening; had someone told her what to expect? Clothed in pale rose, her head high, with a crown of pink feathers in her hair, she swept towards the dais, her maids-in-waiting chattering in Spanish behind her back, resembling a bouquet of flowers, carrying real roses to scent the air. Looking neither left nor right she ascended the dais where two thrones of unequal height had been placed. She seated herself deliberately upon the larger one, all the while keeping up an animated discourse with her friends. And beside them, the Princess Mary seemed more than ever like some butterfly, her attention flitting from one person to the next.

Henry heard the cry. He was not so enraptured that he could not heed a warning, and his drunkenness had passed. Nor was he ready yet publicly to insult his queen. He knew that, despite her eagerness to please, her temper could be harsh if she felt herself abused. After all, she was daughter of an old line of kings, and she was proud. Letting go his hold, he stepped out of the alcove, not even bothering to arrange his clothes, fumbling, as if he had retired to relieve himself. In an instant his chamberlains were at his elbow, whispering earnestly; at a signal, the musicians struck up a new tune, one that the queen preferred. Without further ado, Henry strode towards her, as undisturbed as if he had really been standing in a privy alone.

'Tomorrow we set sail for France,' he cried in a hearty voice. 'Tomorrow brings us victory. Tonight we celebrate.' And, taking a leaf from the duke's book, he bowed, hand on hip, the perfect Renaissance prince, in a trice transformed back to affectionate husband, dignified king, loyal friend, nothing left of the wine-soaked fumbler in the dark. 'I drink to you, my queen,' he cried. 'To the fortunes of war, and love. If you will so honour us.'

She bowed her head in response; the music swelled, the rose-coloured cloaks swirled like thistledown. Henry led out his Spanish queen, looking at her affably. The Princess Mary swung past, still smiling at everyone; Charles Brandon, Duke of Suffolk, chose his own partner too, and began to dance. Hidden in the alcove, Philippa watched them all go round and round. 'Are any of them real?' she thought. 'How do they survive? And how can I get free from them?'

CHAPTER 7

——

In the end the man who extricated her was the only one she might have longed for, and yet would have avoided (at least at this time). He it was of all the court who had had the foresight to shout out the queen's name as a warning; as a means, perhaps the only one, of recalling the king to his real duty, without more scandal. It was he who, snatching up a mask of his own, now strode towards the arras and dragged her out, forcing her to dance with him, obliging her to keep time and not to rush, as he skilfully steered her between the couples towards the exit and escape. She knew who he was at once, although he was not dressed in courtier finery, and his spurs (which he had not even had time to unstrap) dragged at her skirts; he must have just arrived, she thought; did he come here to hunt for me? She thought, he is the only man here to know my name; the only one to know who and what I am, and what my real purpose is; and the only one who can misjudge me for the wrong reasons. Why is it, what quirk of fate, what misfortune, that every time we meet, I am obliged to rely on him, he the rescuer, I the victim!

As he drew her out she watched him beneath the remnants of her mask, those masks now rendering them both anonymous amid the swirling crowds. The threat of king, of queen, fear of the princess's reprisal, shame at the manner of being used, all faded away on recognizing him. I knew he would come when he could, she thought; I knew no barracks or guard room would hold him long. Let the duke laugh and flirt with someone else, avoiding unpleasantness; let the princess ignore us both, pretending innocence, now Lord Montacune has come the world once more is in accord.

But he did not speak. And where once she could not have imagined anything more of delight than to have him hold her, dance with her, suddenly she felt she might have been a stranger to him, and he, like some passing stranger too, was merely taking pity on her. His hand was hard around her waist; his boots tapped out an intricate rhythm like a drum. As hard as steel and as implacable, she felt his animosity towards her, and the tenor of his unspoken thoughts was not that of a lover. How dare you trifle with me, he might have said; and worse, why should I care? Are not all women fickle and vain? Is this what I gave up my career for?

He was dressed in riding gear, and as they came into the light she could see the grime upon his cloak, the layer of dust; she could sense the fatigue. He must have ridden hard, she thought, perhaps bringing reports about the army's mustering. It suddenly dawned on her how it might seem to him, to approach the court in this way, when he might have been here all the time, at the duke's side, as one of his trusted equerries. Armed as he was, despite his lack of finery, he did not seem so out of place in these surroundings as she did. Had he found a partner worthy of him, she thought, he would have danced as nimbly as the king. She thought, it must be one of fate's bad jokes that he noticed me, just when the king did. No wonder he begins to regret his lost advancement.

They had reached the door; one last turn, and he spun her through. His mantle flared, the spurs grated again. She thought, in a moment he will be gone, striding along the corridor, out of sight. If we part like this I may never see him again, and all that might have been between us will go with him and be lost. Almost without meaning to, she called out to him as if he already had started to turn away, 'Wait. I would speak with you.'

And when once more he seemed to move (although in fact he had not moved at all), 'Wait,' so loudly that a servant poked his head out to stare, 'Wait, I have done you no harm. So why should you ignore me? And after all that we have shared; after the way last time we had to part, you owe me speech at least, Lord Montacune.'

'Christ,' he said. 'No names I beg. The walls have ears. I serve like any common trooper, no need to explain who I am. As for speaking.' He was gazing at a space above her head, looking out into the distance, almost as the duke had done. 'What can you have to say to me, or I to you, that has not been spoken of by men of higher rank? What can you want of me, that this great court cannot give?'

The questions were dry; the tone ironic. Beneath the irony ran a bitterness that was new. She felt rather than saw it twist the generous mouth beneath the mask, and make the eyes hard. 'You have learned court ways fast enough,' he was continuing. 'You have no need of me.'

137

She felt the conflict in his voice, she felt the reproach. 'It was not my choice,' she cried. 'I only came here as a last resort. It was not my plan to serve the princess. Nor did I wish to dance with the king. I would have avoided him if I could. It did not please me to be noticed by him. It was . . .'

He seized her arm to put a stop to these indiscretions and hustled her away, searching for some private place. The corridor was lined with rooms, most small and empty, used probably by court officers for official rendezvous. Opening one door at random, Richard shouldered his way inside, slamming it behind him fast as if to keep the world at bay. 'Mother of God,' he cried, 'I have not been confined to quarters all this while, kept in a pen like a caged bear while my wounds healed, only to be tossed aside when I get out, like an empty glove. Is this the way you keep faith? See these scars. I cannot put them off as a glove is put.'

Then calming down, more formally, 'You once were kind enough to say I saved your life. Have you no sense, to throw it away? Well, risk your own safety if you wish, but for what? To persuade a king to help you instead?'

The room was dark and quiet; its thick walls blocking out the distant revelry. The only light came from a pale moon reflecting through the high window, and Richard's tall outline loomed against it, blocking it menacingly. 'That is a game you cannot win,' he was continuing, every word deliberate, as if to force the idea into her head. 'You match with a king whose appetite is endless. One gulp, he will swallow you and spit out the bones.'

He seemed to be working himself into a fresh rage.

She thought, anger is better than silence. Let him rage; he will regret it in time.

'I will tell you what the king wants,' Richard was continuing. 'Did you take him for a fool? Do you take me for one? Here, I will show you what he was looking for, in the dark with you.'

And as if goaded beyond endurance he tore off his mask, tore off hers, took her face between both hands and forced his mouth on hers.

As kisses went it had little of love or loving, much perhaps of jealousy and lust. 'There,' he was repeating; every embrace could have been a blow, every blow a caress. 'When the king has had his fill, when he has begot the heir he is desperate for, princeling or bastard, what matter which, he will throw you to his hounds. Are your lands worth the name of whore? Or did you think he would give them for free?'

She struggled with him as she had struggled with the king, but it was the words she fought not him. The more she struggled the fiercer he became, the harder his mouth, the tighter his arms, until she thought she would suffocate. But although she bent under him, she would not break.

When at last he let her go, and stood panting, wiping his mouth, 'Only you knew me,' she told him in her open way that he had not forgotten. 'No one else. Why should I put you at risk; you are the only friend I have ever known?'

She suddenly tore off the cloak as if it burned, and threw it to the ground, along with the last shreds of the mask, grinding the pieces with her feet. 'I never thought

139

to be called a whore,' she said, 'not by my stepfather, not by you. It is a lie. And you know it is.'

Her voice was low but vehement. 'I stamp that lie out,' she said, 'I stamp out my hopes for us.'

Lord Montacune had stooped to disentangle the rose-coloured silks that had hooked themselves about his spurs. His voice came out strangely muffled. 'I came to Richmond because I was ordered to. I hoped to find you here, but not like this. I hoped to . . .' but he could not finish the thought because he did not really know what he had hoped to do.

'And do you think I wanted to be found like this?' she cried. 'Why do you not trust me? Why should you think the worst of me? I love you.'

Her words rang out like a clarion in the silence that followed them.

He straightened up, twisting the silken threads, running them through his fingers. He was aware of every inch of her as he had never been aware of anything. He wanted to stretch out and take that pale face between his hands and smooth the lines of grief away. He wanted to smooth the web of hair that spilled down her back springing alive from the bones of her head. He wanted to stroke the small ears underneath, and the wide cheek bones, the slender neck, the shoulders with their slanting thinness, that made her seem so vulnerable. 'Oh God,' he whispered almost to himself, all anger gone. 'Oh God, come here.'

He drew her to him so that her reply was lost. He reached his hand down to tilt her chin or did she raise it to anticipate him? His touch was contrite, perhaps ashamed, but running hot beneath its gentleness. He wanted to cover that red mouth and dip deep. All that he had suspected the king of doing, furtively, with jaded touch, he wanted to do himself, but gently, without rush, here in the soft and glowing dark. He wanted to feel the moisture of the lips and the warm skin with its glow of youth. He wanted to swell the buds of breasts into his palms so that the nipples rose, to run his hands down the spine and up the long white legs, parting, searing them. Palm to bone, cleft and shaft, back and forth, until she sank upon him like a bird, and he surged against her, confident. 'So,' he said, 'hush now, my love,' the endearments easy too, each whisper a stroke, each word a touch, hot and damp, fire and rain.

In this fashion, laving away the king's lusts, restoring delicacy and balance, he gentled her, teaching her how a girl may be wooed by a man and a man may woo a maid, until she began to tremble as he remembered from the past. Reluctantly then he stood back, wanting to disentangle himself, not wanting to. 'Gently,' he whispered at her ear, but to himself as well. 'We go too fast. Softly now my love. Wait a while.' But she clung to him, hands entwined in his black curls, her body stretching up to his, alive in every part, the current between them running strong. 'Not yet,' she said.

Pressed along her body's length, he bore her down, taking the weight upon his own. He drew off her clothes that hampered him, threw off his own, together they lay, naked flesh to flesh, until he came to the quick of her and she let him in.

After a long while, he began to smile. 'So this was what you came to London for,' he whispered. 'Shame on you Mistress Philippa, to have wasted time. You could

141

have had it that first time, there in the fields with me.'
He stroked her mouth, running one finger along the
lower lip. 'And now I have found what you want, you
have no need of anyone else.' He watched the play of
light upon her skin, stroking it in graceful curves,
encircling it, tracing out its shape. She shivered beneath
his touch as if cold but he knew that she was not cold,
not with his own body's heat to cover her. Her skirts
were gone, her legs were bare, the inner folds of flesh
spread to his touch. 'There,' he said, 'does that please
you my love to touch you there, does that satisfy you?'
And she gripping him, matching his movements with
her own, wider and deeper and faster, whispered back,
'Not yet.'

So they led each other on, matching stroke for stroke,
equal at last, until the short night was done, and the
early dawn began to brighten the window sill. He rolled
over on his back, one arm still wrapped around her waist,
while with the other he began to reach for his shirt.
'What shall we do with you?' he asked. He almost gave a
groan. 'I cannot regret it my love,' he said, endearments
he seldom used before coming readily to his tongue. 'But
what of you? With the king gone could you stay here?
Would it be too hard for you? The war will soon be
done, I promise you, a little skirmish or two, a great
rattling of swords to soothe his pride, we shall be back
again. But how can I leave you, alone, so far from home?
How can I take you with me?'

For answer she came close to him, as if burying herself
into the shelter of his arms. He watched how the
expression of her face changed, one moment full of hope,
the next sad, as her mood changed. Fear for her made
him helpless, and helplessness was new to him. 'Come

142

sweeting,' he made himself whisper, 'it will not be for long. And if you do not let me go how shall this war begin?' He glimpsed a trickle of moisture on her cheek where the light caught it. 'Nay, never weep for me,' he said. 'I bear a charmed life. And when I return, shall we not ride north to Netherstoke?' He tried a smile. 'As castles go it is small and old, but it satisfies me. When I am rich enough to rebuild its walls and restock its barns, when I can re-seed my fields, would it please you to go there with me?'

He smoothed her cheek again. 'You would like it there,' he told her. 'It is a rougher country than these southern parts, with wild moors, good for hawking and not much else. But the air has a taste to it, like wine, and there are small trout streams. And in the distance you can see the border mountains.' He said, 'My mother would welcome you, and bid you stay.'

She let him talk. She knelt beside him as he dressed, trying to help, his sword and belt too heavy for her to lift, the elaborate lacings of his shirt defeating her.

'I wish I had some gift for you,' she burst out suddenly. 'I wish I had something to bring you luck.'

'Only yourself,' he whispered. 'And that I take without restraint. Wait for me. I promise to come back.'

These whispered confidences, these half promises, half wishes, these lingering farewells were slight things to hold on to, but when he left they surrounded her with their warmth, as strong as any medallion of faith. Outside the window she heard the sound of horse's hooves, as sharp as if they struck through frost. Once more she knew herself alone, with only her wits to rely upon.

And as he returned to the world of men and war, he

took the touch and feel and taste of her, locked away in his secret thoughts for his own pleasure and comfort when he was alone. And for the first time cursed the soldier's life that now would keep them apart, although for so long he had sought it eagerly.

The king had no such reservations. During the next days, Philippa was to see the full glory of his departure, all show and pageantry. In his armour and white surcoat, surrounded by the yeomen of his guard, Henry resembled some crusader off on Holy War. He rode one of his Flemish stallions; before him marched his trumpeters, with scarcely breath left to blow; behind him came his little drummer boys from his new music school in their blue coats. Each of these is armed, Philippa thought; from all over England a real army is converging on the coast, in their thousands. *A little skirmish*. This king means his invasion to succeed even if all of them are sacrificed.

The queen and princess were to bid him farewell in equally flamboyant style, riding with him to the coast and staying to watch him embark. But when they had wearied of their waving to the empty sky they too returned to Richmond in a different frame of mind. The queen surrounded herself with her Spanish confessors whom she kept at a distance when the king was home. The Princess Mary, seating herself by the window, began to chatter aimlessly. Perhaps the view reminded her of past pleasures which might never return; perhaps she thought of the favour she had given to the duke without receiving his thanks, perhaps she thought of a farewell that had had nothing of intimacy for her.

She suddenly looked about her. 'Go to, go to,' she

cried, to the listening ladies. 'You look like crows, harbingers of doom. How dare you seem so mournful.' Petulantly she threw off her golden cap and kicked at her skirts with her pointed boots. 'Are we at a funeral?' she cried. 'Of course the king will win. What about those three hundred ships my brother has? And those guns. Why does he call them his "Apostles" if he does not expect to convert the French with them? He sailed in the flagship, the greatest warship in the world. And the Duke of Suffolk sailed with him. What if our enemies know our plans; the more valour for us to attack them; what if our allies betray us, we fight alone. The duke told me that the French king is old, so sick that he cannot move from his bed let alone lead his army in the field. Like Mars, my brother is the god of war, and the duke will lead his army's van.'

But thought of what that war might also entail sent tears rolling unchecked down her cheeks. 'He will be safe,' she screamed. 'He will, he will. God must grant us victory.' But which 'he' she meant her ladies did not speculate, clustering around her in dismay. Philippa, standing apart, knew which man she herself was praying for. Yet as she prayed a picture kept coming into her mind. It was painted on the church wall and had puzzled her as a child, an old painting, smoke engrimed, of a group of dancers. They sped along on nimble feet; the musicians played; their cloaks swirled, they laughed and gambolled in their finery. Riding along with them, unnoticed by them, unheeded, a black clothed skeleton kept time with them. The dance of death, as then, so now. And only God could tell who would be spared.

But as trickles of news began to seep through the

court, detailing the king's every move, she welcomed them. Each day's advance meant one more day closer to her love, each day's halt one day longer away. *Wait for me. When I return shall I be your champion? Shall we ride to Netherstoke?* Those were the things that seemed real and that she clung to.

But summer was over and the beech trees in Richmond park burned like flame against the sky before the king won the victory he was looking for. The ladies, equally longing for glory, had been disappointed too, descriptions of hunts and feasts, and minor skirmishing near the coast reassuring perhaps, but not exactly examples of martial bravery. The messenger who now came galloping towards them was obviously bearer of more important concerns, and, seeing him, the ladies stood still, like statues frozen into place, models of expectancy.

The queen and princess, wrapped in mantles of squirrel fur, had been strolling along the gravel paths that day, feeding the swans, while behind them page boys romped, gathering up chestnuts to pelt each other. Philippa had been walking in their company, never exactly joining in the ladies' talk, never exactly excluded from it, when the sound of horse's hooves had made her turn. The horseman who rode over the leaf-strewn grass was mounted on a grey mare that had recently been groomed, and his own person, fresh-bathed, fresh-shaved, seemed to exude excitement. He was young, his blond hair straggling beneath an enormous cap, his stout body so stuffed into a French doublet that when he stood up in the stirrups (to give himself height) his coat bulged at the seams. He flourished his hat enthusiastically as the ladies waved back, and pulled up among them with a display of horsemanship that would have done justice to a cavalry charge. But Philippa was among the first to suspect that all was not as simple as it seemed, more by what he did not say than said, as if he were holding something back; as if he were nervous what to present first, good news or bad.

He started with the good news. In flamboyant phrases, reminiscent of the king's own words, he reiterated Henry's constant and pious intent: namely, to seize the throne of France for himself. Then followed a list of small actions, minor events, in which the army had distinguished itself, and so, by degrees, he arrived skilfully at the king's own part. The army was on the march at last, he said, despite the autumn storms (which the king's critics claimed would bog them down). The king himself had forged ahead and reaching a flooded stream, had been the first to ford it, forcing the army to follow him. This manifestation of royal bravery caused the ladies to sigh with relief and clap their hands. But it was only an entr'acte, preface to a greater theme, which the messenger's duty now was to reveal. Philippa, who had continued to watch him as he spoke, noted how, as he came to the next part, he shifted uncomfortably in his ornate saddle with the Tudor crests, and how the moisture glistened on his pink cheeks. True, the day was close, without wind, and under the trees the gnats still bit. But it was not heat or insect bites that made him twitch.

'The king sends greeting,' he was continuing, in the same correct tone, although he eyed the ladies nervously, as if dubious that they too might bite. 'He bids you know that once his army made its move, it won two victories in quick record: first, the battle known as Spurs; second, the siege of the town of Tournai.'

He wiped his forehead as the ladies pressed around him eagerly, overwhelming him with questions where these places were, wanting details of both engagements. Again Philippa watched as he explained how Spurs came to be so called (because the French name was deemed impossible to pronounce), and how Tournai was occupied. Tournai itself was ancient, he explained, a fortified market town, whose maze of buildings were surrounded by miles of walls. Only the king's great guns could have pierced those walls, and so the king had had his cannon, his 'Apostles', brought up, to ensure their collapse. This had immediately occurred, enabling the army to pour inside. These descriptions of attack and counter-attack, this talk of bombarded redoubts and shattered gates, obviously were gratifying, and he would have lingered there had not the rest of his message still burdened him. 'And so, my queen, the king, your loving lord, would have you rejoice with him,' at last he made himself bring out, stiff as the brocade upon his coat. He wiped his forehead again. 'Our soldiers occupy the town, thanks in part to the bravery of Suffolk's men, with whom I myself was proud to serve. The king, our master, has entered in, and the French have submitted to him; in short, the enemy, abashed by their loss, have offered friendship and begged for peace. Which, in his mercy, the king has granted them. He has ordered our so-called allies to withdraw (for they never helped us much anyhow) and alliance with them is at an end.' He gave a cough, to hide embarrassment. 'The betrothal of the Princess Mary with

148

that would-be emperor is not renewed, and she is to put thought of him aside. As reward for gallantry the Duke of Suffolk is sent to Lille, chosen suitor to the Duchess of Austria (his own widowhood having occurred). Those of his men who fought so bravely in the siege are rewarded, as I am, by being made messengers to the crown. And thus I bring my message to its end, God save the King.'

All this last came out in a rush, the words tumbling over themselves; no wonder he sat his horse as if upon a prickle bush. No wonder the queen snatched at her rosary and held it to her lips, uncertain whether to thank God or to ask for compassion for her sister-in-law. The princess herself cried out in disbelief, as did all her other ladies, their cheers suddenly turned to mockery. Philippa, equally bemused by this reversal of plans, had sense to notice how the messenger backed away, relief and regret written upon his face. The title of royal messenger is a favour few men resist but for the first time it occurred to her that a messenger's fate is not always a pleasant one, dependent upon the way his message is received. Philippa thought, perhaps this news benefits the king, but it brings sorrow for the rest of us. It will break the princess's heart. Pray God it breaks not mine.

CHAPTER 8

——

After the princess had been led away in hysterics and the courtiers had trailed behind her, openly mulling over these tidings, Philippa broke away from them, determined to seek out the messenger herself. She found the young man seated in the main hall, drinking wine, his fair hair plastered to his head with sweat, his fair skin still flushed. Off duty, he looked what he was, a country lad, more used to barrack life than courts, at a loss dealing with ladies of high-born delicacy. He was in his shirt sleeves. His embroidered coat, his spurs, his belt and gear lay scattered around him like autumn leaves, although had an enemy appeared he could have snapped them up quick enough. He flushed again on seeing her, mistaking her for one of those ladies who had terrified him, and her direct query took him aback.

'Lord love us,' he cried, fumbling ineffectually for his belt, his brown eyes bulging with alarm, resembling some nocturnal animal startled from its den. 'Know Lord Montacune! Why there's not a maid from here to France who has not heard of Dick.' A remark which, even as it left his mouth, he realized was unfortunate. His good-natured face grew deep red and he cursed beneath his breath. He himself knew Richard well, as one does who serves with another in the same company. He had helped bind up his wounds, had kept watch with him after the ambush at Westminster. He also knew there was some breach between Richard and the duke, although Richard himself had never spoken of it. On seeing Philippa, he guessed at once this was the lady who had caused the quarrel, and he looked at her curiously. He saw a young slender girl who showed nothing of that tendency to hysterics which had so unnerved him today and who revealed her feelings only by the intensity of her look and by the nervous twisting of her fingers behind her back. Her expression however was resolute, reminding him of some raw recruit facing his first battle charge and he felt a sudden rush of sympathy. 'Christ's mercy,' he went on, feigning a smoothness that surprised himself, 'all the world has heard of Richard Montacune. I count myself fortune to have fought with him.'

He shot a quick glance at her under his fair eyebrows, and watched how her dark eyes glowed as if a flame had lit their blue depths. 'Aye mistress,' he continued, taking in her simple style of dress, her simple speech, with its west-country lilt, all of which appealed to him more than the other ladies' elegance. 'He lives, the king has rewarded him. He was the hero of the campaign.'

He saw her pale, her skin like alabaster beneath its normal colouring. 'Both of us are made envoys to his majesty,' he began to explain. 'I here; he in France. He often spoke of you, mistress; he has bid me say he thinks of you. I am to greet you in his name' (not altogether

151

true of course. Richard had been careful in what he said and the greetings had been implied rather than actual). Yet, seeing how the pink crept back to her cheeks and how her tautness slackened, he could not help but feel the deception was justified. He took another gulp of wine, running a finger round the inside of his shirt as if the collar was too tight. But being a simple soul himself (although not always at ease with the opposite sex), and at heart glad to do an absent friend a good turn, he began to tell her all the things he had suppressed, speaking more openly than was his custom, with an enthusiasm not altogether feigned. 'My name is Edmund Bryce,' he began. 'Like Dick, I belong to the duke's guard, and like him, fought in the war. It is true that, if I live to enjoy success, it is thanks to Richard Montacune.' And, encouraged by her obvious interest, he explained how at the Battle of Spurs the duke's cavalry had routed eight thousand French, gaining so many prisoners that ransom money seemed to sprout on trees. And how, too, at the siege of Tournai, those same men had won the town for the king.

'For there we were,' he said, secure of her attention now, at ease with military talk as he was not with diplomatic, 'beyond the outer walls.' He drew the lines of fortifications in the wet rings left by his goblet on the table top. 'And here were the town folk, withdrawn to the inner walls, after the king's great guns had battered through those outer ones. Between the outer and inner lines was an empty space, littered with stones and . . . littered,' he added lamely, stifling all mention of that desolate stretch where the bodies of men and beasts lay sprawled. 'That space had to be crossed before we

152

reached the inner walls,' he went on. 'Most of us wanted to wait until the king moved his cannon up, but not Dick Montacune. "While we wait," he said, "the enemy strengthen themselves at our expense. I, for one, have done with waiting. I had enough of it last time." And shouting out his battle cry which would afright any regular Christian, he stormed ahead, alone, although the enemy poured shot down at him. To a man we followed him. And when we came to the inner barbican we clung there under the gates like limpets on a rock while the tide of war raged over our heads. For after the defenders had had their turn at shooting down at us, so did the king's great guns. The king saw what we had done, you see, and he ordered his guns dragged forward without delay. In this way then, when the gates were burst, we were the first within the town. We were the first to take the city streets and the first to raise the royal flag above the battlements.'

He thumped the table top as if to impress her with that triumph, living it vicariously again through her eyes. 'And when the king left his tent that evening to ride in victory through those gates, he admitted his debt.'

'The king and the duke rode side by side,' he went on. 'Mounted on those Flemish stallions, they looked like giants. "Who are those men?" the king is supposed to have asked, reining back to look up at us where we leaned from the gate towers. The duke had to acknowledge us, although in truth our mothers might not have known us, we were so plastered with dirt and blood. Nay, lady,' once more he cursed his tongue. 'I swear he was not hurt, simple scratches that is all, from where the shot ricocheted off the stones. The duke presented us one by one, giving our names, making sure to point out that he was responsible for our bravery since it was his good judgement that had first picked us out. And that night when he and the king dined in state at a table set up in the main square, we were summoned to attend their graces and dine with them.

'The order caught us all off guard. We were feasting ourselves, not perhaps in state but well enough, with a good fat goose and a cask of wine.' He coughed in time to prevent himself from revealing that not one of them had been in condition for royal visiting, Richard Montacune no better than the rest. But he did tell her what Richard had said.

'After the battle,' he said, 'while we went looking for our friends and refought the war, Richard sat by himself. He seemed to want to be alone, and was in no mood for a royal summons. When he did speak, he talked of that first campaign, which had been so disastrous. "Had I died then," he said suddenly, holding his sword in his hand and rubbing his thumb along its edge, "I'd not expect my friends to mourn me long. But since I live, I mourn them. They were friends of my youth, men from my own estates, my father's guards, whom I persuaded to come with me, promising them fortune and fame. I swore on that Spanish border where I buried them that they would be avenged, and so, today, they have been. I drink to them." And he raised a bottle to their ghosts, then tossed it over the ramparts to shatter on the stones. Only the greatest effort on our part got him tidied up and on his feet, and stuffed into a clean shirt. Off we marched to receive the grateful thanks of our king. His

154

victory pleased him so much that nothing was too good for us. I suppose he forgot that some of us were those same men he would have hanged in defeat.'

This whole incident sounded so like the Richard Philippa knew that had she been in doubt it would have convinced her. Edmund saw her smile break out full strength, and he sighed, partly in relief at having allayed her fears, partly in regret that that smile was not really meant for him, and for a moment he envied his friend. Then a new thought struck him.

'I will tell you something, mistress,' he now whispered. 'It is true Richard remains in France but, mayhap, you can join him sooner than you think.' He caught her arm, to draw her close, taking care that no one was within earshot. 'They say,' he continued in the same confidential tone, 'that now the princess's betrothal to the Emperor Charles is done, the king is looking for a French marriage instead.' He shrugged. 'Why not?' he said. 'France was the greatest power in Christendom until we defeated it, and its king, at least, is king, not some youngster waiting for a crown. Besides, the French king has no sons and his heir must marry someday. Why not an English princess? And when she leaves as Queen of France, you could go with her.'

He eyed her complacently, proud of himself. 'As for that would-be emperor,' he said. He snapped his fingers to show contempt. 'On hearing the news, they said he flew into a rage, typical of him. He ordered his falconers to bring him a hawk and began to tear its feathers out, one by one, in a cold and systematic way. When his councillors berated him for cruelty, "They have misused me," he said, his misshapen Hapsburg chin sticking out like a wedge. "Because I am young, like this hawk, too young to complain, they think to strip me bare. But I shall grow and flourish. Then let them beware. Then let them squawk who think to pluck me of what is mine.'"

Once more Edmund Bryce paused to look around to ensure that they were still alone. 'But all those of us who fought for the Tudors there at Tournai think that a Tudor princess deserves better than him. And a Tudor duke deserves better than an Austrian duchess. We think,' and now he did hiss in her ear, young and earnest and loyal, 'that the duke is sent to Lille to keep him out of the way, and is made to dally there simply because he wants to come home. His wife is dead. She died but recently, while he was away. That makes him eligible to marry again. Why should he not return to court as a suitor to someone?' He put his finger to his lips, and nodded, as if to say, 'And you know who.'

'But until this comes to pass, not a word. And until Dick Montacune returns, he sends you this in courtesy.' He ended his story with a flourish that said much for his oratorical skills (although the kiss he planted on her cheek was entirely of his own invention).

She did not push him away with pretence of modesty, or complain that he was an insolent varlet, as many ladies might have done, feigning displeasure at what secretly pleased them. She merely smiled her full and luminous smile and curtsied to him as if, as her lover's messenger, it was only right that he should give her all that her lover was entitled to. Her smile, her grave acceptance of what was due, won Edmund Bryce's heart, although then he did not realize it. Then, he felt only that he had done the right thing and had unexpectedly blossomed into a man of tact and grace.

In the days that followed, Philippa was to see for herself how Edmund's news fermented gossip, like wine in a vat. Some of the courtiers still placed confidence in the Emperor and made bets on him. Others, remembering the story of the Nun of Kent, dredged up those former Kentish tales and began to list the French advantages as Edmund Bryce had. A third group claimed that the duke's absence was a subterfuge, and that all the stories of his flirtatious wooing abroad were lies, told to discredit him. The return of the king whipped that gossip to boiling point.

Henry arrived as became a triumphant general, with his carts of prisoners, his sacks of loot, his fawning sycophants. He was swollen with pride, so full of himself that he had Te Deums sung and Masses said until he almost bored himself. He never said a word about those marriage plans; never a word about the exiled duke in Lille, never spoke in private or public to his sister to explain or console, keeping everyone guessing. But in secret it was whispered that he continued his negotiations with the French, keeping his messengers on the trot, to and fro from Richmond to Paris, as if he were playing a tennis game and all of Europe was his tennis court. In the New Year he made up his mind. His decision came as a surprise to everyone, a French marriage indeed, to keep the peace and make a new ally, but not a marriage to the young French heir. The Nun of Kent must have been gratified at her success and Wolsey doubly pleased at a coup that kept his rival out of sight and brought himself such renown! For when in January the old French king lost his wife, Henry fixed his sights on *him*.

157

Now among Henry's messengers in this international marriage game both Richard Montacune, and his friend, Edmund Bryce, would have agreed that there were diplomatic reasons for Henry's choice. 'King Louis of France is more than old,' Richard would have said. 'He is so infirm that his late wife once prepared a burial for him, thinking him dead. Having outlived her he wants a new lease of life. What if the princess is a third his age, and he is riddled with disease, racked with gout, given to fainting fits, all legacies of a life of ill repute? Thought of marriage refires his blood. And he still hopes for a son.'

'Especially since he and his present heir do not agree,' Edmund Bryce would have added. 'His heir, Francis, is a scoundrel, even more lascivious than Louis once was, with an ambitious mother who is a shrew, determined that her son shall be king. Louis would love to thwart their plans. Besides, Louis is afraid of Henry. The French king is used to enemies, but none has ever claimed all of France before.' These explanations were diplomatic ones. The English court had other, personal ones that were even more convincing.

Their explanation revolved around the king and queen. Since Henry had returned from France, they said he had had more than victory in mind. Vowing to his friends that youth was too short to waste, boasting he had learned more in France than martial skills, he began to show off his amorous ones. Far from hiding his lechery, as he had in the past, now he openly pursued the ladies of his court, without the help or connivance of his former friend, the duke (although it was also claimed that he seemed to take dark pleasure in repentance afterwards which Charles Brandon certainly never had). If Henry looked for a masked girl he had left behind or if he wanted to beget an heir out of wedlock (being so unsuccessful within it!) his courtiers did not specify. And if, in the absence of the duke, he fell more and more under Wolsey's influence, they whispered that might be because Wolsey persuaded him what he was doing was justified. 'A barren wife is barren,' Wolsey was supposed to have soothed. 'God's will be done. But,' and all the cunning of the world was in that 'but', 'God does not prevent us from helping ourselves and a curse can be put aside. As can a wife.'

Queen Catherine could not avoid these rumours, and she was not one to endure humiliation quietly. Making her displeasure felt, she complained of Henry's philandering to everyone. Among her relatives was that boy Charles, who was already smarting from Henry's treatment. He was the queen's nephew. He took up his aunt's cause avidly. In turn Henry, feeling threatened, sought the French alliance, all the more because it shocked the other European powers. A twisted story then, this marriage bid, of lust and greed, political manoeuvring and personal betrayal. So that when at last the contract was agreed Henry felt obliged to justify it to his own family. And to the world in general.

As Richard had explained, like all Tudors, Henry was sensitive to public opinion, and he basked in public approval. Public good will had first given his father the crown and in the end would help him keep it. Henry had always been generous with his time, granting his subjects access to his court. Now he began a series of open audiences, allowing free airing of the people's wrongs, in the hope of glossing over his. And on the day of the

159

marriage settlement he ordered his family to be present, with all their retinues and friends, to uphold that impression of harmonious family life that he felt was important.

As for the princess, who was the object of all this manoeuvring, for the first time in her life she became a victim. No longer did the king have converse with her, being too busy with his new ideas. Ladies who might have flocked to join her entourage thought of excuses to stay away and the queen, lost now in her own griefs, had scant time for her. This neglect drove the princess wild, the more so that the duke remained abroad, never sending word to her. Philippa, to the contrary, welcomed it. She had no wish to see the king nor to be party to his plans. But come the day when the French marriage was confirmed, she sensed that whether she would or not, she would be drawn into this matrimonial controversy.

That day, the princess's misery broke out at its most pitiful. She lay down on the floor, weeping that she would rather die than be sacrificed. In vain her women-folk tried to pacify her; tried to dress her in her most sumptuous clothes, arranging her hair, her jewels, as if she already were a queen. 'Help me,' she screamed at each one. 'Stand by me. Tell him I refuse to come. Tell him he is killing me.'

But to Philippa she showed her worst side, catching hold of her and pleading with her. 'You can out-talk him,' she cried. 'You did so once, you can again. And you escaped from a marriage plan. You owe me this much gratitude.' Proof not only of her growing dependency upon Philippa, but also of her desire to manipulate her friend.

Philippa had dreaded the king's decision, unable to

avoid comparison with her own life. She guessed that he would never change his mind. Man-like he would beat down all argument, just as her stepfather had done. And just as her stepfather had shown no mercy, nor would he for all his professed love of his sister. Nor, if he should recognize Philippa again, would he be merciful to her. Nevertheless, out of a feeling of sympathy, out of pity and good will, and from some sense of fate perhaps, Philippa was among the princess's little group who joined the court that day, feeling much as she had done when she confronted her stepfather in a similar way.

They say that to think of the devil is sometimes to conjure him. Perhaps it was simply coincidence again; perhaps Philippa should have known that her stepfather was not one to leave well alone and would find ways to present his case; perhaps he had hoped that she was dead.

For his part, revelling in his new marriage and anxious to cut a figure for himself, maybe he brought his new wife to court to present her to the fashionable world. Most likely, hearing even in his rural Devon of the king's good will, and his open audience, Master Higham seized the chance to vent his wrongs without cost to him. It was his bad luck that he chose to bring a suit that dealt with dowry rights and disputed marriage contracts and female disobedience on the very day the king was confronting them in his own life.

Philippa recognized Master Higham and his wife at once. They were in the forefront of a group of suppliants who came pouring into the audience chamber (although she knew they could not see her where she stood behind the princess). Their clothes alone would have made her step-parents conspicuous, not one part of their person seemingly unadorned, their garments embossed with gold, with braid, with jewels (most of which were paste). Aware of the need of catching the king's eye, Master Higham strutted importantly, not averse to reminding the king's chamberlains of the urgency of his request, and beginning to rehearse his speech aloud.

The king had been playing at chance, a game called 'cents' and was in an especially good mood (if happiness means winning money from one's friends). The arrival of the common crowds had caused a momentary fluster which he chose to ignore. If earlier, the princess's downcast face or the queen's aggrieved one had vexed him, he had put that thought aside and concentrated on counting his winnings. He was seated behind a small table, dressed in new French style, rich velvet and silk, multi-coloured. His hair was long, in need of cutting, and his face was flushed with too much wine. When Master Higham took the floor he was probably only half listening, but his later 'What, what?' should have alerted any normal man to be quiet. But full of himself and his wrongs, Master Higham misunderstood. He bleated on louder than before, in the mistaken idea that the king had heard nothing, rather than having heard too much. When he began to re-explain how his ungrateful stepdaughter had fled from home, refusing to obey him; and how he himself, as guardian of her lands for many years, wished to have full right to them, the king reared up, glowering from him to the princess.

It is possible that Henry thought there was some collusion between the princess and this preposterous Devonshire squireling. He may even have pretended to himself that this little country bumpkin was a threat to him. Most likely his conscience pricked and he felt the need to excuse himself. At any rate he bawled his answer to the one as if it was meant for the other. 'She'll do as I say,' he shouted, red in the face. 'I have full rights over her,' an ambiguity which startled his petitioner, and terrified the princess half to death.

In this domestic crisis, perhaps the king missed the duke and felt a rush of petulance with the princess whom he blamed as the cause of the duke's enforced exile. So his sudden snort, 'You'll not have him, miss, not if you live to be a hundred,' was not so unconnected as it seemed. 'He belongs to me, the duke,' he snarled next, 'not you,' as if they were in the nursery and the duke was a disputed plaything. And he jutted his head forward like a lion in his menagerie.

My duke. There lay the crux of the quarrel between the royal siblings. The princess of course understood what her brother meant. So did Philippa and the rest of the court. The petitioners however were stunned, thinking the king had gone mad, and Master Higham's peroration ground to a halt.

Philippa had been listening to this exchange with her hands pressed against her mouth. Her stepfather's appearance had shattered her composure, just as his recital of her 'misdeeds' had burned like red hot brands, making her feel ashamed. And perhaps the princess felt the same way. Suddenly summoning up her strength she gave Philippa a violent push. 'Tell him all the things you felt,' she blurted out. 'Tell him that I have rights; that I am too young to be buried in a tomb; that, as he loved me once, he should not treat me thus.' And, cowering behind Philippa, she used her as a shield.

Philippa saw the king's full hot stare light on her. The other time, in the darkened hall, where smoke and gloom had hidden her, where the great black mask had kept him concealed, she had never really taken full stock of him, and in the same way he had never had a good look at her. Now she was in the open and there could be no more hiding. Her stepfather saw her too, and recognized her. As if a spark had jumped from the fire he stamped his feet whilst his wife cried out, 'Harlot, whore, where have you been?' Goaded out of common sense, goaded into reply, Philippa said the first thing that came into her head. 'All have rights to content and love,' she cried. 'Those rights are found in happy marriages. Without them none can be said to live. And no one can force another to marry unhappily.'

She might have been speaking for herself; she might have been speaking for the princess; she might have been answering all those fathers, brothers, husbands who force their womenfolk to knuckle under to their will. She certainly was speaking to the king, and an appalled silence followed.

Henry recovered first. 'By God,' he cried, 'who are you to bandy words with me?' He seized her arm as if she were a balky horse. Some thought stopped him. He stood still, stared at her again, stooped to snatch a tablecloth from underneath his winnings. 'Speak,' he countermanded himself. 'Now walk, turn here, turn there.' He held the cloth in front of her to cover up part of her face so her voice came muffled through its folds. When he threw the cloth down and put his arms about her waist as if to lead her in a dance, she felt a sinking in her heart that was worse than fear. 'So lady,' the king said almost triumphantly, speaking rapidly, ignoring princess and queen, court and commoners, turning his great stare on her. 'Here you are. I have been looking for you for the longest time. Where the devil have you been that you jump up now to threaten me? And who are you to stand between me and mine? You owe me something.' And before she could turn her head, he kissed her upon the lips, a great resounding smack. 'There,' he said, 'I deserved that.'

Still holding her by the waist he made a gesture which could have meant anything but which his attendants interpreted rightly. One by one they filed out, shooing courtiers and petitioners in front of them. The last sight Philippa had of Master Higham was his shocked look of dismay, while by his side, his new wife marched along, berating him. And she and Henry were left alone.

Henry's mood turned jovial. He rubbed his hands, glancing at Philippa from time to time as if to convince himself she was still there. Plainer than words his expression revealed his satisfaction and delight. She thought, he has me now for sure unless I can outwit him. And she felt a tingle to her fingertips.

She made no move to retreat. There was nowhere to go, the door already closing softly after the last man, the guards retired outside, the thick walls made to keep sounds in.

'My lord king,' she said, keeping her voice neutral. 'You flatter me. *I* thought our meeting forgotten long ago. I have not forgotten,' she added truthfully enough.

He grunted. She felt those small eyes' fierceness

165

encompassing her. There might have been a flicker of amusement behind their intent, as if he saw through her little speech. *He flatter her*! That was a clever reverse of the more usual state of things. She could feel him beginning to relish her. He had liked her last time when she had sparred with him. And he must have thought that in the end she would surrender, as the others did. It was just a question of waiting and he was prepared to wait.

Facing him, she knew she was no match for him, but half his size, a pygmy to a giant. And he was young, the young Tudor king, not yet a monster and she recognized his charm which all the Tudors knew how to exert when they wanted to. It was as much to put those thoughts aside as to prevent his trying to use his strength that she began to speak. But what she stammered out surprised herself. 'My lord king, I have come here with a purpose. And I should tell you it.'

She watched him move towards her, one fast step, snatching at her in the familiar cruel grip, drawing her down with him in his chair, pulling her upon his lap. 'Of course you have,' he grinned. 'Nothing new in that. So do half the ladies of my court. But they do not all win me as prize.'

He was covering her face again, squeezing her like a starving man, thrusting his tongue into her mouth as if to drain it dry. He planted embraces on every piece of skin, trying to pull down the neckline of her square-cut gown, trying to stuff his hand beneath the bodice. But he did all this with a coarseness that was new, with a roughness that perhaps he mistook for French technique and his fumblings seemed both lewd and pathetic now

166

that she had something to compare them with. She might have felt sorry for all that lust, imprisoned in that huge heavy body. Yet she herself remained cool and remote, and when he paused for breath she said in a voice that was also cool and rational, 'How do you know what I want? You do not even know who I am.'

Inflamed in earnest now, obsessed with his own desire, he scarcely heard her, or if he did, he mistook her words for some vestige of maidenly modesty, certainly not for refusal.

'Tell me then,' he was blowing in her ear, breathing down the cleft between her breasts, tearing at her clothes, tearing at his, like a man on fire. 'Tell me all your secrets. I will keep them safe.'

She did not give him his titles but spoke to him straight, woman to man. 'If I tell you, then what will you promise me?'

The elaborate fastenings of her clothes were thwarting him. He could not get at them and he was buckled into his own, as if belted into armour plate. Her lack of assistance puzzled him. By now she should have been moaning in his arms, limp with ecstasy, not passively niggling him with demands. When she saw him naked, his golden body naked like a god, when he had her naked, she would grow hot for him.

She felt him harden beneath her lap, potent like a bull, heard her protest torn out of her, as his hand went up her skirts, gripping her as if to wedge her legs apart, forcing her to straddle him. 'Anything you ask,' she heard him muttering, 'I promise, as a king and gentleman. Just give yourself to me.'

He was thrusting up at her, snuffling, blowing, in

such haste that she felt him hurting her through the folds of cloth. He had only to throw her to the floor with himself on top, that royal rape would have easily been achieved. But he could not wait. He surged up at her, snatching at what he had, in his haste unable to hold himself back, crying out again, 'Yes, yes, yes' the words pouring out of him in great gouts, until he could cry no more.

She sat astride him, face to face, his small eyes clouded with desire, his loose indulged mouth only inches below her own. She felt him slack beneath, and she cool above and she watched him subside, collapsing back into himself. For good or evil what she had been waiting for had begun, and, for good or evil, the king had responded in his own way. Slowly and clearly so that there was no mistake, she told what she had been rehearsing in her mind since she had left home.

'My name is Philippa. That man out there was my stepfather. He covets my lands. But I want them for my father's sake.' And she thought, God pardon him for using me in this shameful way; God forgive me, for using him for my own design. And may his wife forgive us both.

He said softly at first, as if exhausted, 'What promise?' Then more quickly, with a sharpness beginning to reveal itself, as if the world were coming back into focus. 'Christ's mercy, but you gave me little to demand so much. What stepfather, what marriage plan, what lands?'

He heaved himself out from under her, turning from her to straighten himself, beginning to concentrate. Left sitting, feet dangling in the big oak chair she felt drained, a rag doll that he had tossed aside. 'You asked me for something,' he said. He shot a glance at her. 'What father?' he repeated. 'How were his lands lost, that your stepfather claims them first?' He suddenly grinned, that secret grin which hid malice underneath. 'And,' the sharpness defined now, like a dagger point, 'you have not told me all your name.'

You cannot win. She heard Richard's voice warning her. *You play with a king whose appetite is endless.* Perhaps, she answered him, but I am sworn to try. She made herself go on, no way back for her. 'I am a de Verne,' she told the king, with the same touch of pride that Richard Montacune had observed. 'And it is my father's memory I seek to clear; it is de Verne lands that I claim.'

'De Verne, de Verne.' He turned the name over thoughtfully. 'There was a de Verne once,' he said abruptly, 'a west-country man.' He looked at her, comprehension suddenly narrowing his eyes to slits. Then, as abruptly he looked away; she could not tell what he thought, but his silence was ominous.

He said, his face suddenly grim, as impenetrable a mask as that black one he had worn. 'It is the asking that destroys the gift; giving is easy. Had you not asked for anything I might have given it in any case. I thought you different, Philippa de Verne. I thought, God forgive, that we were in tune, you and I, and that you were worthy of me.'

He sounded both arrogant and guileless, almost sad. 'Had you been that someone else,' he went on, 'we might have enjoyed ourselves. There would have been a future for us.' He shrugged. 'As for promises, we may not meet again so how will I know what you want another time, and how will you know if I give it you? You can tell the princess that if she survives this marriage she can have her freedom to try again. And you can try with her.' He looked at her, his face like stone. 'As for de Verne lands,' he said, suddenly beginning to stride away, pausing at the door, to throw a malicious backward glance, 'why, you can expect them back, in the same way your father forfeited them.'

He was gone. She heard his braying laugh outside, his loud boasting, seemingly not caring what his queen thought. Ashamed for him, ashamed for herself, left with the wreckage of her hopes, she crept back to the princess's chambers, her feet carrying her there despite herself. She found the princess in a cheerful mood. 'What did he say?' she cried. 'What did he agree to?' Intent upon her own concerns she spared not a thought for Philippa, nor for her sister-in-law, although Catherine had certainly been more generous to her. 'There,' the princess cried. 'I said that he would listen to you, and he did. I had hoped for more, but this is better than nothing. So I shall pray for the French king's death.' She added in her ingenuous way. 'That cannot be a sin, since God has already spared him to be so old. And when we are in France you shall see your young man. For,' and now her eyes did grow hard, 'I insist you come with me.'

Philippa thought, God forgive me that I wish my name and quest had been other than they are. God forgive me for my father's curse. God forgive me for the wrong done today, even to the poor queen who did no harm to anyone. And God grant the princess true love one day, as He gives me my true love back.

God grants all prayers in His own way and time, not looking for advice how or when. And so the ladies and their lovers were to discover in due course.

CHAPTER 9

——

As the feverish wedding preparations began, Philippa found the queen remarkably forgiving, never speaking of this incident, as if she had put it out of mind. The princess herself alternately preened or sulked. Only Henry, who like many men professed no interest in these feminine concerns and used them as an excuse to absent himself, only he seemed determined not to forget.

Even when he was not there, Philippa felt his presence like an overhanging shadow, never completely eradicated from her consciousness. And when he returned from hunt or ride, or from one of his progressions through the countryside, basking in his subjects' cheers, the 'jovial Hal' who had revived their pride and made England the greatest nation in the world, when he was back at Richmond, she felt his brooding look fixed griffin-like upon her, turning her to stone. She feared another sexual encounter with him, but it was not things sexual he was thinking of. His obsession had become completely political.

He had recognized her name and who her father was.

The Tudors have long memories, especially for those who had done them wrong. He also knew that treachery was like mud; throw it once, it befouls all it touches. Even if he had not met Philippa in the way he had, his suspicions would have been aroused. Now, feeling himself unmanned, angered that she had tried to best him at his own game, he let his suspicions run riot. How had she come to court? Who had helped her? Who had presented her? Most of all, what was her relationship to the princess? All these were simple questions with simple answers. But Henry was not interested in simplicity. Systematically reviewing all the details of the old de Verne plot, he set out to uncover a new one.

He hid his intentions of course, having no desire to seem more of a fool than he had been, nor yet a knave, fabricating evidence where there was none. Even he could not accuse without some proof, although to his own mind he needed none. By Tudor law a man was guilty merely by accusation, the burden of innocence falling upon the victim – whose guilt of course would make him deny the charge (a masterpiece of legal sophistry)! Since obvious proof of treachery was lacking, Henry had to invent some. To do this he relied on spies.

Since his return from France, and perhaps before, Henry had begun to be suspicious of everything and everyone. Now, it was whispered, he had planted informants even in his own household, easy enough these days when so many newcomers arrived to join the princess's train. Perhaps he had learned this trick from the French court, where such underhand methods were commonplace. Perhaps he merely copied the example of Wolsey, whose spying in church matters was notorious.

But such was Henry's desire to be proved right, that he came to believe in his own lies.

Henry's spies were not yet as skilled as they were to become, capable of turning a single phrase into a dozen conspiracies. They hit upon a theme that was over-ingenious, perhaps incredible, but Henry welcomed it. 'My sister never criticized me before,' he argued. 'If she does so now, some wicked influence must be at work to make her turn from me. What can be more treacherous than fermenting unrest in the king's own family?' And so his informants, sure of pleasing him, produced two proofs of Philippa's perfidy, by relating what the princess did. Neither incident had anything to do with Philippa; neither had anything to do with treachery. Such as they were, the princess alone was responsible. But that was what Henry wanted: to use the princess to strike at her friend.

The 'incidents' themselves were small, of human importance only, revealing more human sadness than treachery. It says much about Henry that he had to stoop to such pettiness. And it says much for Philippa that however she might distrust the king she would never have believed him capable of listening at keyholes, while the princess might well have believed she could rely upon her friends, as once in happier times she would have done.

The first incident then. The princess had been examining her wedding gifts, restlessly arranging and re-arranging them. Suddenly in a fit of pique she had pushed the piles of linen to the floor, overthrown the caskets of jewels and ordered seamstresses and jewellers

173

to leave (jewels and linens both paid for out of Henry's munificence, as if he had a Midas-touch; not one sign of normal gratitude, from a sister who had once worshipped him).

'I know how this marriage will end,' Mary Tudor had cried, 'just like those other times when I was wed, always by proxy, you understand, as if I do not merit the real thing' (a slur upon the royal name). She had snatched up one of the embroidered sheets which Henry also had paid for, picking at her royal cypher with her long nails. 'God's goodness suffices me,' she read, tracing out the elaborate stitchery. 'Little good has His goodness done.' (A blasphemy, as well as a reproach.)

Following this suspicious start she had gone on to make a mock of the proxy ceremony itself, whose elaborate ritual Henry had carefully planned; how after the Mass had been said, overseen by Wolsey to ensure no mistake was made, she would have to lie down on the floor under a bed coverlet, while some French lord would be brought to lie beside her in King Louis's stead. 'One of those French prisoners,' the princess scoffed, 'left over from the Battle of Spurs, I suppose, kept shut up since in the Tower. That would economize, since he is already here. And he will lie beside me, grinning, as if in truth he were a husband. But first he will remove part of his hose so he can stretch his bare leg over mine.'

She had given a little laugh, not unlike her childish giggling but without mirth. 'And I shall lie beside him like a block of wood, until he jumps up again. And he will bow, at his most respectful, as if minutes before he had not been pinching me or feeling in indecent ways, all in his master's name of course so I dare not make complaint.

174

'If that is all that marriage is,' she had continued, as if these indiscretions were not enough, 'then I am reemed with it like any whore. For when I have been trundled off to be redressed; when I have been told to enjoy the feast, what is left for me to enjoy, and who shall I enjoy it with? I have a brother who has turned to straw, and a lover who has turned his back.'

She had not spoken in a frantic way, but rather in cold formal tones, as she had been taught. Her words sent shivers down her listeners' spines. Some had crossed themselves, fearful of treason's taint. It was well they did. The taint was there, and Henry's spies knew how to make the most of it.

The second incident followed close upon the first. Prompted no doubt by the same bitter regret, the princess had gone on to complain how she had been only a child when the first marriage offer had been made. Even her voice changed, became low and monotonous, as if she were in a trance (which she might have been). What she revealed was a litany of shame, all calculated to embarrass the king, for what idol likes to see himself turned to clay. And revealing again that malign influence.

'The first time,' the princess said, 'the groom-to-be was that same Charles who will become an emperor. Younger than I am he was in his cradle still, so his men came on his behalf. He did not choose me himself, nor did I him. A loveless marriage is an affront to God,' she had cried, 'as you, Mistress Philippa, have often said. God must have abandoned me.' Disrespect then, added to blasphemy, in which Philippa de Verne concurred, agreeing with the princess, comforting her, urging her to speak her mind.

'When they came,' the princess continued, 'my mother was dead, my older sister sent to Scotland, my father bowed with grief. The only one to stand by me was my brother Henry. He helped me then, holding up the train of my skirt since it was so heavy I could hardly walk, telling me what to say, coaching me on what to respond. He stood by me, hand on hip, like a little courtier, and glared at those ambassadors. Where has all that kindness gone,' she cried. 'Why does my brother forsake me?' And the traitress Philippa, not disputing these lies, had said, 'He will regret it one day.'

The end of the tale was full of dark and terrible mystery. It made Henry's blood surge with a strange yearning, almost as strange as the experience he had had with Philippa, and even the men who recounted it were reluctant to speak. Only the traitress de Verne had not cringed. Openly she had held the princess in her arms and encouraged her. 'When I had answered all the questions that Charles's ambassadors asked,' the princess had whispered, 'whether I said my prayers, whether I could read, my nurse took me away. One of the men followed us, a tall thin man, a churchman. Wolsey reminds me of him. He came into my room and closed the door. I heard a clink of coins. Then my nurse lifted me upon the table top, close to where he stood, so that I was level with his eyes. He had eyes like all churchmen I have ever known, dark and deepset and inquisitive. While my nurse held my feet, he threw my skirts over my head, almost stifling me. I remember how cold it was, and how cold his hands, prying with his thumbs between my legs. And when he was done, "Put her down," he said, "I see she is as well made as anyone,

176

enough for my master to enjoy when he is grown."'

She said, 'When the Spanish marriage was first arranged, my brother Arthur was but a babe in arms. They say the Spanish ambassador examined him in the same way. They did not examine my brother Henry thus, but then he was not born to be a king. And Arthur was an infant, blessed with infant ignorance. I was old enough to remember everything. I remember how cold it was. If that is all that loving is, I shall never feel warm again.'

And the traitress de Verne, not contradicting her, had replied, 'When the time comes, love will keep you warm. I know, and I promise so.'

Who was not meant to be a king; a thing of straw; who has forsaken me. These were the phrases which burned in Henry's mind, more than enough to fuel suspicion into flame. But he did not strike at once, playing with his victim like cat with mouse, wanting Philippa to veer from fear to hope to fear. He meant to make his move just before the princess set sail for France. And so he would have done had not a third 'incident' occurred. This too was the princess's 'fault', if 'fault' it was. But since it was done in public gaze Henry had no need of spies to report what he could see for himself. And, being in public, it forced him to revise his plans.

By now the weeks of preparation were done; the marriage settlements, the dowry gifts, the grants of land, were approved, and Henry had had the proxy marriage performed, as the princess had foretold. He even had agreed to go with her on part of her journey as sign of respect. He had arranged for more than a hundred souls to accompany her, most of whom she did not know,

177

chosen by him to enlarge his dignity rather than to serve hers. He felt that all that money could buy had salved his conscience; he was relieved that it had been done with such little complaint (although of course he had pretended otherwise).

Surrounded by the greatest lords and ladies of the land Mary Tudor was to sail on the king's flagship. The rest of her retinue would pack themselves on other ships, among the crates of goods and supplies, as if France were on the moon, without comforts. That milling crowd assembling on the coast, the lords and ladies and their attendants, the personal servants of the servants, the lesser clergy, bailiffs, horse masters, tutors of French and etiquette, made order impossible and nearby villages and towns were jammed with homeless courtiers looking for beds. Henry had been obliged to seek Wolsey's help.

Wolsey undertook the organization of Henry's peace in the same way that he had organized Henry's war. He had his clerks make lists: lists of people, of rank, role, functions; of goods and gifts, and where they came from; of supplies, and who should use them. He himself supervised the whole, keeping careful notes of his own, until it could be safely claimed that he was their master.

Among these lists, so long they might have contained all of England, two names were conspicuous by their absence. And they were the two the princess herself had fixed upon.

The night before she was to sail she had an unexpected visitor. It was the queen, moving swiftly on her dainty feet, cloaked in her customary black. 'Sister,' she said, standing tall, although she was so small a thing, her lisping English suddenly very Spanish. 'I have a wrong to confess. My jealousy has been part the cause of your grief, although God knows I did not wish it so, and long have been my prayers that I might overcome its sin. For jealousy is a sin I know. I also guess at your handmaiden's distress for I have watched her all this while (although she I think did not know so). I see how she has avoided the king, not thrown herself into his path. And so, to make amends, although God knows I never did you harm, I bring you this.'

She felt beneath her cloak for a sheaf of paper which she had secreted about her person. 'Take it,' she said simply, 'and read. What you do with it is up to you. I myself have made peace with God for this, to right a wrong and perhaps avoid a worse one. My husband is dearer to me than all the world. God bring him back to me,' she cried. 'God send him back into my bed. God right my wrongs for me.'

Crossing herself in her foreign way she left as silently as she had come in. Sitting bolt upright in her great four-poster bed, the princess for once was silenced, although not for long. Recovering, she screamed to have the tapers lit, and summoning her chaplain, on pain of death, had him read aloud the lists that Catherine had dared to bring to her.

The first missing name she noticed right away, by far the greatest, and the one dearest to her heart, that of the Duke of Suffolk. Alone of all the English lords he had not been invited to the wedding in France. She knew his suit with the Austrian duchess long played out; she must have wondered at his absence; now she guessed her brother's command kept him away. She said nothing, turning suspicions in her mind just as her brother did, biding her time too, not willing to let that brother trick her again.

The second missing name was that of Philippa de Verne. Its absence made the princess think, not perhaps for Philippa's sake but for her own. Henry had made a promise. She needed to ensure he kept his word. She was a queen to his king, and she meant to challenge him, to show him that she was as good as he was. Lying there in the dark, on the eve of her leave-taking, she too came to a decision.

The long delay had not disheartened Philippa. Now, on the verge of freedom, she could scarcely contain herself. In France, she thought, she would find Richard waiting for her. What would her lover care that she was penniless? Her lands meant less to him than her. And far from the English court, why should Henry be a threat? In her eagerness she had convinced herself that Henry had no malice left. Just as Henry hoped she would. His dossier against her was complete, and he was ready to savour it, the pleasure of her terror as his guards arrested her more than making revenge complete. When he had her in his prison, he thought, when his gaolers threatened her, then how she would scream for help, then she would not refuse him.

He had waited to the very day the ships sailed, a fine day, although his master mariners warned that the sun would not last. His fleet rode at anchor in the bay, all fourteen ships, newly painted, newly decorated, their royal banners streaming in the breeze. A gallant display, he must have thought, one calculated to impress the French. And even his queen accompanied him, having decided that anger would never win him back. Her offer of truce was gratifying as was his personal scheme to wipe away his own personal shame (too late for the princess to stop, but soon enough to show her too just how powerful he still was). Pleasure therefore was in his walk, his stance, in the very way he lifted his head to scent the air.

On the pier the princess was waiting for him.

The morning brightness outlined her, the morning wind whipped her skirts. 'Brother,' she said without ado, 'I go to France for England's sake, not my own.' She spoke loudly so Henry's companions and the many ambassadors who attended him could hear and would act as witnesses. 'Next time I claim the right to marry to my own pleasure.' Again she paused for effect. 'As you promised me,' she cried. 'And I'll not go unless the Duke of Suffolk meets me there. And Philippa de Verne accompanies me, as God allows.'

Beside her stood the other young woman whom the court was to admire. She was as straight as a stripling, with passionate blue eyes and long fair curls. She did not look down as she had taught the princess not to do, but fixed her gaze on Henry, not beseechingly, but as if she willed him not to shame himself by refusal. And seeing them both, Henry did feel shame, although that too he hid.

Henry was surprised by the princess's attack (although that was just what he had warned his spies to expect). He never believed his silly little playmate would be so shrewd as to study lists or having read them would think ahead as to what they meant. *You promised.* There was that word to strangle him, a weight, wrapped round his

181

neck like a plumb line; would he ever be freed from it. *As God allows*; he was afraid God might.

Caught then by his own trap, not needing spies to relate what all the world saw, Henry turned from his sister in a rage. Back he stalked, refusing to accompany her, his queen and courtiers trailing after him, afraid to comment on his change of mood. Out of sight he howled for his guards to countermand his orders of instant arrest, thwarted by his own cleverness. And doubly certain that Wolsey's efficiency had ruined him, he summoned his Archbishop to answer to him. And as ever, Wolsey came to the rescue.

Henry knew that the Archbishop (who preferred to be called 'Cardinal' in anticipation of a greater honour) was cloistered in his own private sanctuary, paying a visit to that same Nun of Kent, from whom, it was whispered, he often sought advice, under guise of his professional role of spiritual adviser to her, a profitable exchange for both. Since the Convent of the Holy Sepulchre lay not far from the coast the king's messengers had no difficulty in routing Wolsey out. And Henry's message was blunt enough. 'This is your fault. I blame you.'

The Archbishop then was of young middle years, not yet bloated with the corpulence of age, and he lost no time in scrabbling into a saddle to hurry back, cursing the while in un-Christian wise, both the lack of finesse and the lack of tact. Henry soon heard him scuttling through the cold castle rooms, and was relieved, although he threw himself into a chair, his mouth closed petulantly. Under his eyelids he noted how Wolsey forced his features into their customary deference and how he listened, bent head, to the king's loud list of faults. And when Henry could complain no more, having run out of compaints, he allowed his Archbishop to assume control.

'This is what I suggest, my lord king,' Wolsey's voice resembled honey and cream, a tone Henry knew was assumed when the Archbishop wanted to placate but which never failed to achieve its end. 'Let both go to France, queen and queen's serving wench, for thus you promised and thus you must do. But there they stay. One to marry as you planned;' (a compliment this, that mollified the king somewhat for he had not liked that word 'must') 'the other to rot in a Calais gaol.' And when the king still frowned, more persuasively, in that same golden tongue, 'Calais belongs to England still and your law runs there as well as here. A Calais prison will be as firm as an English one, and better hidden if anyone should dare inquire for her.' He tapped the side of his nose to suggest that no one would. 'Better all round to let them sail,' Wolsey went on. 'But before they do, send off fresh orders by special ship, your fastest craft, to arrive ahead of them. Write a new list in your own hand, and prick your seal beside the girl's name, so your agents know to look for her. And when you have her fast, and the queen is delivered to her new husband, why then my lord, you have what you want without being forsworn.' And he smiled, a false smile that failed to light up his sunken eyes.

Henry pretended to hesitate for a while. Wolsey's idea was good enough; the king only disliked being obliged to use it. But time was pressing and the fleet must leave. 'Very well,' he grumbled finally. 'But I add one other name. And a letter to go to Lille.'

The name he added was his own masterstroke, the

Duke of Suffolk's, and the letter to Lille was sent to him. Not to please the princess to be sure, nor even less to gratify the duke, but to torment Mary all the more, to give her a lover she could not have. And to ensure the duke obeyed he baited the trap with offers that he knew the duke could not refuse, to lead the English at the wedding jousts which were to be arranged after the real marriage in France. *Before I was betrothed my brother and Charles fought a hundred knights.* Let Charles try the same trick again, before a queen who had passed beyond his grasp.

Wolsey understood the king, and the king understood him. Both knew the purpose of the game, to make the punishment fit the crime. What Wolsey knew that Henry did not, was that each time the king indulged himself, his satisfaction was less; each time he was driven to greater excess, until in the end there would be little left of the 'jovial Hal' whom the people loved. But that was a risk that Henry took. Except perhaps the king did not yet know how great the risk and what in the end he stood to lose. And Wolsey also knew one other thing: that of the two he still was master of the art. And so in the end Wolsey too played his part.

Not changing the king's orders, for not even he could do that, not showing, by one flicker of those deepset eyes, what he intended, he had the king's writ sent forward at once, and copies made to distribute to the king's men to acquaint them of the king's change of plan. In secret, he added a mark of his own beside Philippa's name. He did not care what Henry's trumped up crime was, nor whether she languished for it in a Calais gaol.

He had recognized her name himself and, not underestimating all of Henry's work, he at once knew who she was and more about her than Henry did. For, not withstanding Henry's claims, he knew, as Henry did not, who her lover was, and what her lover had done to his men. And he had a use for her. Fate which hitherto had stood aside, now was to play its part.

First came a storm. The master mariner's warnings had been correct. Hardly had the flagship cleared the bay when the sky had clouded and the morning breeze had stiffened to a gale. Before the rest of the fleet had time to turn back, the rain had come driving from the east, lashing the sea to foam. The ship upon which Philippa found herself held in front of it, running with full sail. What a moaning now rose from the wedding group, in an instant merriment replaced by seasickness. The gentlemen cowered on deck trying to duck beneath the spray. Down below, the ladies screamed at each surge and pitch, their fears of piracy or monsters changed to a more real threat of drowning. The fleet was scattered, blown off course, so that, when at last the skies cleared again, the ocean stretched as blue and empty as it had been on the day God created it.

Some of the ships were lost of course; most finally limped to shore, their paintwork damaged, their flags torn. The princess, pale green with sickness, could barely crawl on deck, and had to be carried through the surf like a sack of wheat, so much for Henry's triumph. (Although the young man who carried her was rewarded on the spot with title and rank, a fat prize for getting his feet wet.) Philippa's ship, the one she had hoped would bring her to safety and happiness, was one of the luckless ones. Driven this way and that, caught in a fog, its rigging gone, its sails cut loose, it drifted with the tide, almost back to where it had started from. And fate now played its second trick.

The storm had not frightened Philippa at first as much as Henry's anger. Who seeing his face that day would not have felt afraid? Perhaps the sea was in her blood after all along with her uncle's sea-faring skills. Her heart beat with excitement as she felt the suck and roar of the waves. Free, free, free, is what she thought, free of Henry and his court, free to find Dick Montacune, free to marry him. But after days of storm, of rain in sheets and fog so thick that visibility was reduced to a hand's length, she too yearned for land, any land, as long as she could stand upright on it. When the sixth day broke, calm at last, almost warm, but so mist-enshrouded as to make navigation impossible, she felt only gratitude at still being alive.

The captain thought so too. All he could do was cut the tangle of spars and ropes, place lookouts on the bowsprit to sound for depth, and trust that luck would bring them safe to port, even one controlled by the Emperor Charles. Charles would have loved to get his hands on any part of the princess's royal escort. Aware of this possibility the courtiers put seasickness aside, forgot their ruined clothes, donned their armour, and unsheathed their swords, preparing to evade capture. And while the sailors bent their backs trying to make the ship answer to the helm, the ladies, on their knees, alternately baled water from the leaking hold, and prayed. The ship, like some wounded bird, crept along, until, within a hundred yards of land, the fog suddenly lifted.

There were no rocks, praise God for that, no high cliffs, only an innocent stretch of beach curving into a bay, where waves broke steadily on the shingle. But where that beach was, on whose territory, still remained a mystery and the courtiers leaned over the ship's rails, gripping their swords nervously. The arrival of several fishing smacks, rowed round the headland by burly fishermen, resolved their dilemma. The boats served to ferry passengers and crew; the fishermen's speech, albeit crude, was obviously some English dialect from south-eastern Kent, and there on shore, armed men appeared, standing guard. All on board cheered with relief. Except for Philippa. For although the guards were there to help, they spoke and acted in the king's name, and their coats were Wolsey red.

Here then was peril, doubly primed. The soldiers stood in a group on a small breakwater built of stone, their horses tethered behind them. They chatted among themselves, keeping a close watch as each boat returned. Then they hastened forward to help the ladies through the surf, saluting the gentlemen with rough courtesy, ensuring that the boats were turned to make another run. For it was clear the fishermen would have cheerfully tipped courtiers and all into the water to get at what really interested them. And that was loot, all those boxes in the hold, those crates and barrels and casks holding the princess's wedding gifts. The sea is a hard taskmaster, and those who live by it seize what they can. Their lack of welcome paled in comparison with what Philippa faced.

The sergeant of the troops was an arrogant man, of middling age, rough complexioned, sandy-haired, hard-eyed in a handsome sort of way, as were most of Wolsey's guards (a scandal, the ladies now whispered behind their hands, for what do churchmen want with male beauty?). He wore his badge of office over his red padded coat with an air of authority and greeted the ladies in his master's name with impatient restraint, showing a coarse sort of charm when he called the youngest one, little Nan Bullen, a 'Venus' risen from the foam (although she tittered and said she looked more like a half-drowned rat)! He kept a scrivener by his side who could read as well as write, a plum-pudding of a man, as roly-poly as the sergeant was lean. His task was a simple one, to intone aloud from Wolsey's lists, accounting for both passengers and goods, this storm like to lose most of the queen's retinue, to say nothing of all of Henry's dowry gifts.

The scrivener himself was cross, half-asleep in the mid-day sun, pressed into service against his will, and feeling himself ill-used that of all the miles of English coast this was the one the ship had chosen to come aground. He therefore read the names in a bored but fulsome voice, as if picking plums, in no mood to quibble over details, anxious to get home to his own dinner. He would have by-passed Philippa's name without a qualm, even though the list he used was the one to which Wolsey had added his mark, had not a gust of wind, flapping the parchment, brought it to the sergeant's attention.

Sensing danger, aware there was little she could do to avoid detection and yet not certain of being sought,

Philippa had waited to the very end to be brought to land. The sergeant was thorough. 'Your name, mistress?' he asked again, when she had mumbled it, low-voiced. He did not look at her but took the sheaf of notes from the scrivener who was still fumbling with them, and leafed through them (although as a professional soldier he might not have been able to read). Perhaps not, but he could recognize the king's seal. And he knew better than most the secret mark his own master had made, without the king's knowledge.

'Well, well, very well,' he said, whistling between his teeth, and tapping his thumb against the seal. 'So here is a catch after all.' When he looked up there was a glint in his sharp grey eyes that suggested he knew exactly what catch he had been looking for. And when he seized Philippa's arm to stare at her she knew so too. He made her repeat her name, louder, for the sheer satisfaction of hearing it, meanwhile signalling one of his men to bring up horses and sending another ahead as messenger. 'Philippa de Verne,' he cried after this was done. 'Why, that's a name to remember, without reading it. All of England is searching for you.' And he smiled, a self-satisfied smile.

Philippa could have lied of course. She could have claimed he had made a mistake; she could have given any one of a hundred names. That shrewd grey glance warned her that the sergeant was as careful as his master was. Worse, a silence now behind her back from her former companions warned that they too would not tolerate untruths. Why should they help her? There had never been much loyalty from the start. So while they warmed themselves with this new scandal (which they

189

swore they had always suspected) and while the soldiers had those crates and boxes dragged along the shore, the sergeant mounted her on one horse, tied the reins about his wrist and started off in a cloud of dust. He did not tell her where they went, nor why, nor even what was the cause of her arrest; certainly he did not discuss the preference of his loyalties. If it came to a choice between the king and the king's Archbishop, he knew which one to choose. And Philippa rode with him as if she had guessed all along this was what was meant for her.

The ride was not far, inland, through a pleasant stretch of countryside known as the 'Garden' because of its orchards and fields. The villagers were preoccupied with the harvest, and the air was rich with the ripe scent of apples and pears. People had no time for staring after a soldier and a lady, although the lady's dress was water-stained, and she swayed in the saddle like a ship at sea. The sergeant rode ahead, not turning round, still humming complacently, pleased with himself as perhaps he had reason to be. Bad luck was something he knew about, after all, her bad luck would prove his good. He knew also that a search was being made, a specific one for a specific wedding guest, on both sides of the Channel coast. A price upon her head, why should he not benefit? And since she had come to shore so close to where Wolsey was, he had decided to take her there himself. A mile or so further down or up the coast, where men's loyalties were first to the king, Philippa would have found a different welcome. Although for better or worse, fate does not judge differences.

The sun beat down as if there never had been rain or wind. Philippa soon was parched, thirst drying her mouth where the seawater had crusted to salt. Her skin, her hair, her clothes, were caked with grit, as if she had been rolled in sand, and at every jolt she lurched in the saddle as if to fall off. When she asked to drink, warm brandy from the sergeant's flask made her retch. 'By God,' he said, watching her, leaning on his saddle, chewing a blade of grass. 'You look a sad sack. Who would have thought you worth so much?'

But when he swung down to fetch her some water from a nearby stream, she came alive, tried to kick the horse into a gallop. It reared and fought, until she slid off to run on foot, weaving in and out of the currant bushes which grew wild along the banks. Her feet sank into the sandy soil, and her legs seemed curiously stiff, as if she could not bend them, but for a moment she thought she had outrun him. Then she heard him laugh. As she skidded to a stop he pounced on her from behind a bush, catching her fast by the waist and throwing her to the ground, jarring her breath. But when she still tried to bargain with him, through gasps telling him she had friends who would pay him well, 'So say all prisoners,' he grinned. 'They all have "friends". But how am I to know what their price is?' He was crouching on his heels, his red coat covered with dust and she was pinioned half under him. He pulled her round to face him and grinned again, a wolf-like grin, showing a line of yellow teeth. 'My master's credit is good,' he said, not taking his hard stare from her, 'and he pays me double for you alive. He did not say he would mind if I enjoyed you first.'

And he put down his mouth to cover hers.

She bit him. She felt the blood puddle and run down his chin as, with an oath he jerked back, his hand raised instinctively to strike. 'Touch me again,' she cried, 'and I tell him. What would he say to that?'

He wiped his face slowly, still eyeing her as a wolf does when it is circling for a kill but with a kind of wariness that suggested caution. Caution won. He gave a cruel laugh. 'My master couldn't care less,' he told her, his voice gravel harsh. 'Mostly he prefer boys, and so do I. But he needs you; otherwise I'd not bother to take you alive.'

He scrambled to his feet, brushing his jacket down. 'Get up,' he said. 'You've wasted enough time.' He looked at her menacingly. 'I'm no priest,' he suddenly told her. 'How do I know what my master wants? But as he's waiting for you in a nunnery, perhaps he means to keep you there. Perhaps you're one of those new heretics, buried in the king's court like a tick. Perhaps my master intends to root you out, as he does most heretics, and a nunnery'll be the place for you. Locked up there you'd do no harm. But,' and now his voice took on an even harder quality, as hard as his agate eyes, 'if by chance you get out again, then look for me. I've a bone to pick with you.' He watched her pale. 'No, two bones,' he said. He leaned forward and pointed at his chin. 'One, for this. And two, for what happened at Westminster.' He bared his teeth again in imitation of a grin. 'I had two friends I buried there,' he told her. 'And there's been a man I've been a-hunting since. If by chance you know him or his whereabouts, perhaps you'll lead me to him. I have a debt to pay with him. First him, then you. That would please me very well.'

And after that there was no point in saying anything.

The Convent of the Holy Sepulchre where he took her

was large, as became the home of a nun being groomed for sainthood. It stood outside the town of Canterbury, surrounded by meadows and fields which the sisters owned. Like the convent, these farms showed signs of neglect, the fields run wild, the weeds high where once cattle and sheep had grazed. The surrounding walls and iron-barred gates gave tribute to its former power, and once perhaps, long ago, it had been powerful, occupied by ladies of high quality and filled with bustling life. Now, the cracked stones, the peeling plaster, the very listing of the chapel roof, were signs of neglect and poverty, and the diminished numbers of the sisterhood suggested spiritual decay. (All reasons, malice whispered, why the Nun of Kent was so important; what better way to restore fame than gain a saint, and what better saint than one alive, twice the value of one dead!)

The sergeant left Philippa in a nun's charge, in front of a small door that led to an even smaller room, like a prison. It had bare walls, hung with one plain tapestry. The floors were bare, with a wooden table and stool set in the stark centre, nothing else, except a wooden crucifix, no wonder Philippa did not recognize this as a place where visitors were meant to wait. She could not know that behind the tapestry was another room entered by a grating, through which the inmates used to speak to their guests. Nor could she know that the nun who brought her there was breaking every holy rule by speaking with her face to face. But then, this nun had special gifts that set her outside the law.

She threw off her veils as if glad to be free of them, pushing back the wisps of mouse-grey hair. Round of face, her country origins were so pronounced that no

193

elaborate robes could hide them, and she plumped herself down upon the stool as if afraid Philippa would claim it first. The bands around her forehead had left red weals which she continued to rub absent-mindedly, meanwhile staring at Philippa with undisguised curiosity like a child. 'God's my life,' she said after a while, her natural speech resembling the fishermen's down to the very vowels. 'So this be the wench they've been looking for. You've brought warm weather for October after all these storms. But they might have fed you along the way, you do look half starved.' And clapping her hands importantly she ordered wine and bread and fruit; then settled down to their drinking and eating as to the manner born, although in truth she might have been better suited doing the serving. 'I did know they'd find you,' she said. 'I asked God and He told me so.' She leaned back, crossing her arms upon her breast and belched, with a childish sort of glee. 'God told me so,' she repeated more sharply, used to admiration and awe, and uneasy perhaps when they were withheld. 'And God did tell me He'd send a storm to have you disgorged from the sea.' She stumbled over this last phrase, the word 'disgorged' not in her vocabulary, and again settled back waiting to be praised, as if praise had become her due (which, since the success of her first royal prophecy and the French victory, was not unreasonable). The truth was the Nun Elizabeth was in a fair way to be spoiled; what once had come welling up of its own accord, was now prompted by outsiders' advice and taught her, by rote. Nor was she completely at ease with this new role, as she now showed, lapsing back into her country speech as if glad to be finished with the other.

194

'You do seem too young to be a traitor,' she said, biting into a peach until the juice ran down her chin. 'But if you are, God pity you. A traitor's death is not nice; rather you than me.'

There was a stirring behind the grille, a masculine scrape of boots, a cough, such as churchmen use in the confessional, hurrying penitents to conclusion. These sounds recalled the Nun Elizabeth to her task. Hastily she put down the peach, wiped her mouth, and began again, in the manner that she had first perfected in her royal interview. 'It is your duty to repent. A traitor is an affront to God, and whatever penance is imposed on you, you must obey, to wipe away that treason's curse. Our great king's will is God's will on earth, one and the same.' She blinked twice, uncrossed her fingers as children do, trying to recite their catechism. 'And when it isn't,' she added, as an afterthought, 'why then God'll punish him as well.'

She must have misspoken her lines, as a second angry cough reminded her. She jumped up, flustered, trying to catch hold of Philippa. 'There,' she said, almost crossly, 'why didn't 'ee listen to me the first time? I was supposed to say you do risk your soul if you refuse. A soul's a special thing,' she went on earnestly. ''Tis not a thing to cast aside. 'Tis, well 'tis like the pip inside this peach; attached to you under the skin; no way to get at it unless you bite through. Now, I do peel a peach to eat,' she added ingenuously, 'but peeling you'd be a different thing. And you're too young to die; why, youth do sit on you full bloom. Make the most of it, says I. Do what my master says.'

'But what does he *want* of me?' Philippa asked, almost

exasperated into speech. 'Why should you speak for him? Why does he not speak for himself?'

The Nun Elizabeth was in two minds, to be affronted at not being recognized, or gratified at the chance to reveal her fame. 'My master be the greatest man in Christendom,' at last she said, coming closer to Philippa and turning her back to the hidden grille so she could indicate it with winks and nods. 'One day he will be Cardurnel.' (She mispronounced the word.) 'One day he will be Pope, the first English Pope in four hundred years. A Pope be greater than a king by long chalk,' she added naïvely. 'Think of it. I've told a king what to do; this French marriage be my work and doing. But one day I'll be a-giving advice to an English Pope, me, the Nun of Kent.'

Behind the tapestry a chair scraped as if overturned. There was the sound of a rapid stride, the grate of a key in the grille's lock. 'Lord-a-mercy,' the Nun Elizabeth's face creased with fright and she crossed herself. 'He told me to keep that quiet. Drat you, mistress, for making me talk too long. He's warned me afore not to say too much.'

She tiptoed rapidly to the outside door and eased it open, her feet that were made for country walking too broad and flat for treading quietly down cold corridors. 'Just you stay there and listen,' she whispered. 'He's got ways and means of making you, so best give in before he uses them. As I found out. And God comfort you.'

She was gone in a flutter of skirts, her last prayer at least heartfelt. The grille swung wide; the tapestry was drawn back, a man strode into the room, his clerical robes flapping about his tall lank frame like crow's wings. A look of distaste had curled his thin lips and his eyes

196

were dark and penetrating, just as the Princess Mary had described. He fixed his gaze on Philippa. 'Philippa de Verne,' he cried, his voice oiled with old cunning, like an altar lamp. 'You have wondered who I am. Seeing me, are you convinced? Do not underestimate me. Nor underestimate the Nun of Kent. She still knows more about the secrets of the world than most men, revealed to her by God. If she says "repent" then "repent" you must.'

CHAPTER 10

Philippa had only seen Thomas Wolsey once, during the proxy marriage at which he had pontificated. From a distance, clothed all in white, with his glittering gold vestments, he had seemed like a statue on a church wall, reminding her of the one in Vernson to which people prayed. Now, appearing in wrath, all in black, his long face seamed with lines, his face pendulant, he was so like a figure of death that she almost fell on her knees to him.

But Wolsey was not as angry as he seemed. A master of deception, neither age nor advancement had quenched the fire of ambition which had burned in him since student days. He could still out-think most men, and he still could be boisterous, as he had been when he was put into the stocks for levity. He had been enjoying what he saw and heard behind the grille, despite the Nun Elizabeth's lapses of memory, and had she been successful in making Philippa more penitent, he would have enjoyed himself even more. However, he judged that things were progressing well, and his 'Repent' was more to amuse himself than to frighten.

He watched her dispassionately. He knew all about her, all that Henry knew and more. He had seen the skimpy proofs upon which the king had built his case. But he had other holds on her that Henry had overlooked, and these were the ones he meant to use; hence his interest in her.

Seating himself upon the stool, and drawing the folds of his robes about him, he prepared to interrogate her. He was good at questioning, having all the Inquisitorial skills. He knew when to be silent, when to probe, when to let the victim damn herself. He meant for Philippa to submit, and although the Nun of Kent had failed to break her will, he intended to do so himself. And then, he would tell her what was expected of her.

'Since the day you wormed your way into Henry's court,' he began, 'I have had my eye on you.' (Not true, he had only thought of her in the past few days.) 'Despite the storm, the marriage has taken place, and Mary Tudor and Louis of France are now made man and wife. So you have failed to keep them apart.' (Again, something he knew untrue.) 'King Louis swears that he is so in love that he wants his bride all to himself. He has a strange way of showing it! On the day after, he dismissed his wife's retinue, sending all the ladies back to Calais to cool their heels. In their place he has surrounded the queen with ones from his court who will tell him all she does and thinks.'

He watched Philippa from beneath his thick eyebrows with his churchman's stare. When he noted how her expression did not change, he said more sharply, 'But we in England need someone who knows the queen well and is liked by her, who can listen to her and pick out what is important. Louis claims his purpose is to find if he pleases his queen; his real intent is to be assured that the young men of the court do not flirt with her, and that his nephew and heir does not cuckold him. For my part, I am not interested in personal things. I want to know Louis's views on war and peace and what he really thinks about the treaty we have made, and what his future plans are. Now what could be simpler. The queen needs a friend and so do I. So I have chosen you to keep her company, and help me at the same time.'

'To spy you mean,' she said, breaking in upon his rhetoric.

Her bluntness did not displease him. He had already surmised that she was quick and in his eyes intelligence was not a crime, as it had been for his king. 'If not,' he said, 'then you stay here. And if I put the mark of heretic on you, you will be lucky to remain alive.'

And when she still shook her head. 'There are worse things than nunneries,' he said. He fixed his gaze upon her, boring through into the soul. 'A king's prison for one, where Henry meant to keep you.' He paused again. 'Henry's men are hunting for you,' he said, 'Perhaps you should be relieved my men found you first. Perhaps then you would not be so squeamish.

'Loyalty is a fine thing,' he added more persuasively, 'but it does not help you or your friends. But if you were to work for me, why, I would swear that the king would reward anyone who helped promote the peace that he expects from this marriage. Henry needs it to succeed and so do I. Work for me, I guarantee he will pardon you.'

He turned to her, in an instant changing from priest to

200

something else, his lips curling and his eyes glittering. His whisper was almost a snarl. 'But refuse, I will tell him where you are. And I will tell my men where to find Richard Montacune.'

And he watched even more carefully to see which way his catch would jump.

When she asked, 'And what if I refuse?' he knew he had her fast. No one questions unless full of doubt. 'You choose,' he told her brutally, 'your life and his. Or death for both.' And he made a movement as if to rise, pulling at the fastenings of his cloak. Then, fast as a whip he shot another look at her. 'But if you agree, like the sensible wench you are, why then you shall travel in fine style, with my men as escort, as becomes a lady of high degree. The French court will welcome you as the queen's special friend. And when your task is done, you can expect King Henry to award you as is just. Money, titles, lands, all those lands you wanted back, those would be the least he'll give.' He lied again. He never meant Henry to know his plan, and when it was accomplished, and he had no further use for her, he would turn her loose and let Henry's men get hold of her.

He had never learned that more is less: that the more he claimed the more she distrusted him; that the more he pretended friendship, the more he seemed an enemy. But that was a weakness in him.

Philippa realized that she was in a vice that was slowly closing in on her. It had been closing for a long while, since Henry had recognized her. Betrayal of her mistress on the one hand, betrayal of the man she loved on the other, what choice was that? 'And if I do,' she said at last, 'what proof do I have of your good faith?'

201

He almost grinned, not sensing in her words her disgust at him. 'Why,' he said blithely, 'I will send my sergeant with you, you remember him. He will keep you safe, as safe as I myself. And if you do not like his company, you are at liberty to fend him off as you did today.'

Her startled look amused him. 'I told you Mistress Philippa, few things escape me,' he said, growing more expansive now he had his way. 'Do you know why? I dig at the small details which impatient men ignore; I work at them, sift them through, come to the greater events by slow degrees. And I believe in what I do. For there is always some truth even in lies. And what the Nun of Kent says one day will come true. England is on the verge of being great. If I make its king famous that power will also serve me. When I am Pope, as the Nun of Kent has prophesied, no country will be stronger than ours; no people more receptive to my work. And you will be my helper as the Nun herself is.'

God does not need bullies, Philippa thought. He does not need bribes and threats to achieve His will. This man is not the man of God that he claims he is. But, she also thought, if he wants details, I can invent ones that mislead; I can tell him only what is already known, no harm in that. And when I see Mary Tudor again, when I find Richard Montacune, then they can help me break free of him. It did not occur to her that if and when she saw Richard she might endanger him. And before she was to meet him or the queen again, fate had played another trick.

The way she was hurried back to the coast and brought on board one of Wolsey's ships passed as in a nightmare.

202

But while Wolsey's sergeant watched her with his secret grin, and rehearsed her what to do and say so she could pass her secret news on in a simple way; before she reached France by secret means, and, as secretly, began the ride to the French capital, the Yuletide came upon them with a fresh load of misery.

The pace and gaiety of the bride, the games, the rich food, the late nights and early hunts, finally were too much for Louis's age. He took to his bed and stayed there. The first day of the New Year saw his death which the princess said she would pray for. She might have saved her prayers. For King Louis's heir, his nephew Francis, Count of Angoulême, came hastening now to take the crown, prepared to make a bid to marry her. Meanwhile from Lille, the exiled English duke hurried to Paris himself, with perhaps some thought of rescue, although he did not say so.

The duke was not the only one with rescue in mind. Hot on his heels, although he journeyed independently, Richard Montacune came spurring back on a rescue mission of his own.

Richard was not exactly surprised at the turn of events. He had come to know the French court and King Louis well. If anything, he preferred the French king to the English one; Louis at least was a gentleman, and King Louis had grown fond of him, praising his part in this tortuous bickering. But Richard had had enough of courts, and seeing his duty almost done, he had begun to look forward to home again. And to finding Philippa.

The last of his missions had been to the duke at Lille, with Henry's letter. The duke's relief at being recalled almost cancelled signs of his ageing, such as grey threads in his hair and beard, and a kind of hesitation in his voice, a weakness, that was new. During all this time, amid all these hundreds of reports, these detailed envoys, the duke had largely been ignored. Now like a schoolboy let out on holiday he rejoiced at deliverance. And, in his excitement, he revealed what Henry's message had contained.

'They want me back, boy,' he had cried, 'at the games.' (For when he spoke, Louis's death had not yet taken place.) 'They need me to joust for them, as England's champion. We fight the French king's heir, who thinks that he is God's gift to war as he is to love.' He had guffawed and slapped Richard on the back, as if he were a boy himself, not a man on the verge of middle age. In a trice all coldness was gone; he was as affable as he had ever been. 'We'll best him in both before the year is out,' he cried and winked. 'And there's need for you too, lad.' In a few careless words he had told the gist of what Henry planned for the girl who had been the original cause of their estrangement. He did not tell (because he did not know) what Wolsey had done, but he did tell Richard that he thought the girl not good for him. 'Leave her alone, lad,' was his advice. 'She's caused you enough fret as it is. If the king's got his hooks into her, better not to interfere.' Advice that came not from kindness so much as from well-honed sense that had long stood him in good stead. But he said nothing of his own hopes or plans for Mary Tudor.

During all these months Richard had had scant news of Philippa; a few personal messages delivered by Edmund Bryce, who seemed to enjoy the role of go-between. That did not mean he did not think of her. In

204

fact he had come to think of her more and more. But fear that Henry would turn against her had lessened as time passed and the king's cynicism now horrified and enraged him. Leaving the duke without ceremony, ignoring his advice, he had made straight for Paris in the hope of learning news from the new queen. The last thing he expected was to find Philippa on the same Paris road, with the same destination in mind. It was fate's last trick, that he and Philippa should meet again, just as his feelings were overwhelming him, and just when her love for him would force her to deny hers.

They met under the archway of the great main Paris gates, where all of France seemed trying to squeeze past, the news of the king's death shocking everyone. Already the first few flakes of snow had begun to fall, harbingers of the cruel months to come, the worst winter in years. Wolsey's men, in their usual insolent style, had begun to shoulder through the crowds, their sergeant using the flat of his sword to clear a path. Slightly ahead of them, Richard had paused to acknowledge the salute of friends, and was leaning down from the saddle to glean news, any whisper perhaps alive with clues. He was travel-stained and weary from his long ride. One look back and his spirit soared.

Framed in the torchlights under the high arch, mounted on a small palfrey, her hair and cloak powdered white, Philippa already was the object of attention, the epitome of a great lady riding in with her escort of men. But Richard noted their red coats at once, and that made him pause.

She knew him too. For her there could be only one man who rode with such easy grace, who turned with a

205

smile as if to say, 'There you are, jumped up like some half grown weed. What mischief are you about today?' *Mischief*. That word was too slight for what Wolsey had thrust on her. But even if she had not seen him at once, someone would have pointed him out, the young English milord who had won such favour with the French, the English king's envoy. Dressed in Tudor colours with the Tudor emblem stitched upon his cloak, despite the fatigue and cold, he looked what he was. But he was also something else, a man riding in from some long journey, searching for someone, something, some dream perhaps. And finding it now, here, unexpectedly, he fastened a look on her so intense that those nearby commented on it. While she, still moving slowly under the arch, watched him as intently, her eyes like stars. The spark between them, thus ignited, should have burnt to flame, had she not forced herself to look away.

Wolsey's men were still trying to hurry, pushing aside anyone who blocked their progress. Their French was not adequate to express their haste, but they showed all the signs of alarm. They too had heard of King Louis's death and were uncertain what it meant. Their orders had been to find the queen and leave Philippa with her; following that, Philippa's responsibility was to report to them. Unfortunately Wolsey had not taken the king's death into account. There seemed little value to spying on a queen who was herself no longer queen. But where else should they now take their prisoner (for that was what Philippa was, their prisoner, held in Wolsey's name)? What should they do with her? Richard, who knew the French court better than they did, and who guessed at least part of their purpose, forestalled them.

Before they could move again, he had heeled his horse around to bar the way. He did not greet Philippa directly, still wary of what the escort meant, but he did greet them.

'You go the wrong way,' he told them drawlingly, at his most courtly. 'If it is the former queen you seek, her residence has changed, and she is lodged under the care of the mother of the new king. You bring this lady to the wrong gate.'

'Pretend you do not know him,' Philippa was telling herself. 'Say nothing to give him away.' She stared straight in front of her as haughtily as a princess herself, while Richard discussed protocol with Wolsey's sergeant, a man who had sworn to kill him, had he known who Richard was. 'Do not let Richard speak to me,' she prayed. 'Do not let him smile.'

Suddenly she felt his arms about her waist. Before she could protest, he had swung out of his saddle and lifted her out of hers at the same time, deftly turning so that the horse was between her and Wolsey's guard, keeping his arm about her. 'Step aside,' he said brusquely, no longer smiling, 'I will take responsibility for her.' And he prepared to defend himself, making sure Philippa was safe behind him.

The sergeant had swung off as readily, sword still in hand. He stiffened warily, his hackles rising, his grey eyes menacing. 'Wolsey's orders are – ,' he began, when Richard broke in, 'And mine outrank them. My authority is in the king's name.'

It was a risky claim and he waited to be challenged. Caught between both men, each with a hand on her, Philippa felt pulled apart. Already people were stopping to stare. Always on the lookout for entertainment, in these gloomy times they welcomed it. She knew enough of etiquette to sense a new scandal brewing, but did not know how to prevent it. Nor did she know any way to keep Richard quiet, every word he said likely to reveal his identity and his past encounters with these men.

The sergeant hid his confusion as best he could, wiping his mouth nervously. He knew what his duty was but the king's death had changed the order of priority. Presumably he did not recognize Lord Montacune but he did recognize a king's envoy. He might hesitate to pick an open quarrel, certainly not in such an obvious place, but Richard had no such inhibitions. If anything he had old scores to settle and he was determined to ensure that Philippa was safe. So when the sergeant began to explain their business with the queen, now that the queen was left bereft, 'The Dowager Queen,' Richard corrected him, 'and you are a fool if you think to walk in upon her unannounced.' He moved so that the sword on his hip swung dangerously. 'The Dowager Queen is already removed from power and is immured in the House of Cluny close to the Seine. As perhaps you do not know, according to French custom she will remain in seclusion for six weeks, seeing no one, until the days of mourning are done. Or until it is clear she is not with child, which would make a mockery of this new corona-tion. So your haste is unnecessary. Nevertheless, for old time's sake, I will take this lady there myself. Not you.'

Such belligerence could only have one result, and so Richard knew. Philippa felt herself pushed aside as the sergeant leapt forward, his sword raised, his mouth opening on a snarl. Before he could complete the thrust, his weapon went clattering across the icy road, jarring his arm to the bone. And Richard stood over him sword to throat.

'Now,' Lord Montacune said, 'for the last time. Do as I say. As king's envoy here I have the ordering of you.'

His knuckles were bleeding from the force of his blow, but he grasped Philippa more tightly, and prepared to leave, expecting her to follow him. The sergeant was reeling on his feet. When he began to shake sense back into his head, he would recognize Richard's style; he had seen its like before, even if he did not recall where. When he did, he would remember also the man who had used it on him in the square near Tower Bridge; he would remember what had happened afterwards, at Westminster. 'Oh God,' Philippa prayed. 'Stop Richard before he gives himself away.'

'Who are you?' She screamed at Richard, not caring who heard; better if everyone did hear and saw her rejection of him. 'Leave me alone.'

He was so close she could have stretched out her hand to touch his; she could have ruffled his hair; run her fingers along his mouth. She could have put her hands over his eyes to shut out the surprise in them. 'Hold me,' she wanted to cry, 'never let me go.' 'Insolent,' was what she spat out at him, 'presumptuous.' And to him, under her breath so only he could hear, 'You presume on past friendship. Did you think I would waste my life for you? You come too late.'

He might have shouted her down, or spun on his heel to stalk away. She did not expect the sudden tightening of the sensuous mouth, the sudden break of his low reply as if he had difficulty in swallowing. The simplicity of

209

that response tore at her. 'Is that the truth?'

'Truth!' she wanted to cry at him. 'What matters truth if you sign your own death warrant? Keep away from me. I am death for you.'

'I know you not,' she cried at last, as cold as the winter air, as deliberately hard. 'I have never seen you before.' And with all her strength she hit at him.

The blow was not only to persuade Wolsey's sergeant of a truth. It was meant to convince Richard. It caught him squarely on the cheek, so hard that it thrust his head back against the wall. About them, on all sides, women gasped and men muttered aloud at such unseemliness. She did not care. If this were the only way she could conceal his identity and turn attention away from him, she would, although her heart bled for it.

He did not speak at first, fingering along his jaw; his eyes so dark she could not tell what he felt. After a while, 'I crave your pardon,' as distant as a stranger righting some wrong. 'I thought you were someone else. I thought you were someone different,' just as the king had done. And then, low-voiced, 'Had you been other than who you are, I would not have endured such a blow.'

He straightened up, nodded curtly to Wolsey's guard. 'Ride on with us,' he said. 'I take her to where the queen is housed. That done, we part company. You where you will; this lady to join with her.' He spoke of Philippa dispassionately; he shrugged her off, as if she no longer mattered and what had happened here today no longer was of concern to him.

He swung back onto his horse, moved ahead not looking around, the crowd parting to make room for him. And such was the force of his personality that slowly

Wolsey's guard followed, Philippa in their midst, while their sergeant, cowed into obedience, brought up the rear. Philippa's hand was caked with blood, his blood or hers, what was the difference? She felt the icy wind pick up the snow and send it swirling in white clouds so that their footprints left a straggling line along the street. She thought, this then is the end for us. And her hopes died as his must have done.

In the palace of Tournelles, where King Louis had given up the ghost and where his queen had lived so short a while with him, the heir to the throne was being prepared for his crowning day. Tall and dark, with expressive eyes that he used to good effect, his long Roman nose hooked over a full-lipped mouth, he was admiring his image in a looking glass while the barber trimmed his beard in a style that set a new fashion. He turned this way and that, well pleased with his reflection. Even half-dressed he looked what he was, a young man full of life, so lecherous, they said, that no woman was safe from him, equally at ease in squalid garret or lord's mansion, wherever there was a maid to break in or a wife to seduce. His uncle, the dead Louis, might well have been envious of him. He was thinking now of his uncle's wife. He had counted on his charm to win her over, and was depressed that his tactics had failed. They had never let him down before and he still did not know why. This failure in fact was clouding his happiness at the thought of his coronation day. For the more he had pursued the new queen ardently, tantalized by her rejection, the more she had withdrawn, inflaming his ardour anew. His obsession had so alarmed his councillors, that they in turn had alerted the one person he listened to, his mother, whom he revered and feared. She had borne down on him in wrath, berating him for stupidity, to no avail. And it was his bad luck that now, today, in the midst of these preparations for his crowning, she should take it upon herself to confront him on the same issue, pushing the attendants in the room aside, although they tried to keep her out.

Louise of Savoy had ridden hard from her home in Cognac, and her gouty legs were aching from being jogged up and down over miles of rough roads. Stubbornness was written on her, from top to toe, from her slate grey eyes and curly wig (which she kept tied on), to her large men's boots, designed to ease her sore toes. Since her son's birth she had had one aim in mind, to make him king, and to that end she had devoted herself, body and soul. Louis's marriage had been a blow; his death so soon, a blessing. Only one thing was left to disturb her satisfaction, and she had come to settle it. She did not mean to let Francis jeopardize his claims by hankering after his uncle's widow.

'*Eh bien, mon gars*,' she said on entering, too shrewd to tackle him head on, speaking in the common French of her own land, in a coarse, familiar way (which, people sneered, her son had inherited). 'How does it feel to be a king?' She gestured to the servants to withdraw, and taking up a towel began to dry his fine white skin, as if he were still a child, her 'Caesar', as she called him, destined to wear a crown.

Francis pretended to bask in her adulation, but in reality he was alarmed. Only two things interested him, hunting and lechery, but although he seemed stupid, he was not so stupid that he did not know when he had acted irresponsibly, or when his mother had wind of it. He let her speak of the late king's funeral, suggesting ways to hurry it; he listened to her suggestions for the coronation feast at Reims, waiting for her to get to the point. Reims, she was saying, was where French kings had been crowned for over a thousand years, not a murder among them, thank you; no rebellions, or plots or uprisings. And each king descended in honourable line; no upstarts either, praise God, unlike those English lords, forever at war, killing each other off like flies. And their women cold as fish. Why, that Mary Tudor was an insipid thing, no wonder the courtiers' name for her was 'White Queen', like a rabbit with her protruding teeth.

'*Calme-toi, ma mère*,' Francis yawned, resignedly. He sighed and scratched under his new shirt. He recognized a lecture in the making and braced himself.

'What's to be done with her then?' Louise sounded exasperated. 'We can't keep her shut up and we can't let her go, not with all those French lands that your wretched uncle gave to her. French lands; that means your lands, my son; she'll keep them all unless you look sharp.'

Francis sighed again. The theme was a recurring one of which his mother never tired. 'And suppose I marry her myself,' he ventured tentatively, as he had done before. 'Suppose I leave poor Claude' (for such was the name of the young wanton's wife, although he seldom lived with her). 'Suppose the Pope gives me a divorce; suppose I take Mary, lands and all; suppose . . .'

'Suppose fiddlestick,' Louise snapped. 'Poor Claude indeed. The people love her, you fool. They'd never let

213

you put her aside, not to marry with that *sale anglaise* whom they despise.'

Francis shrugged. The idea had appealed to him and had been worth one last try. Now he sat back and listened to his mother's advice. Poor Claude indeed; Francis's wife had as little hope of him, except perhaps a yearly visit to beget a child. She might as well have let Mary have him for all the pleasure she got from him.

Louise began to limp back and forth, debating with herself. 'Now look here,' she burst out, 'if you've been a fool and bedded her and if there's a child then you're done for. Any child of hers will seem, must seem, Louis's get and that means it'll become the heir, not you. If you don't want to be displaced by a bare-bottomed brat, find her a new husband quick.' She poked her son in the ribs for emphasis. 'Who'd know the difference?' she said. 'I mean, who'd tell if the child were Louis's, or yours, or some new husband's? But it'd have to be done at once, before the six weeks are out or everyone'll suspect what you're up to.'

It took Francis a moment or two to unravel what she meant and when he did his face lightened. He never denied or accepted the original charge but he certainly appreciated her concern. It would be more than awkward if Mary were to produce a son and although he was convinced the old king had been incapable of fathering it that was something that was hard to prove. So he watched Louise of Savoy fumble in her pockets for a sheet of names, all loyal to French interests and therefore suitable suitors for the ex-queen. He fingered it, practical details boring him, more interested in working out his night time escapades. So when his mother added, mean-ingfully, 'And there're other problems too,' he let her speak of them, showing a concern he did not feel. 'First there's that English duke,' she said, 'turned up like a bad *sou*. They say she once was hot for him. And then, there's the young man Louis was fond of, what is he still here for? Best keep an eye on both of them. Although since the duke has been in Henry's bad graces he's not likely to trouble us.'

She rolled the parchment up, deep in thought, pre-tending the idea was her son's. In fact she was well content with the outcome of this interview. For the most part she did not condemn his adventuring, provided he kept it under control. 'As for the young English miss,' she said, noticing how he pricked up at that piece of news, 'they say that she has the backing of Wolsey, no less. So, I suggest we allow her to attend the queen as a token of our good will. Wolsey is more tricky than a weasel. Best keep on his good side. And best not to offend Henry either if we can avoid it. If the thought sticks in his skull that his sister's been taken advantage of, that lump of a king could make trouble.'

So she marshalled her son, using intrigue as well as politics to forward that one aim of hers. In time she was to receive the English duke, letting him flirt with her, although she was old enough to have mothered him. She eyed the younger Richard, rather fancying him, confi-dent she had all in hand. She did not take their determi-nation into account. Nor did she count on the loyalty of a young girl to outwit her. But by the time Richard and his cavalcade had wound their way through the snowy

215

streets towards the Palace of Cluny, she had sent the word to let that English girl inside.

'I leave you here,' Richard told Philippa, straight-backed, an officer saluting a lady of rank, as if he had never seen her barefoot in the mud on a country road. 'But first I have a suggestion.'

He had left Wolsey's men huddled in a group at the bottom of the stairs and had come on foot to help her climb their slippery steps. At the top he looked down at her. The mark on his cheek had faded but he still was pale, his eyes fathomless. And, wiping her face where the sleet had beaded into drops, she thought he will never know why I cried for him.

'Tell the queen the duke is here,' Richard said. 'Tell her that we can be relied upon. When you have joined her, make some sign that can be seen from the outside. We shall be waiting. And one last thing.' His face was stern, unyielding. 'Next time you break faith with a man, do not choose me. Remember, trust goes both ways. Break trust, you break yourself.' He paused, then more briskly, 'Watch your back. Francis is as pliable as a hollow reed, and Wolsey no more trustworthy than his king. And we are cut off here from everyone.'

He brushed past her, his boots catching at her skirts. She watched him clatter down the stairs and mount his horse, dismissing Wolsey's men as if he had in truth authority over them. Perhaps he had; a king's envoy commands respect. But when those men were on their own, in their own quarters, when they began to rehash the events of the day, surely their suspicions would rise again, and they would send to their master for advice. The blizzard at least might delay them for a while, no weather for man or beast abroad. Richard would seek his former patron to offer his services again, his duties for the king finished with. And she would find her mistress. *Loyalty is a fine thing*, Philippa heard Wolsey sneer. She thought, 'And bitterly have I paid for it.' And when the doors of Cluny closed and the oiled locks slid back in place, she thought again, 'Today I have lost the only friend I had; the price was not worth the loss.'

It was cold inside the old palace, once used as a religious house. The very straw spread on the stones seemed to freeze, and the walls dripped like some icicle. When she breathed the air steamed, and the black mourning cloths were stiff with frost. Fumes of dark smoke from inadequate fires hung about the ceilings, choking her. The French ladies whom Louise had left in charge were ice-like too, correct and cold, all dressed in black. They surrounded Philippa like starlings, gliding noiselessly across the hall, strange gaolers for a king's widow. The chamber where that queen was kept was large, its windows shuttered so no light could penetrate, only a flicker of fire for warmth, and one four-poster bed to fill the space. The queen, the ex-queen, the dowager queen, lay huddled beneath the coverlets. Her pinched face and frightened eyes reminded Philippa of someone, her mother perhaps, waiting for her stepfather. And so perhaps the queen watched, dreading the return of those French ladies whom she could not understand and who never left her alone. Seeing Philippa she held out her arms in a childish display of affection.

'Where have you been?' she cried almost poutingly. 'I have been looking for you. Send them away. They will kill me here with their dislike. Have you come to take me home?'

But later at night, when those French ladies withdrew, protestingly, and the queen had time to speak, words spilling out of her as if dammed up, Philippa went quietly to the windows and as carefully unfastened the shutters. Six weeks will be too long to remain here, she thought, for Mary Tudor or for me. There must be some way out.

Beyond the window was a walkway, where in ordinary times a sentry paced. Tonight it was half-covered with snow and deserted. She stood listening, craning through the soft white mist as the snow continued to drift, the first of the storms that were to block the city streets. There was no sound, except the small crackling of ice falls from the roof, like miniature avalanches. She could see neither sky nor ground; there was no colour, every-thing was white. But presently somewhere below she heard the strike of a boot upon a stone, not exactly a footstep, but a scrape, as if a heel had caught and its wearer had stopped to stamp it clear. Accompanying that sound came a voice raised in cheerful disharmony. Some drunken roisterer perhaps, late to bed, was defying the storm's effect, and ignoring court mourning (although who would be out on such a night was hard to imagine). The song itself was haunting, a tune she remembered, the words setting her heart thumping.

> There was a knight sought out his lady fair,
> She waited him her castle within,
> Trela, trela, trela

There was only one man she knew who knew the song and who would sing it in such a way, almost careless of personal consequence. She crept back into the room, and seizing the candle stub, relit it from the fire and set it on the window sill. It guttered there for a moment, but perhaps the watcher below would take it for a sign. After a while the singing stopped, then presently resumed, dying away fitfully. For a long while Philippa leaned from the window, until the snow had drifted inside the room and made small piles around her feet. The thought that Richard Montacune was still in Paris, even though he had not stayed for her, gave her the sensation that spring had suddenly come to keep her warm.

The queen's story was soon told. 'I do not like any of them,' she said. 'The king was kind perhaps but he was like a father, not a husband. His courtiers used to scoff and called me *parvenue*. They said my father had all his children married to foreigners so we would be accepted by old established royalty. That was why my brothers were married to the same wife. That way too, his grandchildren would have less excuse to dispute the crown.' She bit her lip. 'Once,' she said, 'when the king was ill in bed, Francis came to talk with him. He pretended to speak about hunting just to amuse the sick man, but under the cover of the table top he tried to put his hand on me. When he felt between my legs, I opened them.' She gave her mirthless giggle. 'And when I clamped them shut his hand was caught.' She laughed again. 'He looked a fool,' she cried, 'sitting there with only one hand. And I think my husband guessed. He began to speak of a fox whom he had seen trapped by its tail. And then even Francis blushed.'

She said, 'I prayed for Louis's death and God answered me. Let the duke know I am ready. It is my right to wed with him. My brother shall make good his promise to me. And God will grant me the love that I deserve.'

CHAPTER 11

——

While Philippa and the widowed queen were shut up inside the Hôtel de Cluny, their fate was debated hotly on the outside. Richard himself was perplexed. The quarrel between him and Philippa had flared so suddenly and unexpectedly he did not know what to think. He knew of Henry's intentions; he did not understand Wolsey's part; he would have staged a rescue on the spot had Philippa herself not prevented it. But he still knew a rescue would be necessary. Just seeing the way Wolsey's men had behaved proved that. And in the days that followed, as he watched how they stood guard outside the palace, as if they were the king's official representatives, he guessed they had some secret purpose in mind. Equally he was sure it involved Philippa and made them a threat to any plan of his. For he had a plan. The problem was making the duke accept it.

For one who had been so jubilant before, the duke had become strangely indecisive. True, the situation had changed since his leaving Lille, and true, he had brought few men with him, in his haste riding with only his personal guard. But their ranks had been swelled by other English who, caught in Paris by the snows, had gravitated naturally to the Suffolk faction. Among these was Richard himself and his old friend, Edmund Bryce, to whom he revealed his concern. 'The French will never let the ladies go,' Richard said. 'Once Francis puts that crown on his head he'll hold on to it, and them. He'll make an international lottery of the queen, although with what right is beyond me. And when Henry complains, as he is bound to do, he'll throw Mistress Philippa to him as a sop to keep the English quiet.'

Which as a guess was not far from truth. Except he still could not understand Wolsey's part.

'Aye.' Edward was succinct. 'Then we act first.'

But while Richard and he went to survey the disposition of that old building where the ladies were kept, while they examined its outposts and its battlements, noting how the guards were placed: the French above, Wolsey's men below, the duke himself kept quiet, almost morose. In vain his younger companions tried to rouse his enthusiasm; he criticized everything they did, obviously reluctant to commit himself. Richard's temper began to rise. He knew that once the news reached England Henry would be obliged to react. Their only hope was to take advantage of the weather and move fast. So daily as the weather worsened, shutting roads, making normal travel well nigh impossible, he found ways to have horses hired and lodgings arranged outside the city gates. And when, with Edmund's help, all was prepared, he himself confronted the duke.

'My lord,' he began without preamble, 'they say that soon, tonight perhaps, the snows will return. Our best chance will be to use the cover of that storm to try to get the ladies out.' He did not mention Philippa explicitly, although in truth she was much on his mind, nor did he speak of what he hoped the duke would do (although in private he had already admitted to his friend that the duke's support was essential to success). Nor did he say, 'If need be I go without you, my lord,' but the duke knew he meant to.

The duke heard him through, gnawing his lip. Richard's plan had all the marks of good military strategy and its simplicity pleased him, although he did not say so. A rescue like this, at dead of night, through a storm, appealed to the duke's romanticism. But he still quibbled, finding fault at every turn until he finally revealed what was on his mind. 'You know of course,' he said, 'that what you do will set us at odds with everyone. French king, English king, councillors, all will be howling for our blood.'

'So much the worse for them.' Richard was adamant. 'With or without permission I mean to leave, and when I go I take Mistress Philippa with me.'

'Even if she's spurned you?' The duke was shrewd. At Richard's look he shrugged and gnawed his lip again. 'If only you knew . . .' he began, 'if only I could explain.' At last he broke out partly exasperated, partly ashamed. 'Henry has me fast as well. I am under oath to him.'

The story was a familiar one. It seemed that when the duke's wife had died, even before his first embassy to Lille, the king had become suspicious of him. Exiling him had not allayed those fears and the events in Richmond had only strengthened them. Finally Henry had made him swear, in writing no less, never to

223

approach Mary Tudor, or make overtures to her 'on pain of death', although he had used a more elegant phrase. Since Mary was married, and the duke himself had been in exile that oath had seemed of little importance and the duke had ignored it. Now it had returned to haunt him.

'There it is, lad,' the duke said, almost apologetically. 'He got the better of me. As for "getting the ladies out", simply "getting out" will not be enough. Someone'll be after them in a flash. Nor is the queen exactly a prisoner. She may not come unless I ask. And unless she comes willingly she comes not at all.'

He did not explain what it was he might be expected to ask, but he implied it. After all there was only one thing that Mary Tudor had ever wanted from him that he had previously been unable to give. But the duke also knew Richard Montacune, and how determined he was. He knew for example that the night before Richard had again strolled down the city streets, walking in the same drunken way, singing the same drunken song, or a new version of it.

When the river freezes and the snow blows,
Trela, trela, trela,
I shall be waiting there for my lady fair,
Under the window where the candle glows,
Trela, trela, trela.

Last night there had been a fitful moon, and the river banks had been edged with ice. Rumour said that packs of wolves had begun to spill across the Seine right to the city gates, and the very air seemed glass thin. Richard's wavering steps had matched his wavering voice and he had made no attempt to hide himself. Luck was with him again; neither the French nor Wolsey's guards had attempted to meddle with him, a poor drunken sot, like to freeze to death before the night was out. The time was ripe then, the rescue party planned, presumably the ladies warned – 'Then I warn you,' the duke snapped. He drew a breath. 'I am with you to this extent. Rescue them, both of them. Use my name only if you must, as a last resort. If you are discovered or if things go amiss, then I disclaim all knowledge. But I promise to help you if I can. On one condition.'

He slapped Richard on the back in his old way to take the sting out of his words but his face showed a new cunning. 'You have been a messenger, lad,' he said. 'Why, you know all about royal marriages. So who more expert than you to report the end of this one.' He smiled, the smile of a Mary Tudor, lacking mirth. He did not have to elaborate what he meant by 'end', nor dwell on the risks he was asking Richard to take, in telling the king what his sister might have done. Nor did he have to add one last thing, although he did, for it was most on his mind. 'I told you once I would claim a favour back, double fold. Now I have.'

'The queen will need a companion for the ride,' he continued, 'and Mistress de Verne will do as well as anyone. But if all fails, or if you and I cannot come to terms,' he shrugged, 'Henry will take care of her. After all, she cannot mean so much to you, that you would risk your life a second time. There are other women in the world, boy, no point crying over spilt milk.'

Perhaps he meant this to be kind. But he also meant it as a threat, one that Richard was obliged to accept. It became a weight about his neck, similar to the one Philippa bore. And, like her, he made himself carry it, out of honour, loyalty and pride, a fatal mixture.

The next day, as predicted, the sky darkened and the wind rose. Soon snow was falling again in great gouts, turning the city into a waste land, where nothing stirred. All through the day the blizzard blew, keeping the French sentries indoors and driving Wolsey's men under the surrounding porticoes. Richard was ready. He needed the cover of that storm, that empty sentry walk, those empty streets. And relying on the zeal of Edmund Bryce, who hated them, Richard planned to stage a minor disturbance to lead Wolsey's men away. He persuaded the duke to station himself beneath that same portico, where he was to remain in the background, hidden beneath his cloak until his presence was required.

The weakness of the plan was the ladies' approval (as the duke had pointed out) and the duke's person would convince them, if need be. The most difficult task, that of approaching the ladies directly, Richard reserved for himself, hoping he could talk them round. It says much for his feelings that although he still did not understand, he trusted Philippa and relied on her good sense for support. And Edmund Bryce, who acted as his second-in-command, was of the same opinion.

In the darkened room, where the French kept their widowed queen, Philippa's thoughts ran in similar lines. She might reason that Richard had every cause to abandon her; her emotions told her otherwise. Recognizing his voice, his walk, the meaning behind his song, her

226

instincts warned her to prepare, although she did not tell the queen. For every day saw the queen grow more nervous. Twice the new French king had paid her a visit, abusing his privileges to harass her, warning her that he was still considering who to chose as her new husband. He had tried to kiss the queen passionately, fondling Philippa at the same time, setting the queen off in hysterics. These visits had put Wolsey's men on guard, making them hound Philippa for news. But the queen meanwhile took such a dislike to all things French and screamed so loudly when anyone French appeared that the ladies Louise of Savoy had left in charge were obliged to withdraw and Philippa immediately took advantage of their absence.

Still not telling the queen what she was about she drew back the thick mourning draperies, opened the shutters and again leaned out into the cold. Down below she could hear the muffled shouts of Wolsey's men as they fended off the 'revellers' who were intent on pestering them. The shouting died away to silence. Philippa put her fingers to her lips to quiet the queen. 'Hush,' she said. 'Someone is coming.'

The man who came stumbling across the windowsill was so covered with snow, his cloak plastered with it, his sword encrusted with it, it was difficult to know who he was. Scattering snow like goose feathers he heaved himself upon his feet, and ran a hand across his face. He had no need to introduce himself, although had he been anyone else Philippa would have been ready for him, a sharp knife clutched in her hand. Yet if Richard saw the knife, he never mentioned it. He addressed the queen, speaking hastily but formally. 'Lady, if it is your

227

pleasure, then I am bid tell you the duke awaits below. Time is of importance, but if you wish to come with us we are ready to escort you.' And to Philippa, equally brisk, 'Can her majesty clamber down a wall; can she ride in skirts? Can you?'

His hands were cut and bleeding from where he had scaled the wall, so ice-encased that he had slid back more than once, not an easy climb at the best of times, hard in the dark with a drawn sword. But he led the queen with easy grace to the window so she could look down. For a moment she resisted him, glancing sideways from him to Philippa with her sharp Tudor eyes. 'So,' she said, 'you are the gentleman I have seen before. I recognize you.' She gave her little self-satisfied smile. 'I rescued you last time,' she reminded him. 'Or my guards did. Now it is your turn.'

She looked around her once more, seeming to hesitate. That hesitation, that quick glance, seemed to say, 'I was a princess then. Now I am a queen. Shall I relinquish all that royalty? Must I give it all up?'

Perhaps the consequence of what she now contemplated began to dawn on her; perhaps she began to weigh what she would lose or gain. Little beads of sweat darkened her upper lip and she gripped the sill with both hands. Seeing these symptoms her companions exchanged dismayed looks, aware themselves how much now depended on her; one scream from her, and all would be lost.

In the street below the duke was suddenly as anxious. He stepped out of the shadows where he had secreted himself, throwing off his nervousness as easily as he threw off the cloak that had kept him hidden. He

228

beckoned to a page boy to light a torch, as if he meant to scorn disguise, as if he meant to show his true self. Its dripping wax guttered and spat in the wet but revealed him clearly enough, a fine figure of a man, who once had been called the most eligible bachelor in all of England. The torch light also showed him for something else, a man who, when all else was said and done, could no longer be relied upon.

He pulled a length of silk from his belt and held it up, a fine beaded scarf, stitched with pearls which glinted in the light. And seeing it, Mary Tudor leaned forward and waved back. Perhaps it was the sight of that gift which recalled old memories, perhaps it was the sight of him, but she made up her mind. She turned abruptly to Richard. 'Very well,' she said. 'I come with you. But you must promise me something.' She nodded from him to Philippa. 'I take you both under my care,' she cried. 'And when I marry, if I do, so shall you.' If she was aware of her irony she did not show it, nor did she look at her companions again. But like the duke she thought ahead, making a condition of her compliance, like him using it to save herself if she had to, and sure enough of her companions that they would be obliged to honour it.

She gave her hand to Richard, never more queen-like than in the moment of relinquishing it. 'I know you,' she crowed at him. 'And I know her. You deserve each other. And I shall make it so.' And without further ado, she skipped out of the window, blithe as a bird.

Soon all three were picking their way cautiously along that deserted sentrywalk, at times having to crawl beneath other windows where lights flared and people talked and laughed. Sometimes they lost their footing on

229

icy patches and began to slide. The wind blew the snow in gusts, blinding them, and the cold froze them through their clothes. When they rounded the last corner, where the ground rose up as on a slope (a defect that any good defence should long ago have remedied) the full force of the blizzard caught them and only Richard's body shielded them. But that lower lie of the terrain served them well as he had meant it should.

The duke and the rest of his men were already stationed below to lower the ladies by means of ropes, attached previously when Richard had climbed up. Once on the ground the queen held back again, although they tried to lead her towards the horses tethered out of the wind. She threw up her head as if catching breath. 'Thank God,' she cried, in almost her old way. 'One more night inside that place would have smothered me.' She looked at the duke and gave her little moue. 'Well Charles,' she said, as confident as if she were twice his age instead of he being twice hers. 'This is a foolish thing we do unless we are sure of it. We had better make it right so my brother Henry will not be able to undo it.' She put her head on one side and said almost plaintively, 'Henry gave me the right of choice. But I have little confidence in him. Shall I trust you?' She jutted out her jaw. 'You told me I should,' she said, 'long ago, when I was a child. But that was before you went to Lille.'

She watched how the duke's colour changed from red to pale to red again. 'If that was what Henry made you do,' she cried, 'you could show him what you really are and what you really want. You could marry again to please yourself. As I can.' She smiled at him. 'You could marry me,' she said, 'as you always promised you would.'

230

And the duke, throwing up his hands as if helplessly, laughed, as he had not laughed in months, and agreed.

A marriage ceremony had not been part of Richard's plan, but the queen insisted. Indeed she refused to move further than the city gates (where the city guards had been bribed to let them through), unless a ceremony was performed without delay, and so perforce, it was arranged. It was a quick, furtive affair, in contrast to those other marriages, the proxy one and the real one at Abbeville, no gaping crowds, no fawning courtiers, no great lords, just a small dirty church with a frightened priest, dragged from his bed. The wedding guests were armed men, most still battle-grimed from their skirmish with Wolsey's guard; the brides shivering with cold beneath their fur cloaks; the grooms accoutred for war and expecting it. Brides, grooms . . . here was a surprise for everyone, but that too the queen insisted on. 'We owe it them,' she persisted. 'They owe it us. I promised them. Why not, they have waited almost as long as we have.'

Now whether the queen meant well, acting in her naïve way and not caring who she embarrassed, or whether, thinking that a double ceremony would distract from the enormity of her own, she persuaded the duke to echo her. As he did, with only a momentary hesitation. 'Two for the price of one,' he cried. 'Why, lad, that's a bargain you can't miss. And when you tell the king of my wedding you can announce your own.' He urged the reluctant young man forward, while the queen pulled at Philippa. To say that the second bridal pair hung back would not be an exaggeration. Both were bewildered, both angered, and in secret both ashamed to be made such fools, for what man likes to marry because he is forced, and what woman would not prefer to be asked first. Both knew their quarrel unresolved, both felt the fault for it. Then too there was the weight of Wolsey's plan for Philippa, there was the duke's threat hanging over Richard. Although each attempted to laugh the idea aside, neither dared look at the other. The princess continued adamant, and the duke, beginning to see the advantage to him, something he too could hide behind, urged her on. So the trembling priest married both couples at the same time, the queen prompting him when he stuttered out of place, leaning on the duke's arm in such a way that had he been obliged to draw a sword he would have cut her in twain.

Mary seemed to enjoy herself more than at any other wedding. On the way to the altar she paused to thank the duke's men, giving them her hand to kiss. And when the marriage vow was fully sworn, although how valid it was she never stopped to inquire, perhaps not at all, she turned back to the scanty congregation and cried in triumph, 'Witness what we have done. And witness them.' And she pointed again at Richard and Philippa, obliging them to acknowledge the cheers (which in truth were enthusiastic, Richard being popular and the lady seeming beautiful beneath her wraps). So what the queen had begun perhaps in jest was ended now in earnest, for better or worse. And the fates of both were joined.

Standing there in that old church, Philippa felt Richard's hand on hers; it was steady, firm, unyielding. She could feel the calluses on the palm, the cuts and weals. And he could feel her trembling. Neither said a word, two strangers, saying 'yes' to the priest's faltering, or two

232

lovers who dared not reveal the full extent of their feeling. But they did say yes, and under cover of the dark and cold, the spark between them surged.

When it was over the duke, married for the third time, smote the young man on the back and told him of the delights to come, while the queen, the ex-queen, now become a commoner, cried, 'So, will love keep me warm?' and blushed prettily. Philippa's silence matched with Richard's but her joy matched with the queen's.

The digression done, they had to ride fast, yet still not as fast as they should have. The snow that was to hide their tracks and prevent a search party finding them, now hindered them. They were obliged to walk at times, leading the horses, and deep drifts forced them into long detours. The duke seemed unable to hurry. He and his bride rode in front, the duke leading her horse and whispering to her. Perhaps he had many things to say, or explain, of such importance that delay seemed relatively of small account. Or perhaps she had things to say to him, her Tudor energies all concentrated on him; her flightiness suddenly focused on him.

Lacking the duke's leadership, Richard was forced to go ahead to break a trail, anxious that they did not lose the way, fearful that, despite his care, they would be pursued. He knew they would not be safe until well out of France, and perhaps not then, depending on what Henry had in mind for them. To say he did not think of what had happened would be untrue, yet when he did it seemed unreal, something which he did not know how to deal with. He knew of the princess's whims, but never one like this. Most of all, though, he thought of Philippa. He could not put the image of her slight body, her downcast eyes, her trembling, out of his mind; they obsessed him more than the inconsistencies.

Left behind him, with the men, her skirts kilted up out of the drifts, Philippa rode with similar thoughts in mind. Although she seemed obliged to fend for herself, she did not feel alone. She had been conscious of Richard's presence ever since he had entered the room, as if she were attached to him by strings, or he to her, so that wherever he moved or whatever he said, she was aware of his thoughts. She knew without being told that the horse she rode was his, that the cloak tied on the saddle, soldier style, had been left there by him. Had she stumbled or slipped he would have been there to break her fall. Like him, she knew a reckoning due, and she welcomed it. None of that seemed to matter. All that mattered was him.

Just before dawn, still so dark that it would be impossible to know when night ended or day began, the little party came to a halt. The horses were exhausted and so were the men, the ladies half frozen in their cloaks, the snow deepening at every step. One of the chosen resting places was close at hand, a modest inn, well off the main road, selected for its remoteness (as well as for the loyalty of its host, who, being English bred, might be expected to shelter them). Although he did not ask, he recognized a royal party when he saw one, and his hospitality rose to the occasion. He also recognized fugitives, on the run, and he acted accordingly, removing his family to the barn out of harm's way, himself acting alone as servant and groom, all smiles, but also cautious and wary.

The snow still fell in flurries. The warmth, the food,

the smiles, together with the smallness of the place and its situation, deep inside a wood, added to the feeling of security. The duke and the queen withdrew at once occupying the upper rooms; the men bedded down gratefully wherever they could, in the stables and on the kitchen floor, rolled in their cloaks, on benches in the main dining room. A place for everyone then, all carefully thought out beforehand, a masterpiece of planning. Except for one thing. And when Richard was gone to set a watch, to oversee the provisions and quartering, Philippa told Edmund Bryce what it was.

She had not spoken to him since her days in Richmond but she remembered him well. And hearing of his part in the attack on Wolsey's men she had wanted to thank him. When she came to the point of her domestic concern, to her chagrin at first he laughed, looking at her with his boyish grin as if to say, 'Why Mistress Philippa, or is it lady now, we left the best place of all for you.' He was standing with some of his companions, drink in hand, preparatory to taking leave of her. Suddenly serious, his fair hair plastered to his head, his forehead scored by some glancing blow, he began to realize her difficulty. 'We meant no harm,' he started to say. 'But I, for one, thought you belonged to him.'

He suddenly looked at her in his forthright way. 'Where else should you belong?' he asked. And when, in a sudden fit of nervousness, she cried, 'But suppose he resents being tied?' 'Why should he?' Edmund's voice was sharp. 'Nay lady, trust me, he'll not mind.' And without telling her Richard's present fears, he did tell her of his past ones, and of his long and fruitless search for her. Nor did he tell her what else he thought, that given half the chance, he would have leapt to fill Richard's place. And he showed her where she should bestow herself in private.

It was more of a servant's cubby-hole than room, but there was a grate, and someone had spread straw upon the floor. Left to herself Philippa looked at it ruefully, not much in truth for a wedding night. If Richard chose to join her, that is. Wearily she seated herself upon the floor in front of the meagre fire, resting her head upon her arms. And when she heard his voice outside, a panic froze her where she was.

He lifted the latch carefully, then barred the door. He was carrying his cloak over his arm and as he shook it out the flakes of snow fell to the floor in showers. Snow had blocked the one small window and the day was overcast so it was as dark as night and for a moment or two he hesitated. Then he began to move more purposefully, unbuckling his belt and sword, struggling to unstrap his spurs. It was the grate of the rowels on the hearth stones that made Philippa sit up; he was so close he might have stepped on her. Her sudden movement must have startled him, her head almost on a level with his as he reached to unfasten his boots. He looked at her. She could just see the gleam of his eyes where the faint firelight caught them but she felt him close to her, bent almost over her. The cold had made his face pale and when his hands brushed against her she could feel the ice in them, so that she wanted to hold them to give them warmth. For a moment he did not say anything. Then, 'Is that the only bed you have, on the floor?' he asked, pulling at his cloak, and reaching over for hers.

'Let be,' she said. 'Let me speak with you. We have

236

not spoken in so long a time I have almost forgotten what it is I have to say.'

She felt him stretch beside her, his long legs almost crowding hers, and it seemed to her that he was smiling. 'Speak then,' he said. 'If you wish. I had other things in mind.' She could feel his heart beating, could smell his breath upon her cheek, could sense his presence like a flame. 'If I do not presume, that is,' he was whispering against her ear, 'if my wife has room for me.'

Wife. 'Is that so?' she cried. 'Are we wed? Do you wish it so?'

'Do you?' he asked, and again she had the feeling that he was smiling. And when she cried, 'Yes, yes, yes,' he laughed out openly and put his arms about her. The cloaks were rumpled in a heap but he spread them fur side up so that they had a place to lie. His hands were warmer now against her skin, smoothing down her cheek, along her neck, like honey running molten. He unfastened the dress, parting it, so like two halves it slid off her back, like an outer skin, baring the fruit between. He heard the cry she gave as his hands followed tracing the whole, peeling the fruit to get at the essence of her. And like a current the flame sparked.

Where else should you belong. 'I cleave to you,' she cried, and he cradling her, showed her how, until he gave a cry himself. And when he surged towards her in triumph holding her, when he covered her, settling down on her, she wrapped her arms about his back, as if never to let go. 'Hold me,' she whispered as she had that first day, 'Take me with you; I will follow you.' And when he had showed her the way she did not linger. That was their wedding night then, their wedding day, one and the

237

same. They loved them both away. The wedding might have been hurried, furtive, the loving that followed it was open and generous. They slept only to wake, they woke only to love and when they had loved they slept; all through the day they kept each other company; no marriage, royal or not, could have been more richly endowed.

But as the hours passed, and their first desire slackened, there was time and need to speak of many things. They lay entwined, her head resting on his breast, his arms enfolding her, and of the things they spoke, some were old, some new, some revealed with wonderment, some with regret. They never mentioned at all the people and events that had shaped their lives and still had power over them. Only once did Richard say, 'To find you in Paris was like some miracle; I never thought you could turn on me.' And she, holding him tighter, suddenly covering his face with kisses as if to wipe away the blow, cried, 'I could think of no other way. Forgive me, love.' And for a while there was no time for saying anything as he showed her how he could forgive.

And in the rooms upstairs, the little one-time princess and queen learned too what love was, and what power it brings.

But the world outside could not be shut out for ever. Back it came in the end. The snow was still falling, lightly now, tapering off. In a few hours they must be ready to move again. There were supplies to think of, armaments, food; the new duchess imperiously began to cry for luxuries that this humble establishment had never heard of. The lovers passed each other about some task, the slightest touch, the slightest half glance, set that flame alight; and when they came together again in their little room, they might have never known what parting was. And in the end Richard revealed what lay ahead.

'My love,' he said. She was lying as he liked to have her lie, upon his lap, so that his body encircled hers and his hands were free to roam at his desire. 'My love, I have a thing to confess. For honour's sake I cannot relinquish it.' And he told her what the duke had demanded of him. And when he was done, she in turn told him what Archbishop Wolsey had demanded of her, and for a moment that small place seemed filled with old venom, like an evil smell. Richard tried to comfort her. 'We cannot stay in France,' he said. 'And even England may not be safe. But the duke has lands and estates there where he can keep himself, until Henry's will reveals itself. And so do I. Once my mission to Henry is done, then we can go north.'

He stroked her breasts, cupping them, curling her hair about them like a net. 'I am just a messenger,' he said. 'No danger to me.' He did not add, 'But for you, my love, Wolsey's reach is long,' but he thought it. And when she began to shiver as if with cold, he wrapped himself about her to keep fear out, and to let love in. 'I keep you safe,' he cried, 'here is my seal. I set my mark on you.' And feeling him deep within her, so deep she felt him reach into her womb, she held him so that he too should be safe in her where no other harm should come. In the outer world, their enemies were waiting for them.

The third day the duke was impatient to be gone, although for caution Richard would have advised a longer wait. Love in a garret had not impressed the duke much, albeit his bride was ecstatic. But even she would have preferred to have had friends and servants to wait on her, and a court to display her happiness. What she and the duke discussed, what their plans were, they never said. Having set his mind to leaving, the duke reverted to his usual careless self, scornful of detection. He rode openly, not caring now who saw him go, secure in his Tudor wife. And she, equally content, would have had trumpeters if she could, to go ahead and blare aloud her news.

Philippa could see the anxiety beginning to furrow Richard's brow, but he said nothing to her, as was his way concealing his concern. She noted, though, how all the men had armed themselves, and rode alert, as if expecting attack. Richard set the ladies in their midst. Before they left he stopped as if to tighten the saddle girths on Philippa's horse, but in reality to mutter a warning. 'We ride fast,' he said, 'although the duke would have us loiter. I think we shall be safe until we near the coast, but surely there Francis will have posted look-outs.' He hesitated. 'But if trouble comes,' he said, 'do this for me. Break clear. This horse is trained to run. Do not look back, do not try to defend yourself.' He tried a grin, 'Although what you could do with a knife perhaps would win a war,' taking away her frightened look with a jest. 'If Francis's men are like him,' he said, 'they will be too busy with their lady loves to track down fugitives; no harm in them.' It was not Francis's men he feared, it was Wolsey's guards. And knowing now, for the first time, what their hold on his wife was, he was sure they never would let go. Wolsey's wolves were well named. And they would be out hunting for her, and him.

The first hours passed without incident. Although the snow still lay in drifts and tree branches were snapped off by the weight, the air was not so cold, and from time to time a gleam of sun appeared from beneath the heavy clouds. Those who were weather trained sniffed the air and promised themselves more snow but today was clear and they made good time. They had avoided several larger roads, bypassing any that seemed to lead to villages or farms, and had come to a crossing where to the right a path had been trampled down. Away in the distance there was a faint spume of smoke as from a fire, and the temptation to turn towards it was great. While they debated, the duke and his lady all for rest, Richard all for pressing on, there came a cry to their rear. They all spun round. Galloping towards them, one of the Suffolk guards was shouting to them, waving his hat to make them stop. He plunged into their midst unsettling the other horses, almost unable to control his own. 'My lord, my lord,' he cried, his voice breaking between excitement and fear. 'A band of men is following, riding fast. I spotted them a scant half hour ago.' And to their questions, 'Yes, my lord. They know where we go. The innkeeper must have told them so.'

CHAPTER 12

——

There was no time for discussion. Even the duke was silenced as they veered as one man, taking the path towards the spume of smoke they had spotted in the distance. There was not even time for thought, the trampled snow flying behind their heels, clods of ice falling in clumps where they brushed against the over-hanging bushes and trees, the horses' breath coming in great white puffs. This was the only cover for miles and they had to use it. Set in their midst Philippa felt the wind bring tears to her eyes, felt fear riding with them like a spectre.

The farm itself, such as it was, was small and squalid, a scattered group of huts set within a broken wall. The gates themselves were gone but the stone pillars were ancient and must have been handsome, perhaps part of some castle tower. As they funnelled through into a muddy barn yard, littered with old fencing and brush-wood piles, scrawny goats scattered amid frozen straw and a dog snarled on a leash. 'By God,' the duke cried, as they skidded to a halt, 'this is a sorry place.' He reined back savagely, as if, for a moment, he saw his handsome body with all its charm and wit diminished into a broken heap like these wooden hurdles. Richard made no reply. He was already wheeling his horse round with that cold look that Philippa recognized, searching for a place to defend.

The peasants had come tumbling out, the women and children screaming in French, the men sullen, armed with scythes, ready to protect themselves. When they understood that there was no threat to them they retreated back into their hut and barred the door, dragging their goats with them. Some of the duke's men had already dismounted to block the gaps in the wall with fencing and brushwood, a hopeless task as nothing was large or firm enough; others scoured the remaining huts, driving out their occupants, a pig or two and some chickens that went scrabbling through the snow. A sorry place indeed.

'My lord duke, our stand is best outside the walls.' Richard made the decision. He too reined up in a splatter of mud. He had his helmet on but not fastened and his breastplate shimmered beneath his cloak. 'The ladies must retire to that barn.' He pointed to the largest structure facing the entrance, a ramshackle building, the only one with a door. He paused. But if he expected the duke to shout, 'By God lad, am I a woman? I stand with you,' he was disappointed. Without a word the duke led the way inside, ducking his head under the beam and pulling the duchess's horse after him.

Philippa and Richard looked at each other, no time either for farewells. Richard's voice had that calm note she also remembered. 'They'll do you no harm,' he said, 'not with the duke and duchess here. But if they break through do as I said before, give the horse its head and run. Take this.' He handed her a small purse. 'Buy your way home,' he said. 'Go north to Netherstoke and wait for me.'

She thought, if they break through that means only one thing, your death. And mine. Why would I run anywhere without you? As if he guessed what she was thinking he said. 'But they'll not get through.' He took her hand between his own, held it to his lips. 'God keep you, my love,' he said. Then abruptly he heeled his horse aside. She heard him ordering the gateway to be narrowed with farm ploughs and hoes used to clear a space in the yard for a last stand, and a few men to be stationed at intervals, armed with pikes (although horsemen were not trained to fight on foot, and they were too few to hold a charge). Then, gathering the rest in a group on either side of the gateposts where the main thrust would come, he drew his sword and waited.

Inside the barn, where there was barely room for one horse, let alone three, Philippa left the duke and duchess to themselves. The duchess was weeping, tears of fright rolling down her cheeks, and the duke was staring out of the door, morosely watching the men he should be leading prepare to defend him and his wife. The inside of the barn was dark and damp, long fallen into disrepair, but under its rafters there was a kind of loft where wisps of hay still hung. Philippa clambered up to it on a set of rungs attached to a post. There was an opening at one end under the pointed roof and when she had crawled towards it she could look out. She could see over the gate posts beyond where Richard stood, down the track they had just ridden along. And when she saw the first spumes of snow beaten up by horses riding in a troop she leaned out of the gap and screamed a warning.

Richard did not wait. Followed by some dozen men he rode out to meet them. The track had widened as it approached the farm into an open place edged with thickets, and as the first riders burst into the space he and his comrades charged at them, two by two, keeping their backs to the farm, and themselves between it and their opponents. And as the enemy horses now came tearing out of the lane each pair of defenders rode them down.

The first horsemen were taken by surprise, and went under at once. The duke's men then wheeled smartly back to charge again, never going far from their main post, allowing some to escape if they led too far off. The soldiers they charged against were not English, as their shouts and uniforms soon proved. They were part of the new French king's guard, out in force, making up for their negligence by trying to win back the 'prisoners' they had let escape. But although there were many of them and they were persistent, they were not the real threat.

After their first ranks had been cut down, the remainder drew back out of reach, stationing themselves among the bushes that edged the track. Philippa put her hands to her mouth to cut short her cry. For there, thrusting forward aggressively, eager too to be avenged, Wolsey's men came at a gallop, in their resplendent red. And at their head rode the sergeant who had been tricked again.

Seeing him, Richard gave a yell and drove his horse on; behind him came all those men he led, the duke's guard, who now risked their lives for their duke and his wife. Towards them rushed that enemy, men Philippa also knew, who had brought her here and with whom she had been forced into daily converse. Down below her, the duke swore unceasingly and beat his fist against the door-jamb so that it creaked in a smother of worm-eaten wood.

The two groups met with a crash, a thud, a howl that merged into one dull roar. Swords gleamed, lifted, struck, lifted again; horses neighed; there was a choked-off scream, a shout, a sudden rattle of harnesses, little puffs of snow as horses slipped, downing those who had got through. In the swirl of mud and snow it was impossible to distinguish friend from foe. Riderless horses plunged away, one dragging its rider after it. Two red-coated men, their faces masked with blood, tried to retreat towards the entrance; the men stationed there cut them down. Once Philippa had watched Richard fight alone. Now, surrounded by his friends, the flower of the duke's company, she saw what he could do in a fair quarrel.

He thrust and thrust again, never pausing, never giving way, pivoting his horse with his knees, letting the reins go, using both hands to heft his sword. When a man crowded close to strike under his guard, he seized the man himself by the belt and unseated him. And after fending off the attack so well that he forced Wolsey's men to withdraw under the shelter of those same trees, he and his men drew back also, too tired to shout for victory but grinning among themselves.

They reined up between the gateposts, where their companions rushed to help them off. Some were wounded and limped away; one sagged in the saddle unable to move. The open place in front of them was covered with another kind of clutter, some dressed in blue, most of whom would never move again. But Richard was not hurt. He had raised his helmet to ask questions and answer them, seizing a piece of snow to quench his thirst, keeping a careful lookout for attack and Philippa could see his face clearly. She thought, he has held them off this time. They will come again. The next time will be harder.

Richard must have thought so too. He withdrew all those whom he had set on the walls, having everyone mount, and holding them all in readiness. And down below in the barn, Philippa heard the duke shout, 'Good lad, but watch your back,' as he too waited for a flanking attack.

Moments lengthened, passed. It was obvious that the attackers were assessing strengths and weaknesses before deciding what to do. Richard knew his weaknesses as well as they did. He was outnumbered by three or four, and he had no reserves. They had the king's whole army if they chose. His position was flimsy at best; he had no food, few supplies, a hostile terrain surrounded him. Added to which he had women to protect, and an English duke who was no help at all. These were facts that a clever enemy could use. The only real advantage he had was his own and his comrades' ability and courage. That counted for something with the French, whose hearts were not so much in fighting as simply following instructions. Wolsey's men on the other hand had more at stake, and were not likely to give up so readily. It was easy to imagine how the arguments went back and forth, the

French for staying still and keeping watch until reinforcements could be brought up, Wolsey's men for attack.

Richard knew that a concerted drive would be harder to resist. If he had been in command of the enemy he would never have made a frontal assault in the first place, and he knew where the main thrust ought to come without the duke's telling him. Most of all he knew the value of what he defended, and the price put upon its head. As he had done in other emergencies he tried to think his way out, never giving up hope until hope itself was lost. What he did not expect was the flag of truce.

An officer came slowly out from under the trees. He was one of the French guards who had been stationed at Cluny, and he advanced in high court style, with all his braid and lace and epaulettes as if on parade before his king. True, his finery was tattered about the edges, and the gold fleur-de-lis on his saddle cloth was blood-stained but he saluted Richard with deference, doffing his hat, bowing deep, pivoting his horse right and left as to a crowd. When he spoke it was with such French flourishes that had Richard's comrades not been in so tight a place they would have laughed. Certainly Edmund Bryce did. 'God's mercy,' he said in a stage whisper. 'He squeals like one of those pigs.' But when the elegance had been reduced to its briefest terms the message it contained was not amusing.

'My Lord Montacune,' he began, formality in every line, 'my lords all, I bring you greetings from my king although you have given me slight chance to present them. My master, *François Premier*, Francis the First, bids me tell you that I am not come to cast blame, although stealing away in the night is not exactly what

248

French courtesy is accustomed to. My king has sent me to ascertain that the former French queen is not harmed, and is content. I find it surprising that she should be here, in such a place.' And he waved his hand disparagingly, taking in the hovels, the dirt, the broken walls. Cleverly he never mentioned the duke, although he must have known he was there, and he never spoke of what Francis really needed the queen for. Nor did he try to explain away his first attack.

Richard interrupted him, sitting straight in his saddle. 'The queen came of her own free will,' he said. 'And she is no longer queen. She has put that title aside. But she still is princess of English blood. At her request we take her home.'

Before the French officer could reply, there came a startled shout from the barn. Mary Tudor came riding out towards them, pushing forward importantly, the duke riding behind her as if to stop her, his face all frowns (although how hard he tried was for his conscience to decide). 'You speak of the queen of France,' she cried. 'Here I am. But I have another name. Henceforth call me by my new title, Duchess, wife to his grace, the Duke of Suffolk.'

'*Merde.*' The French officer was startled out of elegance. He reined back. 'The king knows nothing of this,' he said after a while. 'This is news to us.' And to Richard, 'God's life man, couldn't you have kept it quiet? That's set a cat among the pigeons.' Whether he told the truth (and he might have done, a terrified priest not likely to blab of a service that had been forced on him, and few others abroad on such a night), his surprise at the duke and duchess's appearance was not feigned. He

249

never expected them to throw away their trump card. But, on reflection he may have seen it as a way to salvage a delicate situation without losing face. After a moment's pause he saluted the duke and the new duchess with even greater flourishes.

It was the duke's turn to speak. 'Tell the French king,' he began grandly, 'that all we require of him is safe conduct to the coast, for me and mine. And for your pains, our thanks and a queen's reward.' His courtier's delicate touch this, not exactly a bribe, but a hint. And again it made the French officer hesitate, weighing opportunity. At last he replied, carefully correct, 'My master bids me greet you and escort the queen as is just. He did not specify in which direction. If the queen does not wish to return to Paris, I and my men are at her command.' He bowed once more, turning back to Richard to add, 'My quarrel is not with you.'

'But mine is.' Spurring up behind, with his men in line, came Wolsey's sergeant, his face livid with rage at what he took as betrayal. 'Mine is,' he shouted again. 'I have been looking for you, Richard Montacune; you owe me much. And I claim Philippa de Verne as my captive as is my right.'

A hubbub broke out, everyone shouting at once. All, that is, except the duke and duchess who kept strangely quiet, although one word from them could have settled the matter instantly. The obvious claim that both Richard and Philippa were under Mary Tudor's protection, and the duke's, was never made, although the duchess had promised it, and the duke should have enforced it out of gratitude and respect. Richard's angry roar was therefore doubly loud. 'The lady you speak of is my

250

wife. Give her title as is correct or I thrust it down your throat. And tell your men you and they answer to me; I too have a score with you. Collect your own as best you can. I will kill you first.'

The poor French officer was out of his depth. He wiped his face, horrified by this burst of violence contrary to all the laws of truce. 'My lords, my lords,' he began to bleat, 'we should keep calm, no point to this. I suggest . . .'

'I order.' Again Mary Tudor's voice broke in, overwhelming his. 'My husband and I are ready. Escort us, as you are meant to do. As for the rest, leave that to those whom it concerns.' And ignoring Richard, all that latent Tudor selfishness rising to the surface, she pushed towards the French officer, giving him her hand to kiss, smiling at him. The duke hesitated for a second. The words were almost forming on his lips, 'Christ's bones lad, I fight with you.' And his men leaned forward expectantly. He hesitated too long. 'Come Charles,' his new duchess said, without turning round. 'We keep these gentlemen.' She never said a word to those others she had made such a fuss of before; she gave no explanation or regret, let the French guard surround her as they had often done in the days when she was queen, and went off with them, the duke still riding in the rear, abandoning her friends she had pretended to be so fond of.

Wolsey's wolves raised up a cheer, and drew their weapons. Those left behind looked at each other, consternation in their eyes. The men Richard had been leading were not in fact 'his men', although they might have felt so, having grown used these past days to having him in charge. But they belonged to the duke. Their

251

loyalties therefore were torn, between leaving with the duke as their commission held them to, or staying. Only one man cried out decisively, and that was Edmund Bryce. 'By God,' he shouted, 'here is a disgrace that the Suffolk Blues will never live down. Desert a comrade in distress! Never.' And he came forward to align himself by his friend's side. Two against a troop is still not enough, but his offer made Richard's face light up, the more so that three more quickly followed Edmund's lead. The rest withdrew in shamed silence, and Wolsey's men let them go, parting ranks scornfully so they could pass. 'Now,' said their sergeant softly, 'We shall see who kills whom.' And without another word he threw himself at Richard.

Left in the loft, Philippa had already begun to scramble down the ladder. When she ran out into the yard the fight had begun, the last fight between the remnants of Suffolk's men and Wolsey's wolves, the fight with his rival that the duke had always sworn to win. Once more there were the same shouts and screams, the same intermingling of friend and foe, blue coats and red so besmirched that both seemed grey. Even the peasants in the hut came creeping out to watch, standing with Philippa beside the gate posts. Wolsey's men outnumbered Richard's but at each stroke the numbers decreased for Richard's men fought with the fury of those trapped.

They did not charge this time, but faced their enemy in a mass, letting their enemy charge at them. To and fro they swayed, as the weight of their opponents pushed them forward, pushed them back. But they held firm. And when one of their members was wounded, or even killed, the press of the struggle held him fixed in place.

Not until the remnants of Wolsey's men drew back, did the true carnage reveal itself.

Wolsey's guards were decimated. Perhaps five remained whole enough to ride again. Only two were left on Richard's side, himself and Edmund. Both were wounded, bleeding from a dozen cuts but strong enough to defend themselves if the attack should begin again. No one in his right mind would have expected it to. But the sergeant was still alive, and he still wanted vengeance.

Back he surged as fast as his tired horse would allow, screaming out his curses full of hate, and behind him his four companions dragged themselves. They were professionals, trained to fight, no French fops mimicking war. But Richard and Edmund were trained too. They backed between those gateposts which perhaps had seen many such stands, forcing their opponents to come at them one by one. The first two they cut down as they came, sending horses and men stumbling in front of them, making entrance even more difficult. And blocking the way out. And in that instant the sergeant suddenly saw his chance.

Setting his most reliable swordsman to keep Richard and Edmund occupied, he and his remaining companion made for the wall, clearing it easily, breaking through the brushwood like straw and storming across the yard in a clatter of hooves. Attacked from the rear, pinned down in front, Richard and Edmund were driven apart, caught in the smaller enclosed space without room for manoeuvre. They still had the advantage of speed and agility and they could have broken out. What stopped them was the sergeant.

He had spotted Philippa. One swoop, he had her fast,

hauled up against his saddle bow, his bloodied sword thrust against her neck. 'Now yield,' he screamed, 'or I kill her.'

He was quick, Wolsey's sergeant, a veteran of many wars. But Richard was quicker. Not breaking stride, relying on Edmund to hold back the other two, he thrust his horse forward so that it bounded on springs, sending it crashing upon the sergeant's in a welter of feet and teeth. From the saddle Richard launched himself with all his force, knocking the sword aside although it cut him to the bone, bearing rider and captive to the ground. He fell heavily, but the sergeant fell heavier still. Philippa landing on her side was not hurt except for a nicked vein in her neck which bled freely. But, bruised and shaken as she was, she would have been unable to crawl away had not the peasants, taking pity, run out to drag her to safety. Amid the snow and ice Richard and the sergeant rolled and struggled with their bare hands, locked into a death-like embrace. Their swords were gone, their helmets gone, their heads, one fair, one dark, coated with mud. Richard was younger, lithe like whipcord; the sergeant tough and wily. The outcome might have been evenly matched had not the sergent's men come to his rescue.

One of them kept Edmund at bay; the second sent his horse careening over the spot where the two men fought, trampling Richard underfoot. He turned to make another pass; Edmund's sword caught him mid-stride. And before the last man could swerve back to do the same, Edmund had turned to cut him off. The odds were narrowed then, two against two, two on horseback, two on foot. But those on foot were panting for breath, trying

254

to pick up their swords, scarcely able to haul themselves upright.

Richard's ribs must have been broken and his left arm dangled at his side. Blood streamed from it so that each time he moved splashes fell in dark patches. But the sergeant was hurt as well. 'God damn your soul to hell, Montacune,' he had breath to hiss, as he crawled towards his sword. Richard's foot hooked out and sent it sliding under a pile of straw. And before he could try to stretch for it again, Richard had caught him with his right arm and held him fast.

The horsemen were as well matched: Edmund eager, foolhardy, young; Wolsey's man cautious, coldly professional. He reckoned on finishing the young sprig off, then returning to his sergeant's aid. And he would have done, cleverly drawing Edmund further away out of the yard, had not Edmund also known a trick or two. With a quick movement he had reversed directions, the pursuer now becoming the pursued, until with one final lunge, he had him pinned against the gate post. 'That for my lord,' he shouted and thrust. And wheeled back to help Richard.

'My sword.' Richard's speech was slurred but he was on his feet, leaning against the wall. 'Give him his. To the death he said. So be it.' He seemed scarcely able to take a step and his hand was sticky with blood. The sergeant, gathering up his weapon, allowed himself a grin. It was the last grin he ever made. Summoning his fading strength Richard made one last mighty sweep, the movement that the sergeant remembered well. It sent the sergeant's sword flying in the air, arching in a parabola while Richard's own sword traced out a similar arch to reflect it. He and his opponent folded together, toppled to the ground like two bundles of rags. The sergeant never moved again, and Richard lay like one dead.

They dragged the dead man off the living, although the living scarcely breathed. With the help of the peasants Philippa had him carried within the hut whose owners squatted in a corner and watched anxiously. Edmund, himself bleeding from a dozen cuts, tried to bind the worst of Richard's, until one of the women dared come close. She stretched out her hand gingerly to touch his arm, dabbing at it with a dirty smock, meanwhile shouting in her own tongue for water and salves. She worked quickly and efficiently, used to nursing wounds, binding the broken bones with soft cloths and making splints from pieces of wood. Something about her forthrightness brought the real world back. Philippa suddenly sat down on the dirt floor, her legs no longer capable of supporting her. And after a while, when she could move again, she came to sit by Richard's side, holding one of his hands in hers. Another long night stretched ahead, the future looked darker then ever.

It was many hours before Richard stirred, his swoon having deepened into sleep. Meanwhile Edmund who himself had fallen into an exhausted doze, had wakened to the realization of how vulnerable they still were. 'They'll be back,' he told Philippa, his face puckered with alarm. 'I know them well, those French. They speak smoothly, but they're as forked as an adder's tongue. What of their dead? Won't they return for them? And seeing what has become of Wolsey's men, won't they try to accuse us of ambushing them?'

All through the night, whilst the men had slept,

Philippa had heard the peasants outside the hut. Now Edmund realized what they had been doing. The ice-crusted ground had made digging difficult so, using the hurdles as stretchers, they had dragged the English corpses and gear into the woods, leaving only the French ones. Their frantic activity almost done, they were preparing to leave themselves. Carrying their children and rounding up their animals, they were gathering their little possessions up, all in silence without complaint, as if they were too afraid to complain. Clearly they wanted no part in this struggle which ill-luck alone had caused to happen on their land. It meant nothing to them, and yet they knew they might yet be blamed if there was no one else left to blame. They knew it behoved them to be far away before Francis's guards came back.

'They mean to hide,' Edmund told Philippa. 'Some safe place they keep for emergencies. When they go, we go with them.'

He said persuasively, 'Dick cannot stay here. True, the journey could be too much for him. But if they find him here, he will assuredly die. And so will we.'

Persuading the peasants to let them come was not easy, especially since his knowledge of French was limited. But he used the horses as bribes. There were plenty still loose in the courtyard where the peasants had left them alone. Peasants in these parts were not accustomed to horses, and this farm was too poor even to own an ox. Choosing ones with the duke's brand, Edmund had the boys round them up and harness some to a kind of sled made from hurdles. He had Richard placed upon the sled, wrapped in cloaks and hidden under piles of rags. Finally, selecting the best three, he and Philippa mounted up, leading the third. The rest were driven into the forest to forage for themselves, with the understanding that when all was quiet again, the farmers could have first claim on them.

All this took time and taxed his strength, so that he too looked as pale as a ghost. But before the day was an hour old the peasants had started out, following an overgrown path that wound under the trees. The huddle of huts was left behind, as had happened many times in the past.

The path was one only the peasants could have known. Once under the trees they scattered so their trail was lost. Some doubled back; others began to drive animals to and fro to hide the prints of human feet. They continued in this way until the snow began to fall, not heavily as before, a light dusting, but sufficient to hide them and to cover the worst evidence left behind in the barn yard. Then they made more haste. In any case they did not go far. Deep in the woods there was a ridge that ran along a small river bed, now frozen solid. Under the ridge were caves hollowed out in the cliffs, long used as summer quarters when there were cattle to fatten in the river meadows on the other side. Some of these caverns stretched deep underground, large and wide enough to hide a company, and there they set up their camp.

They allowed the three fugitives shelter in the driest part of the cave, shared what food they had, little enough; gave good advice on which roads to take and roads to avoid, not much of it accurate since they seldom stirred beyond their own land. Once their ancestors had been soldiers, or so they claimed, and once a greater battle than this had been fought, so fierce that even now

258

ploughs sometimes turned up pieces of bone or scraps of buckles and mail. The old name of the place was 'La Croix' they explained, because of the graveyard crosses that once had been raised there. And when Richard finally opened his eyes, they suggested that their welcome was over and all three should leave.

By now several days had passed. Edmund was almost fit again, although stiff and sore. The snows had tapered off and it was no longer cold. No sight or sound of pursuit had been heard and the peasants, creeping back from time to time to spy on their home, had reported that the French guards (who had returned as Edmund said they would) had left immediately. The time was right then for departure. If the sick man could ride.

Richard's broken ribs alone should have kept him immobile, to say nothing of his other wounds. He made no resistance to the idea that they should all continue on; he only resisted coming all the way with them. 'We go together to the coast,' he said, his tone harsh, although he spoke in a whisper. 'With Edmund's help I can ride. When we reach England you and he will go to Netherstoke, where I will join you as soon as I can. After I have been to Richmond.'

At Philippa's cry, he said in an even harsher voice that could not be argued with, 'You did not think I would leave that task undone? What if the duke abandoned us; I do not abandon my word. Besides,' he tried to grin, a faint imitation of it to soften the meaning, 'I wish to alert the king that I too am a married man and my wife belongs to me.' And nothing his companion or wife could say could change his mind.

These discussions alarmed the peasant folk. Not used

to strangers they could not understand, they had grown restive at close quarters with them. They had promised to let them come with them; that did not mean keeping them indefinitely. If the young English milord rode out before he could stand did not all lords ride before they walked? Let them go, before their enemies came hunting them. They gathered in corners, not smiling now, anxiety furrowing their foreheads, suspicions making their eyes sharp. Forced into leaving then, Edmund and Philippa had no choice but to accept Richard's decision. But privately they agreed that he could not make that journey on his own; if he went to Richmond they went with him. But they kept that thought between themselves.

They left therefore sooner than they meant, Edmund in front, on guard, Philippa leading Richard in the rear, where she could help him. He could use his right arm to guide the horse but not to put any pull on it and he had to rely on his friend to heft him in and out of the saddle. His face was white and drawn, but he still could smile. Nor would he show weakness even if it should kill him. And letting Edmund lead the way, they began the long trek home. Philippa thought, he has left France like this before, wounded, in hiding, and her heart bled for him.

During those days in the cave Philippa had had time to think of many things. The fight, the deaths, the violence, had blurred into nightmare, although she would always have the mark left by the sergeant's sword. Mary Tudor's perfidy had cut deeper. Although, on looking back, through all these months she had known her, Philippa realized that possibility of betrayal had always been there, held in reserve. Now fear and hostility had released it. To think that Richard Montacune would risk his life for a man so treacherous as the duke seemed to her incomprehensible, so incomprehensible in fact that she did not believe it. She was convinced that Richard had other plans in mind and watching him now as he rode along, not whistling as he often did, simply concentrating on staying on his horse, she tried to imagine what he thought. He was not a foolish man, obsessed with revenge as that sergeant had been; he knew his enemy. What then would take him back to Richmond into his enemy's stronghold? These questions nagged at her unceasingly. But when they reached the coast at last, then they nagged no more. For they found there what would resolve some of the doubt for her.

CHAPTER 13

They had made good time, good that is for a sick man who was as weak as a kitten, and for a woman who would have found the ride hard under any circumstances. But Richard and Edmund knew this region well. They had traversed it often; in their role as messengers it was the route they would have taken if they had been with the duke as they had planned. The out-of-the-way inns in obscure villages were still available to them, and Richard's money could buy them anonymity. The snows which had hampered other travellers were almost gone and the roads were clear. At times the sun almost shone and every day saw Richard's recovery assured. Had their mission not been so hazardous, had Richard not held firm to his purpose, they might even have been happy. But on the coast the ports were still ice-bound, the boats trapped at their moorings. And when they arrived at Calais they found the duke and his duchess there.

The duke and duchess had made no secret of their return. Escorted by Francis's guards they turned it into a royal tour, staying with lords and abbots along the way, as if on a triumph. They had been in no hurry it seemed, content to enjoy themselves. Installed in the royal castle, their French escort gone now they were on English soil, the duchess and her new friends had begun to celebrate the wedding in fitting fashion. Amid such merriment it was not difficult for three more English to slip in after dark and find a room in a town where everything seemed English.

The duke however was in a sombre mood. Married to the woman he had always sworn to have, basking in her warm regard, he should have been happier than he was. He had lost weight, slept badly; his hand shook, the hand that had once earned him the reputation of the best swordsman in England. Thoughts of his brother-in-law had returned to haunt him, that brother-in-law in whose castle he now resided and whose messengers were waiting for the first sign of thaw to take fast ship to report the news. Sometimes as he looked at his new wife, when she slept, or when she chattered with the hosts upon whose hospitality they had thrust themselves, he began to find her small pouting mouth and dark eyes not as innocent as they had once seemed. And other things bothered him. He could not get the thought of Richard out of his mind, someone whom he had counted as a friend. He had not dared ask the French what had become of him; he almost did not want to know. And another characteristic he had begun to dislike in his wife was her refusal to speak of the young woman. But the duke thought of her. The last thing he wanted was to be confronted by these ghosts of his conscience.

Richard said nothing when he realized that the man who had betrayed him was here in the same town. And it was still difficult to know what he thought. In these days of travelling he and his wife had grown close, sharing the same fears and simple pleasures, sharing the same friendship with Edmund Bryce. But that night, when it was dark, Richard stood up, and buckled on his sword. 'Take care of her,' he said to Edmund before he left; nothing more. And Philippa who knew him well enough by now not to protest, guessed at once what he was going to do. She said nothing either, but when he had gone, she begged Edmund to follow him.

Richard walked with difficulty and his left arm was still strapped to his side. The last day's ride had wearied him but he refused to let his weakness show. He caught up with the duke just as Charles was entering the castle gates after being entertained by the Governor of the town. The duke's men recognized Richard first and would have crowded round had he not waved them back. And so it was he and the duke came face to face under the portcullis where the wall torches flared.

The duke gave ground. He did not say anything either, simply drew back into the shadows like a man afraid, drawing the fur collar of his cloak as if to hide himself. Nor did Richard address him by rank or title, but spoke abruptly to the point. 'I was looking for you. I supposed I would find you at Richmond. I had two messages to deliver there. One was on your behalf, although since now you blare it so openly I think it will not be news when I get there. The other concerned my wife. Your wife owes her life to mine, and until recently held my wife as friend. You brought both into intimacy (and in that sense may be held responsible for their relationship). I am here now to give fair warning what my message is.

The Archbishop Wolsey promised my wife just pardon. I say "just" since he knows, and you and I and the duchess know, that my wife has done nothing wrong. I mean for the world to know. I shall tell the king so. And I shall make claim on her behalf for her lands, as the Archbishop bribed her.'

The duke gaped at him. In all his life, he had never been spoken to with such a show of contempt, and it stung his pride. He growled with anger and reached for his sword. In a moment he would have been in a public brawl with a man who scarcely could move, let alone defend himself, had not Edmund Bryce rushed in between. 'My lord,' he shouted. 'Hold back.' And to Richard, 'Dick, you fool, you cannot fight him in this state. Let me fight him in your stead.'

The effort to draw his own sword had left Richard gasping for breath, so that he had no words to berate his friend as he deserved. As for the duke, suddenly realizing who Edmund was, he cried out, 'You too. Then is she safe as well?'

'No thanks to you.' Knowing who the duke meant, if anything Edmund was more blunt. 'And if you survive you can thank her yourself.' He rounded on the duke, all his young eagerness suddenly spilling out for the last time. 'We fought them, as we always said we would, and we bested them. You did not even stay to watch.'

'No.' The duke's answer was as blunt. 'And you cannot best him, lad. Wolsey has the jump on us. He is now the king's chief councillor, his right hand man, more powerful than I ever was, privy to all the king's secrets. If anyone can intercede for me with Henry, he can. I do not dare offend him. I shall throw myself upon his mercy too, and pray he persuades the king to favour us.' He suddenly cried out, 'It is not easy to be thrust into exile, made second where you have long been first. It is not easy to be wed to a queen, who is sister of a king. But what I can do for you I will. And what my wife can do for Philippa de Verne I swear in her name, as my own is Charles Brandon.'

He looked from one young man to the other. 'I swear then,' he corrected himself bleakly, 'in the name of our former company, which once was as dear to me as you.'

Perhaps at the time he meant what he said; perhaps he thought he could persuade Mary Tudor; perhaps he believed he had some honour left. Neither Richard nor Edmund believed him. And the duchess felt the same way. Her eyes grew close with spite when she heard what had occurred. She did not like to hear herself criticized. She had enough on her mind as it was, she cried, keeping her husband's spirits up; no need to have new promises made on her behalf, nor reproaches for past ones. Did he think she intended to let her husband diminish himself, arguing with two hot-heads, not worth the time of day?

But later that night Philippa came close to where Richard lay, speaking softly to him. 'My love,' she begged him again, 'I wish that we could leave at once. I do not trust them. I want never to see them again. I care nothing for what was my land. It is only you I want.'

'I care,' he said. 'It is the least that I can do for my wife who has suffered enough because of them; and for her father whom I felt I knew. The rest I admit is pride, for myself.'

'I prefer you alive,' she cried. 'Now you will be as caught as I am.'

'I already am,' he whispered back. 'I was caught, long ago, when I saw you first and stole you from my men. They were right to say I had. And when we get back home, you shall tell John of Netherstoke yourself. As now you shall show me.' And under cover of the night, she did, his wounds this time not hampering him.

The next day the thaw began, with great creaks and groaning from the ice, which in such an unusual way had kept the boats in port. Now all those ships that could be commandeered were readied to sail with the tide, for, despite the blizzards on land, the sea had been calm. The duke and his lady departed in grand style, as if, now the die was cast, they meant to brazen it through, as if defiance was their best hope with the king. Behind them, Lord Montacune and his wife and friend sailed in a smaller boat, more like a fishing smack, but sufficient for them. And although it was true that, as perhaps for the duke, what would happen when they reached shore was not yet clear, they accepted that, confident it would be the last obstacle before they reached home.

On the harbour wall, the king's men were waiting for them.

The list of indictments against them both was endless, as the ducal party had given testament. Theft, murder, capture of a queen without her consent, ambush and collusion, treason, any one of the accusations could have hanged them. They listened almost without comment; so much for Charles Brandon's word.

The guards held Richard fast while these charges were read, supposedly because he was most dangerous –

although one look at him could have shown how unable yet to raise defence. They left Philippa on the edge of the quay, presumably a girl not likely to do them harm, and they ignored Edmund Bryce completely since he had not been named as accomplice. For the last time Edmund Bryce acted as go-between.

'Run, run, my lady,' he screamed, pushing between her and the guards. He had his sword out, flashing dangerously, forcing them to retreat along the quay on the seaward side, their prisoner with them. And hearing Richard's own voice shouting the same command, with one startled look, Philippa slipped over the landward side, where the ground below was flat and firm.

She began to run in earnest. She probably could not have gone far, for Edmund could not hold six men at bay, even those hampered with a prisoner, and she would not have known which way to run had she not by good fortune jumped to the side where the soldiers' horses were tethered. She was used to horses now. It took but a moment to untie one, and set the others free. Then scrambling up she turned again with some thought perhaps of riding the soldiers down. One look at Richard's face as Edmund fell to the stones, a sword buried in his chest; one shout from him, 'Ride on,' made her swerve away. Kicking the horse forward she plunged through the village at a gallop, with no thought in mind except how to rescue her husband, and how to help his friend.

She could not say how long she rode, nor in what direction. She gave the horse its head and trusted to its good sense. All she could see was Richard's face, all she could hear was Edmund's scream. But presently as sight and hearing came back, when her tears were done, she began to recognize the sleepy lanes and rich orchard fields as ones she had seen before, when on an autumn day she had ridden through them with the sergeant of Wolsey's guard. And because there was no other way to go, and she knew no other place to hide, she came at last in the evening to the Holy Sepulchre, where she had been brought those months ago.

She recognized its outline before she came to the main walls, and a quick search revealed the same small side door. Fastening the horse outside she hammered with all her might. It had begun to dawn on her that a nunnery was a place of sanctuary. As long as she remained free perhaps she could help Richard. And at the back of her mind there lingered the idea that Richard had had of approaching the king and challenging him openly.

The nun who answered finally was not pleased at this late hour intrusion. An unknown lady who was travel-stained, who shouted for the Nun Elizabeth and would not be quieted, did not make a welcome guest. But once Philippa had ascertained that the Nun was still there, and was alone, she insisted until at last she was let in. And while she waited, suddenly all the things she needed to know started to throb in her brain so that, like a man who begins to drown, she felt a wave sweep over her. And seeing the Nun Elizabeth at last emerge from behind the grating, she burst into frantic pleas for help.

'Lord love us.' The Nun sounded motherly. She sat Philippa down upon the stool and wiped her face. 'You're back,' she cried. 'I didn't expect you so soon. You've led my master a merry dance. It's just as well he's not at home.' She gave what could have been a grin. 'So we'll make do without him,' she said. And more at ease since the grille did not conceal a hidden spectator, she had food brought and a chair, and lights, all comforts that Philippa was too weary to enjoy, too full of her own story to notice. But when that story was finished with, the Nun sat back, arms crossed upon her ample bosom and stared at Philippa in amazement.

'You mean,' she said wonderingly, 'that the French king died. God never told me so. That do seem unfair of Him; how's a body to guess a thing like that. And you mean that you and this new husband of yours have been made out proper fools, tricked by the queen and her new husband; lord, it does make the mind to reel. But I know about trickers and their tricks.'

She suddenly cast a shrewd look that had nothing to do with prophecy. 'I've had my share of them,' she said. She thought for a moment. 'But no use your staying here,' she said briskly, 'and I don't know where else to suggest (although were I in my own village, why there's plenty there would shelter you). But a pretty wench like you shouldn't cry; time for crying when you've tired of the marriage bed. And a fine young man like your lord is meant for love not death.'

She turned and turned about like a dog pacing up and down. 'I always liked the looks of you,' she said at last. 'And I feel sorry for you. You never let on about your wrongs last time; no wonder I couldn't turn them aside. But if they're true, which I don't doubt, why you've had a life to make you sad. And I think God meant us to be glad.'

She brooded for a while, sucking the end of her veil, and tapping her foot on the ground. 'I don't know much about sanctuary,' she said. 'But there be things that I do know. And one, 'tis not right to hound poor young folks into their graves, for no fault of their own. So I'll help you with what I can.

'In my earlier days,' she went on, waxing eloquent now she had Philippa's attention, 'when I was young, Lord bless us, how God spoke to me. Every night He came to the foot of my bed and the words rolled out. Now, I'm not so sure. Sometimes I think He's forgotten me. But if I pray, and you pray too, why, perhaps He'll put the thoughts back on my tongue just as He used to do.'

Without further ado, she spread her skirts and plumped down on her knees, resting her head upon the table ledge, her hands folded piously as children's do, her mouth moving up and down in some private litany.

It was quiet in the little room, and still. The candles burned steadily, casting shadows against the plain white walls. All the hard sad day rose before Philippa like a cry of pain, then seemed to fade, as pain is forgotten once its course is run. When the Nun Elizabeth moved, a scent of flowers stirred with her, like lavender perhaps or roses. A garden might have been unfolding in that room, where fir trees stood like sentinels, and white birds fluttered over the red Devon soil. And Philippa might have been a child herself, praying in the old church where her ancestors had worshipped through long centuries. There are many kinds of loyalties, she thought. And one man's life cannot encompass them all. Man is made for joy and love, not for wickedness and sin. When my child is born, let him grow to God's delight. And when the Queen of England conceives let her no longer

271

be counted barren, but like a flower, blossom into fruit.

She rested her head on her arms and slept, a sleep full of hope although in all things else the future had not shown any. The Nun of Kent rose from her knees, brushing her skirt hems free of dust, briskly preparing to go about her own business. Her face wore a smile that could be best called angelic, although that word sat ill with her full red cheeks and coarse skin. But when she had risen to her full height she suddenly stooped again as if a lance had pierced her side, and a look of terror undermined her smile. She stuffed her hand into her mouth as if to dam up the words that now came out. 'But the fruit of guilt and deceit is cruel,' she seemed to cry. 'Let the House of Suffolk beware. One day a child will be born of them, a Nine Day Queen, to make the Tudor line tremble.' She wiped her face, sweat starting on her cheeks in drops, her hair matted with it. Beside her, still leaning her head upon her arms, Philippa slept on, unaware.

With the morning the Nun was her usual self. When Philippa awoke, stiff from sleeping in one cramped spot, she was free with advice for salves and potions to relieve the soreness and bruises of many days. 'How white your skin is,' she said, rubbing it. 'How soft your hands for all that you have been riding like a man. Well, that is almost done. When you have said Mass with us, and broken fast, mount on your horse that you have tied outside. Take up the reins for the last time and ride to Richmond as your husband was sworn to do. Never fear. Your young lord will yet be safe and his friend still lives. This much I do for you.' And speaking hurriedly she told Philippa what to do and say, and how to use

272

Wolsey's weaknesses to turn him into an ally. 'But hurry,' she said. 'When my master knows what I have done, my days too may be numbered.' And again a look blurred her face, as if the future were hiding there.

Philippa rode openly to Richmond, not trying to conceal herself. No one seemed to notice her, all intent upon the greater news of Mary Tudor's marriage to a duke, and the arrest of a young traitor, who was held responsible. The court had never known such excitement, more than equal to the first announcement of the French marriage.

The day was mild and Henry had been strolling with his councillors along the river bank. Wolsey had been listing all the advantages of a new French alliance but he had only been half listening. The cold weather that had frozen France had left England untouched and the smell of spring had made him think of hunting and jousts, those pleasures which had never seemed the same since Charles, 'his' Charles, had been gone. He did not know whether to be relieved that he was back, or angry that he came in such a way, after promising not to do the precise thing that he had done. It was the break of faith that angered him, more than the marriage itself, and so far he had refused to let Charles come to court. Let him sweat fear out a while. Just as the young man should.

He remembered Richard Montacune. There was a man whom he had rewarded and made much of; a brave soldier, his own envoy, that treachery then seemed especially personal. Well, the Tower had him fast, him and his friend. But the girl had got away, ever slippery like an eel, impossible to pin down. He never thought to see her coming towards him bold as brass. For a moment

273

he closed his eyes, and made the sign of the cross.

'My lord king,' Philippa's voice was neither loud nor soft, but rang out clearly as it always did. 'It seems you wanted me. So I have come of my own accord, having nothing to hide or regret. And I have come to find Archbishop Wolsey,' for she had spotted his dark robes in the background. 'I wish to report to him all that I did in France, as he asked me to. And beg him to speak on my behalf as he promised.'

Wolsey began to splutter, sensing danger, unexpected and real. Henry looked at him suspiciously. Suddenly many things about his councillor began to fall into place, things which had puzzled him and which he saw needed looking to. But he kept that thought apart. 'What could Wolsey promise you?' he asked softly for he did not want the world to hear. 'A traitor's end is what you deserve. And what you'll get, Wolsey or no.' And he suddenly shouted, 'Why did you turn Mary Tudor against me?'

'My lord,' she said, in that quick way he remembered and, on hearing, could not decide whether he liked or not, 'her majesty did all you asked. You yourself promised her free choice when her first husband died. But what she does is not my fault. And that is not why I came to court.'

'You came to get your father's lands,' Henry cried. 'Is that what Wolsey promised you? If he did, he took too much upon himself. He is not king yet.' He stared at her, remembering too how she had caught him out before in argument. He wanted to justify himself, bellowing aloud all the 'facts' his spies had collected. All he could remember was how the feel of her had possessed him so that he had to have her fast. But overwhelming her in a prison cell was one thing. Displaying himself before the world, in public, would make him look foolish. And kings do not have to argue with their subjects.

He grew cunning. 'I promised you a thing,' he said. 'I told you you could have your lands back, as your father lost them. They are held in forfeit to the crown. Claim them. Fight the crown for them.'

His courtiers who had been straining to listen began to titter, thinking he spoke in jest. Much of what was said was lost to them, but this was not. And Wolsey who had been on tenterhooks saw his opportunity. He gave his blaring laugh. 'A woman fight,' he cried, 'I suppose they will be jousters next. Women in a joust is all we need.' But Henry was not joking.

'Rather a joust,' he said coldly, 'than lectures. Since Suffolk left I have not had one good partner nor one day free of hectoring. You, Archbishop, do not know horse flesh, I think. Unless your father butchered it.'

He watched the Archbishop flush. He turned back to Philippa. 'If Wolsey gave you good advice,' he said, 'ask for it again. Explain to him how it was you came to marry and urged my sister to the same course. Tell him what you would do to get your lands back.'

'Nothing,' she said. 'I only want my husband free and my friend.'

That was the final straw. 'You shall have him,' Henry howled. 'And he shall have you.' He shouted for his guards, sending them scattering. 'Haul him out,' he screamed, 'drag him here if he can't walk. Let them face each other once, and we'll have the truth out of them. Lock her up.' Off he stalked, disappointment and rage gnawing him. Philippa was not dismayed. She remembered what the Nun of Kent had advised and held firm.

One other man was distressed by this turn of events although he did not show it openly. And that was Thomas Wolsey. His grudge against Philippa and her husband had grown, the more since news of his sergeant's death had just reached him. He had always meant to toss Philippa aside, the question had merely been when. Now it occurred to him that she knew more about him than he cared to have known. A chit of a girl, what could she do? But she had already done much, and she had a husband. If he could have silenced her, a quick stab, a slit throat – he had done as much before, but never so obviously. Round and round Wolsey's thoughts went, trying to save his own neck first. He had seen Henry's frown; he had known what Henry's insults meant. In the end he did what he had done before; he compromised. Compromise was his advantage.

'My lord king,' he said in his obsequious way (which Henry hated yet had come to rely upon). 'I have been thinking. Your sister and her new husband have returned to England. They would have gone somewhere else, if they meant you harm. The people have welcomed them back as part of your family. It would be a hurt to them to cut your sister off, your only heir and next of kin.' He let these thoughts sink in, cleverly keeping his real intent to the end.

'As for this Philippa de Verne.' He shrugged as if to say, 'She is not worth much, certainly not worth your regard.' 'Her husband is a noble man,' he went on. 'In the north where his family is well known, he has friends. He has been young and foolish perhaps but not I think treacherous. Or if a traitor, more to the duke than you yourself. A day or so in the Tower will have cooled him off. Have your joke with him.'

Wolsey did not have the duke's ready skills, nor his charm. But he was shrewd. He too knew how much to dig and when to smooth. He left the king with these half thoughts in mind, not enough to incriminate himself, just enough to steer along. And satisfied his work was done, he went next to see Philippa. As spiritual adviser to the king it was not difficult to arrange.

Richmond was the king's own residence, not meant for a gaol. Philippa had known worse lodgings during the past months, and she was not exactly frightened. She had partly expected Wolsey's visit. And he, with that same sneaking regard for her intelligence that he had felt before came to the point at once. 'If you tell the king what I did,' he said, 'you will destroy me and break my hold on him. He will kill you. For if he suspects me, if he lacks confidence in me, the only one he can confide in, Henry will strike at everyone. So whether you will or no, our fates are joined. As I said before, help me, and I will help you.'

He looked at her, wiping the sweat from his face, suddenly seeing his own ruin, just as the Nun of Kent said he would.

'The king has jousts much on his mind,' he went on, using his cleverness now, helping her to help himself. 'He needs to be distracted, missing his old partner. Claim the right of trial by combat, an old custom that will amuse him. Let your innocence be decided in an open duel, your champion riding against one the king will choose. You select the man who bested Charles Brandon. Have your husband ride for you. And since Charles Brandon is forbidden the court no one can defeat Montacune. But the prospect will mollify Henry and will offer you a chance of success. In a legal trial you have none. The charges are too many and weighted too heavily for you to hope for release.'

Stifling the thought of Richard's wounds, beating down the panic that these words caused, Philippa did as the Archbishop said. She knew him wily as a fox, but she sensed some truth in him this time. She sent word to the king that since the charges against her were all false, she would rely on God to give her justice. Let God decide if she were true or false, as used to be done in former times. And Henry, intrigued as the Archbishop had foreseen, agreed.

When next day Philippa saw the tourney field, just as Richard himself had described, lined with courtiers all agog at this spectacle, when she saw the queen take her place, she almost lost her courage. She herself had been placed at one side of the lists with her back to the river. She was dressed in black as became a prisoner whose life was at stake, for whom these elaborate rituals had been revived. Surrounding her on a dais were the king's councillors, dressed too in black, as became judges in a trial of such magnitude. They did not speak, simply folded their robes as if resigned to a custom most of them privately would have termed barbaric, dating from olden times. At one end of the lists stood a black horse which Richard was to ride. She had not seen him. But she prayed that he was well. If no harm had been done to him in the Tower perhaps he was strong enough to fight.

278

She knew he was not strong enough to defeat the charges laid on him. As a soldier his skills at least could serve them both. Better she thought for him to die a clean death in a fight, on a battle field, than the death the king had planned for him. But she did not think he would die. For who in England was there to challenge him?

The trumpet sounded, once, twice, thrice, the call to arms. Even the councillors sat up, thanking God no doubt they never would have to judicate in such fashion again. There was Richard striding out. He wore jousting armour all encased, but he could walk, he could climb into the saddle without help. And he had seen her. Down the lists he came cantering, his sword held up, as if in salute, as if to claim justice, she could not tell. She thought, suddenly ice cold, so it was in a dream I had, the river flowing past, the dark clothed men, Richard weighted down. God in heaven, do not desert us now when we have most need of you. God keep us safe, Richard most of all. God let him defeat the king's champion.

At the opposite end of the list the gates opened. A man on a huge horse rode out, his red hair flying in the breeze, his small eyes narrowing with glee. 'Hah,' said Henry Tudor pulling on the reins. 'So you're the man who wants the girl. Then you fight me. The prize, well, what would be fair? Kill me you get her, lands and all. Kill you, and I claim both your lives.'

What a cry now broke out, women screaming, courtiers on their feet, councillors flapping in their long black robes, trying to reach the king before he threw his life away. Richard drew his helmet off, running his hand through his curls, suddenly looking young and perplexed with his face white against the dark. Left in his seat, Wolsey ground his teeth in rage, outfoxed by Henry in the end, an impossible choice, kill a king or be killed. Philippa caught his glance as he looked wildly round. I never expected this, that look said, and he clutched the crucifix on his breast as if praying himself for guidance.

Did God or the Nun of Kent hear him? Did God in truth speak? Among the ladies on the balcony the queen had been sitting to one side, surrounded by her Spanish friends; they interested perhaps in this fresh example of English stupidity; she trying not to watch. Now she stood up and came to the edge of the lodge, a small figure tending to plumpness, her black hair already showing signs of grey. She leaned forward gripping with both hands as if to give herself courage. 'My lord,' she cried, then louder, 'Henry, wait. I have a thing to say to you.'

Her voice was not loud but it was commanding and it made her husband look up. What a god he seemed himself, that Tudor giant on his giant horse, like the sungod he thought himself, like the god of war he had wished to be, not the petty tyrant that he was to become. 'Henry,' said Catherine of Aragon, her Spanish lisp almost gone, 'I do not wish you to fight today. Come back to me. I do not wish there to be bloodshed on so fair a day. I wish the husband of my child, peace and prosperity.'

The silence lengthened. 'Child,' Henry said at last. He had come crowding to the barricade and was looking up at her. He stood up in the saddle stretching for her hand. 'Child?' he asked again. The people watching took up the word; it flew from mouth to mouth in a hiss of syllable, the child he had been waiting for; the child that God had withheld from them; the child that would make her barrenness blossom from flower to fruit. And she, leaning down said, 'It is so. And on such a day when we should rejoice with God, let all be forgiven and at peace. Let there be mercy for all men and women, royal and commoner, in this place. And let these prisoners have your full pardon to go home.'

And Henry, suddenly his own face bathed in tears, shouted, 'Amen, amen.'

CONCLUSION

—

This general sign of rejoicing was shared by everyone, even by old courtiers who perhaps had looked forward to a spectacle, although never one on such a scale. Certainly the ladies of the court were relieved, the queen's compassion in asking mercy for this girl (whom she must have known had once attracted the king) only surpassed by the king's own generosity. His jovial shout, 'Set them loose, give them title, estates, lands, what they want; let them go where they will, I make them free with my kingdom,' was followed by an even more welcome one. 'Order wine and food, bring out my trumpeters, sound the bells,' showing him again at his most gracious, the well-loved prince who had his people's interest at heart, and knew how to play to the crowds . . . Only two men were not impressed. And one of those was Richard Montacune.

He and Philippa had remained behind, he on his horse, she on the dais which was virtually deserted now since the councillors had flocked to the king. Nothing stopped them from leaving. He looked at her, and she at him, a long slow look that had in it all the things that lovers feel and think when disaster has parted them. Then a realization washed over her, so cold she might have been back in France. She knew without his saying so what he meant to do, and she knew she could not stop him. He had removed the great jousting helm before. Now he wheeled his horse around and shouted loudly, above the hubbub and the excitement, stilling it, 'My lord king, it is not yet finished with.'

Henry swivelled about himself and his courtiers were suddenly hushed. And, sure of their attention, Richard Montacune drew himself up as straight as his broken ribs allowed. Days in the Tower had not dimmed him although they had diminished many lesser men, nor had sight of his wife slackened his purpose. If anything he felt it even more poignantly.

'I praise God for pardon,' he said. 'For as God knows there was nothing to pardon. But I have things left to settle. My wife has lost her lands and reputation through no fault of hers. And I lose my honour if I am foresworn. And so my lord king, although your offer is most gracious, still it cannot be, unless I run a course with you.'

He had perhaps never looked so proud as he did then, nor perhaps so young and arrogant, putting even Henry the sun god in the shade. And Henry felt the contrast. His courtiers on the other hand were shocked; what fool, having had his neck saved, would thrust it back into the noose? Or who would push luck so far as to rely on Henry's continuing good will? But Henry was in an expansive mood, suddenly full of hope. Richard's sense of honour appealed to him. Gone in that moment was all his spite; he and his queen again were the god and goddess of love; all should be as fair and sweet as that fun-loving princess once had believed. Most of all, his child to be, his heir, would turn Wolsey's gloomy predictions to straw.

'Done,' he said. He pulled his helmet down, edged his horse back along the track and turned to face Richard at the other end. He did not say what the wager was, or if it had changed, and no one asked, overwhelmed by the temerity of the challenge, by a challenger who but moments before had been called a convicted felon.

But Richard did not put a helmet on. He rode bareheaded as if to show his face to the world. Seizing a lance, he steadied it against his thigh, couched into place upon the elaborate breastplate. Nor did he wait for the heralds to begin their proclamations. 'God protect you Henry Tudor,' he cried, 'for today I fight in the name of all the dispossessed, for those who have been falsely accused and for those who are innocent. God protect them likewise. And me and mine.'

Down the barricade he thundered as he had described before. And down towards him Henry came, riding on that great stallion which had been the start of Richard's court experience. Left in the balcony with her ladies, the queen sank back, hands clasped upon her breast as if in a faint. And Philippa, reaching out her arms as if to encompass her husband, cried, 'Go with my love.'

The Flanders stallion trod on air, its royal rider so firmly wedged into the saddle only a thunder clap could have unseated him. Richard Montacune rode a black horse, black for penance and woe. But his face wore a smile; he clasped his lance against his side and thrust with all the weight of God behind him. He could not rock Henry from that horse's back, nor turn the horse from its stride, but he caught Henry's lance mid-stroke.

It splintered against his, steel sparking in the sun, the sound like a thunder crack, the sight like a lightning bolt. And stunned by the shock, reins gone, hands flailing helplessly for control, Henry reeled in the saddle while his horse bolted.

Richard had equal difficulty reining up his horse too. But when he had steadied it under him and held it firm, 'God's will be done,' he cried. 'And so is mine. And now it is time to go home.'

Back he rode at a gallop towards his wife, drawing up with a clatter in front of her. 'Lady', he said in formal terms, 'will it please you to ride with me?' She smiled at him, no need to answer.

Men still speak of their leaving. They bid no one farewell or gave thanks again, simply took themselves off as they were, the pages running to unstrap his jousting gear, he struggling with the straps himself until the ground was littered with pieces of metal. He threw off the black veils she wore, black for mourning and widowhood, wrapped his blue coat around her to keep her warm. Paying attention to no one but themselves, they paced along the river bank, leaving Richmond far behind. And when they had ridden long enough to ensure that no one was following them, he tethered the horse under one of those willow trees and lifted her down. 'Now my love,' he said, 'at last you shall make me welcome.'

The sun burned bright in the sky, a spring sun that had in it the taste and scent of summer. The grass was soft, the tree so low that no one could have seen under it. He drew her into its cool embrace, unfastening the lacings of her black gown. It fell on the river bank for the next high flood to drown.

Sunlight dappled her flesh, sunlight outlined his, with the new scars blue against the old. 'Come home with me, sweetheart,' he said. And folding him into her embrace, surging onto him, she cried, 'Here is my home.'

What Henry might have done to them, perhaps wanted to do when he first recovered, impending fatherhood made lenient. He laughed it off, the jovial 'Hal', the noble soul, the generous heart, who was the pride of England. 'Let them go,' was all he said. 'And if they squeeze her lands out of the Devonshire squire, good luck to them.' What he thought of his councillor Wolsey he did not say, but that too he stored in memory: Wolsey's advice that was more self-seeking than was wise, and too arrogant for a councillor. He summoned Brandon back, a humbled Brandon too, at least he could still joust with him. And in time he received Mary Tudor, although they never regained their early affection.

As for Wolsey, the other man who found Henry's behaviour beyond the pale, he took himself off in high dudgeon, his pupil suddenly proving his master. Back he went to nurse his wounds, having the Nun of Kent administer to him, her flattery persuading him that he had not lost his touch. If he knew of her betrayal he did not say so then. And if she guessed that in the end it would be Queen Catherine who destroyed him she kept that thought secret.

Richard and Philippa rode north, when Edmund Bryce was recovered enough to ride with them. But before that they made their promised visit to Vernson Hall. The roses were in bloom again, the famous white and red roses that sailors smell out to sea, and the old house stood undisturbed. Master Higham and his wife and his bailiff and all his servants had fled, not one willing to face a real lord with a real sword, and Philippa had her lands back as she had always wanted them. She left the Devon countryside with regret, promising to return each spring, using its wealth to rebuild her husband's home as her mother had used hers. Richard seldom went far again. 'Netherstoke is where I belong,' he used to say. 'The king's commands have no charm for me. My house and lands, my castle gates, my sons to inherit them, are all I need. And my wife to share with me.'

Philippa, locked into his embrace, could only agree.